Praise for

A Time to Speak

This book is a romance, murder mystery, political statement, and family drama all rolled into one, and it pulls off all facets in fine style. Amelia is in the closet, so far back in it she could see Narnia. Dominique is a great blend of strong with a hint of vulnerable. Alongside the two leading women, Scott has also created portrayals of some key figures in the town. When I first started reading these multiple points of view I feared I'd get lost in all their stories, or that it would be spread a bit thin. Groundless fears, it turns out, as Scott's masterful use of these points of view only adds delicious richness to the story. It is fantastic writing, brilliant weaving of a story, and I couldn't put it down. Highly recommended.

-Rainbow Book Reviews

I really liked the tone of the book. It would be too easy to have created a dark story of inner turmoil and grief, with negative emotions and a violent display of ignorance and discrimination. Riley Scott, however, tells the story with almost a confidence that, even if it is only possible to win the fight with one person, then that one person is important.

-The Lesbian Review

Backstage Pass

Backstage Pass is a celebrity romance with an out-of-control rock goddess and her new PR rep. It's a little grittier than I'm used to seeing in celebrity romances, and it works well. Reading a new-to-me author is always an adventure because I never know if I'm going to like them, love them, or walk away and never look back. I had never read anything by Riley Scott before, and I was more than pleasantly surprised by how much I enjoyed this book. It's very well plotted and perfectly paced, and I found myself wanting to shut out the world so I could just focus on *Backstage Pass*.

-The Lesbian Review

This is a great read. Strong personalities, a solid and well-drawn setting and a plausible and well-constructed plot. Riley Scott fills in detail on a wide range of characters as well as Raven and Chris, creating a good grounding for the plausibility of their interactions. Their behaviours are believable, and even when Chris breaks her own rules we can see how she has been swept up in the rush of life on the road.

-Lesbian Reading Room

ON THE ROCKS

Other Bella Books by Riley Scott

Backstage Pass
Conservative Affairs
Small Town Secrets
A Time to Speak

About the Author

In addition to having published poetry and short stories, Riley Scott has worked as a grant and press writer and a marketing professional. She holds a degree in journalism. Riley's love for fiction began at a young age, and she has been penning stories for over a decade. Her days and her writing alike are fueled by strong coffee, humor, people watching, and just enough daydreaming to craft imaginative novels. She lives in Pensacola, Florida, with the love of her life and their four beloved dogs.

ON THE ROCKS

Riley Scott

2021

Bella Books, Inc.
P.O. Box 10543
Tallahassee, FL 32302

This is a work of fiction. Names, characters, businesses, places, events and incidents are either the products of the author's imagination or used in a fictitious manner. Any resemblance to actual persons, living or dead, or actual events is purely coincidental. The publisher does not have any control over and does not assume any responsibility for author or third-party websites or their content.

Printed in the United States of America on acid-free paper.

First Bella Books Edition 2021

Editor: Medora MacDougall
Cover Artwork: Heather Dickerman
Cover Designer: Judith Fellows

ISBN: 978-1-64247-183-0

Acknowledgments

A story like *On the Rocks* can only come to life with the support of a team. I'm incredibly thankful to my therapist, whose insight and guidance has helped me to become a stronger and more open-minded human as well as a better and more authentic writer. I'm grateful for the advice that was utilized in illustrating the personal growth of these characters.

Additionally, thank you to the entire team at Bella Books. When you took a chance on a young author years ago, I couldn't have imagined the support I would receive and the inspiration for growing and succeeding as an author. I'm thankful to the community of fellow lesbian authors for their encouragement and the openness with which we share our journeys. I'm especially grateful to the late Erica Abbott, whose belief in me came at a time when my imposter syndrome was at an all-time high and whose love and support helped to shape me as a writer.

Thank you to my Twitter family whose humor, advice, and support helps me get through each of my writing and editing days. I'm grateful for every once of you. Also, I'm incredibly grateful to Medora MacDougall, whose insight and wisdom in editing this story has strengthened not only this story, but future stories as well.

Most of all, thank you to my wife—the love of my life and my biggest supporter—for encouragement that never wavers, for dinners on nights when I'm holed up with a manuscript, for always inspiring me on my personal journey of growth and mental wellness, and for loving me through every step of this bumpy life.

Dedication

To my wife, who taught me firsthand that love doesn't wait for a *right* time to shake up your life in the best possible ways. To my friends, who have supported me through every season in life—the hectic ones, as well as the amazing ones. To my readers, who allow me to continue sharing my stories and inspire me daily with their love for strong lesbian characters. And to everyone struggling with anxiety, depression, or mental illness—may we all seek the healing and support we need to keep going.

CHAPTER ONE

Hip-hop music thumped from the loudspeakers near her head, and Lennon closed her eyes. The music coursed through her as she danced unashamedly. Throwing her head back and forth with the rhythm of her circling hips, she loosened her shoulders and smiled, content with the daze swirling through her brain.

"Cheers!" She heard her best friend Grant's voice boom through the crowd, as he approached and shoved another lemon drop shot in her direction.

Shaking her head, she grabbed the shot and raised an eyebrow. "You know I hate these fruity drinks." She scowled but softened it to a smile and mouthed "Thank you," so as not to appear ungrateful.

"I know," he said, rolling his eyes. "But if you'd for once stop worrying about acting tough and just drink it, you'd find out it's actually delightful."

It was a conversation they'd had a hundred times, and given their propensity to go out on Tuesdays, when Lucky's—the local gay bar—ran a special on lemon drops and Vegas bombs, it was one they'd likely have a hundred more. As she gulped down the shot and returned the plastic cup to him, the beginning notes of a Cher number came over the speaker.

Behind her, Grant and a dozen or so other gay men yelled and headed for the dance floor. Laughing, she beckoned him over to dance with her. As she turned to welcome him into an embrace, she caught sight of a brunette sitting in the corner. Pulling Grant closer, moving her hips along with his, she looked over his shoulder, analyzing her—someone who seemed as out of place there as a flower in a snowstorm.

Amidst the crowd of sweaty dancers, leather- or flannel-clad lesbians ranging in age from thirty to fifty, fit men in V-necks and tight jeans, and an array of partiers of all genders dressed casually as Lennon was in her jeans, Chucks, and a Halestorm concert tee, sat the tall, slender woman dressed in many colors. Her multicolor paint-splattered, light-wash jeans contrasted yet somehow worked seamlessly with a newspaper-printed shirt and a vibrant, yellow scarf. Lennon moved Grant out of the way, and as he bobbed his head sideways, he followed her glance.

His eyes danced, and he laughed. Grabbing her face in his hands, he directed her gaze into his eyes. "Don't," he said gently, leaning in to kiss her forehead.

He was right, she knew. But, nonetheless, she pushed his hands away gently. "I'm going to grab a drink," she practically yelled over the loud music.

"No, you're not," he said, shaking his head, "but I'll see you at home."

She could see him mouthing the lyrics to Peaches' "Fuck the Pain Away" but ignored him. It had been his latest go-to in his attempt to create a soundtrack to her life, despite the times she'd insisted she wasn't in pain. She'd put that all behind her already. True to her word, she stopped by the bar first.

"Angel's Envy, double, neat, with a splash of water," she ordered when the bartender nodded in her direction. As he poured her drink, she glanced back to the seat where the woman sat. Finding the spot empty, she let out a sigh and reminded herself it was likely for the best—for both of them. Grabbing her whiskey from the bar, she made her way to the lounge chair in the corner and pulled out her phone. She heard a familiar ding and opened up Tinder.

"Shit," she muttered, seeing a message from last night's hookup asking for another date. A pang of guilt pierced her heart, but her fingers didn't hesitate in pushing the Block button on the screen. Leaning back into the chair, she smiled, replaying the previous night's encounter. It had been fun, wild even, but that didn't mean it warranted a second night.

Work's too busy right now, she thought, rehearsing the line she knew she'd give them if they happened to pop into her bar. It was busy, of course, but that wasn't the reason. Even through a fog of alcohol, she couldn't lie to herself.

As if on cue, her phone lit up with an incoming call—from her most recent ex. Seeing her name pop up on the screen sent a jolt through her. *Too little, too late, Leigh. Too late.* Shuddering, she hit Ignore.

She closed her eyes to ward off tears. She could call her back, get some answers to the questions she had, and find closure. Or she could do what she knew would feel better in the moment. Letting adrenaline fuel the willpower she'd been missing for too long, she swiped through her contacts to find her name, finally blocked the number, and then shoved her phone angrily into her pocket.

"Hard pass on that one, I see."

Lennon jumped and stood upright. Looking up, she gazed into the deep honey brown eyes of the woman she'd seen across the bar. Lennon forced a laugh, trying to catch her breath. "Uh…" she started. "I…just an old friend," she said. "Well, *former* friend." She cleared her throat. "I'm Lennon, and you've got to be new to the area."

The woman leaned back, a mixture of surprise and arrogance dancing in her expression as the corners of her brightly painted red lips lifted into a slow, broad smile. "That I am," she said, raising an eyebrow. "I take it you're the welcoming committee. Do you serve the whole town or just the gay bar?"

Lennon raised an eyebrow. "What's your name?" she asked, ignoring the question. She grabbed her whiskey and downed the entire glass.

"Alex," she said, looking Lennon up and down brazenly.

"Well, Alex..." Her reply was cut off by Alex's lips descending on her own. They were soft but she was anything but gentle as she pressed against Lennon's mouth, dragging her teeth across Lennon's lips. She felt the sigh escape her before she could stop it.

"Damn," she said, pulling away. She leaned back, eyeing Alex sideways. Used to being in charge, she had been shaken by that display of confidence.

"Do I get the tour or not?" Alex asked, her eyes smoldering with passion from the kiss Lennon had cut short.

A little thirsty, Lennon noted, but with her arousal growing under each passing second of Alex's gaze so was she.

"I suppose I've got the time," Lennon said, winking as she signaled for Alex to follow her up to the bar. "What are you drinking?" she asked, looking back over her shoulder, taking in the long, dark hair cascading down around Alex's full breasts, her high cheekbones, and her perfectly crafted smoky eye and winged eyeliner.

"Cab."

The bartender in Lennon couldn't help but analyze Alex's simple answer. *Good in bed. Artsy. Decent taste in music. Maybe just a touch crazy.* The wine order, paired with their brief but telling physical interaction, told Lennon she was in for a fun night.

Out of the corner of her eye, she watched Alex while she ordered their drinks. Alex bit her lip, and Lennon shivered. She couldn't wait to feel those full lips against every inch of her body. She was fairly certain she'd found someone with the force to make her relinquish control in the bedroom for once. The possibility both excited and scared her, as her mind momentarily raced back to summer days, too much beer by the pool, and the thrill of giving in.

She straightened her shoulders and smiled at Alex.

"Just Alex, or is it short for something?" Small talk was a risky game. If you talked too much, sometimes they got attached. Worse yet, sometimes *she* got attached. But she couldn't help herself. Alex seemed just as ready as Lennon was for a drink, a quick fuck, and the parting of ways.

"Why do you care?" Alex asked, playfully running her fingers up and down Lennon's arm and cementing Lennon's assessment.

"Fair enough," Lennon answered, handing the wineglass over to Alex before she paid the tab.

"I don't usually accept drinks from strange women," Alex said.

"Suit yourself," Lennon said. "It can be risky, for certain, but I can assure you this one's safe."

Alex pressed the glass to her lips and smiled before taking a sip. "Alexandra." Her eyes shimmered with glints of mischief. "Alexandra Daniels." She ran her finger across her bottom lip.

"Well, Alexandra, where did you come from before you decided to pop into Lucky's tonight?"

"California." She sipped her wine and looked away.

"You're a long way from home," Lennon noted. "Vacation, business, or relocation?"

"We'll see." Alex shrugged. "Could be all three."

It was a game. Lennon knew as much, but her body tightened each time Alex sipped her wine, each time she looked into Lennon's soul with those brilliant eyes. She'd play the game, because she wanted…no, *needed* Alex's touch.

She tried to focus on her drink. When she'd left the house this evening, this hadn't been her intention. She glanced at Alex and ran her finger along the rim of her glass. Intentions be damned, because she wasn't about to miss out on this adventure.

"Nice," Lennon said after a moment. She nodded and sipped her whiskey.

"Lennon as in John Lennon?" Alex asked.

"The one and only."

"You look a little more rock star than hippie," Alex noted.

"Oh, a Beatles fan by birth. Lazy rock star vibes by choice," she said, pointing at her clothing.

Alex laughed and set her now empty wineglass on the table. She pulled Lennon close. "Take me home," she whispered in Lennon's ear, her voice thick like honey, before biting her earlobe.

Her body tensed, and she could feel the wetness forming between her legs. She pulled back and downed her drink before leaning into the embrace. "I think I will," she said, running her lips over Alex's neck. She saw Grant watching and laughing in the background over Alex's shoulder. "Told you so," he mouthed.

She smiled at her friend and spun out of Alex's arms. "Let's get going," she said, putting her hand on the small of Alex's back and leading her out of the bar.

After a quick stop for a slice of pizza on the walk home, Lennon unlocked the front door to the two-bedroom coastal Craftsman she called home. She allowed Alex to enter first, then shut the door and pressed her against it. This was no time for small talk, both of them seemed to have silently agreed. Alex's body melted in her hands, and she let out small moans of pleasure as Lennon kissed up her neck and back to those luscious lips.

In the background, she heard a man clear his throat. Sighing, she pulled back.

"I thought you were still out," she hissed through clenched teeth, looking to the living room, where Grant was staring at her. She questioned for the millionth time why they still were living together this long after college even though they could both afford to live alone, then reminded herself that this was their dysfunctional version of a family and that it kept some of the loneliness at bay.

"Everyone left," he said, turning away from her and turning on the television.

"Sorry," Lennon mouthed to Alex. She shot a glare in Grant's direction before grabbing Alex's hand and making her way to her bedroom.

To her surprise, Alex wasn't upset but instead was laughing. "I feel like I'm in high school all over again, sneaking around just to get laid."

"Oh, you think you're going to get laid?" Lennon teased as she shut the door behind them and turned on her music to keep noise from spilling over into the living room.

"I think it's a pretty safe bet," she said, turning off the light, taking control, and pushing Lennon back onto the bed. Straddling her, Alex began grinding against her.

"So much for not drinking with strange girls," Lennon laughed as Alex quickened the pace.

"I think I'm getting more than just a drink out of the deal," Alex said, kissing her again. Placing her hands on Alex's hips, Lennon hungrily pulled her in harder. In a tumble of passion, they worked quickly, ripping each other's clothes from their bodies and tossing them to a heap on the floor.

Alex kissed her way down Lennon's curvy body, taking a hardened nipple into her mouth and sucking gently before kneeling between her legs. She teased with her tongue, and Lennon bucked her hips in pleasure. Savoring the decadence of Alex's tongue, she threw her head back and laughed in surprise. Of all the women she'd shared a bed with, few had so expertly and so swiftly found the perfect spot and rhythm. She felt her body tense. *Not yet.*

"My turn," Lennon said, using her hips to roll Alex over to the other side of the bed.

She smiled as she reached down, feeling for the first time the wetness between Alex's legs. She gasped as she plunged inside, causing Alex to arch her hips and cry out with a mix of shock and delight.

"God, I've needed this," Alex cried out through her moans.

"Me too," Lennon answered, pressing her lips to Alex's and speeding up her pace.

Thrusting with her hips to keep the rhythm, Lennon moaned at the sight of Alex's enjoyment. Alex tightened around her fingers, wrapping her long legs around Lennon's body and scratching her nails into Lennon's back before going limp.

Deterred for only a minute, she turned in the bed, now face-to-face with Lennon, and smiled. "I'm not done with you yet," she said in a sultry tone, returning to her place between Lennon's legs. She smiled as she slid her fingers inside, thrusting and somehow answering each of Lennon's unspoken pleas. The same wavelength, matched energy, whatever the hell you wanted to call it—it was pure ecstasy as she continued to pump in and out, moving lower and using her tongue in tandem.

"Oh God," Lennon cried, balling the sheets in her hands as she felt herself lose control slowly, then all at once. She tried to hold off but couldn't resist. Her orgasm hit, bringing wave after wave of pleasure.

Smiling, Alex sauntered forward, bringing their lips together again in a sweet and tender kiss. "Rest up, because I'm still not done with you," she whispered.

Lennon sucked in a breath, and Alex pulled Lennon's body close to hers, wrapping her arms around her. Lennon stiffened. Cuddling wasn't in the cards normally, but she needed a minute to gather her thoughts. With her back pressed up against Alex's body, she exhaled quietly.

No one had ever brought her to orgasm on the first try. Her head swam with questions and confusion swirled around like a Tilt-A-Whirl. She tried to keep her breathing rhythmic so as not to disturb Alex, who was gently wiggling back and forth in the embrace, a clear sign that she had been correct about not being done just yet.

Throwing caution and confusion to the wind, Lennon closed her eyes. She didn't need to sort this out. This wasn't anything more than a one-night stand with multiple innings. Reaching back, she gently caressed Alex's perfectly round backside and then gave it a gentle pat.

"Mmm," Alex moaned, throwing her head back to make eye contact. "Are you ready?"

"Ready as I'll ever be," Lennon said, flipping her over and diving in, consequences no longer seeming relevant.

CHAPTER TWO

Plain, dreary white paint on walls unadorned by even a single piece of art seemed to capture all that Alex felt inside. In an adjoining room, she could hear the sound of a baby crying and a young mother unsuccessfully trying to soothe it with a lullaby.

She pulled the pillow tighter over her head. She was never meant to be here—not in this hotel, not like this. Fresh tears fell on her cheeks, and she yanked the pillow from her head and threw it against the wall. It made a pitiful thud as it smashed into it. Damn! She couldn't even get the bang she had hoped for, she thought, pulling herself upright. Sitting on the edge of the bed, her elbows on her knees and her face in her hands, she decided that the memories bouncing around in her head were far worse than the infant's cries next door. Forcing herself to stand, she walked the bathroom mirror and stood expressionless.

She stared at the reflection, allowing herself to smile briefly at the bite mark on her shoulder, a small souvenir from the night before. Her head pounded from too much alcohol, and she longed for the warmth she had found in Lennon's arms. She shook her head. She had no need to seek warmth if it meant relying upon another person. There was no freedom in that.

She closed her eyes but immediately was greeted with the ghosts of her past. Opening her eyes with a jolt, she took a deep breath and started the shower. The cries continued on the other side of the wall, and she let the water hit her skin, washing away the smells of sweat and sex.

You match the energy of your surroundings. She replayed the statement in her mind as she showered. This wouldn't do. She might have fled, but she wouldn't continue to punish herself.

Out of the shower, she used the edge of the towel to clean the steam from the mirror. Smiling at her reflection, she steeled her emotions. Even if it was a façade, she would roll with it.

Last night, she'd let the combination of being in a new town and a couple of drinks fuel her to be a bit bolder than she might have been otherwise, and today she'd follow suit. It was a week for taking chances, making the first move, and taking what she wanted.

"House hunting today," she said, nodding to herself. "Tomorrow the world." She laughed at the stupidity of the notion. She didn't want to have the world. Just attaining some bit of genuine happiness would be enough.

She slipped into a bright striped dress, applied mascara and a spritz of patchouli, and headed for the door. In the parking lot, she squinted, fishing her sunglasses out of her purse and taking a moment to drink in thick air that smelled of salt and sea.

"I'll never get used to this," she said to no one in particular, noting the way the humidity clung to her, causing her freshly showered and dried skin to go damp.

She hopped in her car and looked in the backseat, piled high with all her important belongings, and sighed. Her tiny sports car hadn't been the most practical for moving purposes, but she'd remedy that today.

Putting the car in gear, she cranked up the volume of the 80s pop station she was listening to and floored the accelerator, determined to make today the start of something—anything—better.

With the windows down and the wind blowing through her hair, Alex almost felt human again, instead of like someone who was living on autopilot. The heat of the early August sun beat down on her skin, and she relished the sunlight, wondering why she'd kept herself from it for so long. Her normally tan skin was shades paler than it had been in years.

The phone ringing beside her in her passenger seat snapped her out of her stupor. *Not quite human yet*, she thought, hitting the Ignore button. She wasn't ready to talk to anyone—not even her friends back home.

Glancing once more at the home screen, she checked the date. Five days of driving. Five days beyond her hometown, her home state, the world she had once known. With one night of passion and a fresh start on the horizon.

She'd come pretty damn close to running out of land to drive through before deciding to hole up in Perdido Key. Although the town was small, it had plenty of ocean nearby and a decent gay bar that looked to be fairly new from what she could tell, and she'd seen some galleries as she driven in from Mobile.

Perched right on the Florida/Alabama border, Perdido Key seemed to be in a world of its own. An Internet search from her Mobile hotel had detailed a quaint, friendly place with all the amenities needed to enjoy a laidback, beach lifestyle. Beach shops—advertising T-shirts, blow-up water toys, and souvenirs—dotted the streets, alongside seafood restaurants and a couple of nationwide chain stores she recognized. Small beach condos gave way to sprawling mansions on the water. It really did seem to check all the boxes of things she might need. And with Pensacola and Mobile both nearby, she figured she'd be close enough to anything that might be needed from a larger city.

It wasn't quite the Florida she'd seen in movies or on TV. It was touristy, but there were no gators and fewer palm trees than she'd expected. Just emerald waters, white sand, and Southern twangs in the voices of the few locals she'd encountered.

Her lips twisted into a grin, as she wondered if all these Southerners moaned with a slight twang when they came or if that had been a Lennon special. Turning up the music another notch, she drowned out the thoughts. As much fun as it had been—and God, it *had* been fun—she needed to get the girl with the big blue eyes, large, round breasts, and playful curls out of her mind.

One night was fine. Anything more than that would be a mistake. Second encounters too often led to third and fourth ones. Before long, you could get yourself swept up in something. Damaged was no place to start something new.

After spending a morning searching fruitlessly for houses or apartments to rent, Alex needed a break. She made her way through the town, found a real estate office, and snagged a flyer to peruse over a drink. Looking around, she spotted an old brick building with a wooden sign out front proclaiming it to be an establishment called Alibis. Chuckling at the name, she gave it a once-over. Rustic chic had never quite been her vibe, but even so, something drew her to enter. The industrial metal and rustic wood decor provided a cohesive, yet unfinished look. Adorned with whiskey barrels, repurposed wood, and antique chairs, this place definitely had charm. The scent of strong spirits and fresh fruit filled the air, and the sun streamed into the shadowy interior, adding an aura of rebellion to day drinking. Gentle sounds of The XX over the speakers soothed her soul. She couldn't pinpoint what it was about the place, but she felt suddenly at home.

At home in a bar. What a surprise! She shook off the negativity and stepped further inside.

Opting for a seat in the sunlight at the bar so she could read her flyer, she hopped onto the barstool.

"What can I get for you?" Alex raised her gaze, and all thoughts ceased. She saw the same dark hair wildly tousled with curls and those same piercing blue eyes from last night staring at her. Lennon wore a smug smile. Her red sleeveless button-down shirt was plain but couldn't hide the voluptuous chest that Alex knew lay just below the buttons, and her tight black leather pants left little to the imagination. In a job based off tips, Alex figured she did pretty well.

"Shit," Alex muttered under her breath. She heard Lennon let out an amused laugh, letting Alex know her comment hadn't been as inaudible as she had hoped.

When Alex didn't answer, Lennon's smile grew, showing off dimples. "I guess I should have told you I own one of the town's most popular bars," she said, stretching out her arms to display the shelves of liquor behind her. "Pick your poison. Looks like you could use a drink."

"What are you, a therapist on the side?" Alex leaned back, unsure whether to give in to the feeling that she'd just been slighted.

"Of sorts," Lennon said, flipping her jigger up in the air and catching it expertly, never breaking eye contact. "But I deal in alternative medicine—as I think I showed you last night," she added with a wink.

Despite herself, Alex laughed. But what she felt was no laughing matter. Even when she joked and acted aloof, Lennon's gaze made Alex's heart skip a beat. Remembering how she tasted, Alex broke eye contact. "This place is great," she said, searching for anything to change the subject.

"Thanks," Lennon answered. "I'm pretty proud of it." She handed Alex a menu. "Front page is cocktails, and the back page is mainly spirits. We have a wide, unique selection of tequila, rum, and whiskey, which is what we're known for."

Alex looked down at the menu in front of her, trying to take it all in. She should run. There were other bars.

"I have wine, if you'd rather," Lennon continued, calmly waiting for Alex's drink order and acting as if nothing had happened between them. The thought stopped Alex in her tracks. Was she *that* forgettable?

"I'll take a single," Alex cut Lennon off as she was explaining a craft cocktail from the menu. "Dealer's choice."

Lennon raised an eyebrow. "Feeling adventurous, I see." She beamed as she reached up behind her and poured a shot into a glass over a few cubes of ice. As she placed it in front of Alex, her smile grew. "This one's on me if you answer a question for me."

Alex nodded.

"You sticking around?"

"I don't know," Alex said, holding the glass and sniffing the bitter, brown liquid inside.

"What's that then?" Lennon nodded toward the real estate flyer Alex had laid on the bar in front of her.

"I thought you said one question," Alex shot back. She let out an amused sigh and answered anyway. "I'm not really sure honestly. Just looking for a place to stay for a while, to find a new start."

"There's a place for rent down off Second Street, if you're still looking for something," Lennon said, casually wiping down the bar. "Good neighborhood, cheap rent. I used to live in the area," she added, scrawling a number on a bar napkin. "Call Gwen, and tell her I sent you." Without another word, she walked toward the sink in the far corner.

Alex drank the whiskey in front of her, thankful for a moment to think. Why had she fucked someone on her first night in town and decided to stick around this tiny place? She could still leave, but did that mean accepting defeat? Where would she go? Back home was off limits.

Taking a deep breath, she slapped a ten-dollar bill on the table as a tip, grabbed the napkin, and stood. "Thanks for the drink and for the suggestion," she called, hopping off the stool and heading for the door. The sweet, husky sound of Lennon's laugh filled the air, and Alex fought the urge to turn back to it. Driven by the determination to move forward, she tapped the number Lennon had given her into her phone and set up an appointment.

* * *

Holding the keys to her new place, Alex stared at the quaint little condo. It was small, but natural light spilled into every room, brightening the place up. It would be the perfect space to create, and the water nearby was just what she needed for a little healing.

She'd unloaded all her belongings from the car, made a mental note of the priority items she'd need to purchase from the store, and ordered a bed to be delivered by Amazon.

Bold moves for someone without a plan. She sighed and tossed the key into the air, catching it as it fell. It was impulsive and probably had been done out of sheer stubbornness, but here she was. Come tomorrow, she'd shop and decorate. For today, she was spent, though not spent enough to fall asleep on a floor so early in the evening. Tonight, she wanted to celebrate and let loose. Then she'd return to her humble abode.

Given that she didn't have any friends, an acquaintance would have to do. She glanced at her phone. It was a Wednesday evening. Hopefully that meant the bar would be crowded enough that Lennon wouldn't think Alex had come in just for her, and maybe Alex would have the chance to meet some other people.

She shook her head. She could go back to Lucky's. But that could just serve to put her back in the same position with someone else. She straightened her shoulders. She'd go back to Alibis.

She would keep it casual. Nothing more. After all, if she was going to stay here, they'd be bound to run into one another, and the only way to remove the awkwardness was to establish Lennon as a casual acquaintance.

Her mind made up, she strolled the three blocks toward Alibis and stared at her reflection in the glass of the boutique shop next door to the bar. Applying her lip gloss, she smiled. Before she could change her mind, she strode into the bar with an air of false confidence so great she almost fooled herself.

She had been right. The bar was bustling with activity, and while she spotted Lennon, it was clear this wouldn't be a time for chitchat. Customers lined the bar, and chatter filled the air. What had once been quiet and sexually charged was now as comforting as any other bar would have been. Grateful for a change in the atmosphere, she took a seat at the far end of the bar.

Taking a deep breath, she hooked her purse on the hook under the bar, happy to find such a convenience, and pulled a menu from the stack on the center of the bar top. Perusing it closely for the first time, since she'd been so distracted earlier, she chuckled at the names of cocktails. Lace and Leather, The Tipsy Kitchen Witch, The Midnight Rambler.

Lennon was clever, she had to admit. She was good in the sack too, but that was something Alex would have to work to forget since she was going to hang around. She needed to focus on healing.

Healing. She let out a sad laugh at the thought, thinking back to her alcohol-fueled rebellion of late. Shaking her head, she focused her attention again on the menu in front of her.

Lennon had said they were known for tequila, rum, and whiskey selections, she remembered, running her finger over the expansive list on the back side of the menu.

"What can I get for you?" she heard a deep Southern voice ask. She looked up. Her heart sank, her mouth went dry, and she felt the heat of blush on her cheeks. She was face-to-face with the man she'd seen the night before in Lennon's living room.

She could tell by looking at him that he remembered her as well. He flashed her a dazzling smile, his ultra-white teeth glinting in the overhead light. "Tequila," he guessed, pointing a finger in her direction with one eyebrow raised as he poured her a glass of water with the other.

"Sure," she managed, taking a gulp of the water as he walked back toward the wall of liquor bottles. She set the water glass down on the coaster he'd given her and put her hands in her lap. Gripping them together, she took a deep breath. She felt steadier by the time he returned, holding two bottles in front of her.

"If you like margaritas, I recommend this one," he said, doing his best Vanna White while unveiling a bottle of clear liquid adorned with flowers. "If you like your tequila straight, with an orange chaser," he added with a devilish smile, "I recommend this one."

"An orange chaser sounds like a nice change of pace," she said, nodding at his suggestion.

"You won't regret it," he said, giving her a thumbs-up sign as he turned away to set the rejected bottle down. Shimmying his hips to the beat of the country music playing on the overhead speakers, he smiled at her before turning his attention down the bar to another customer who was shouting out a drink order.

Leaning back in her chair, she took it all in. Glancing from face to face, she wondered what had brought them all out tonight. The straight couple beside her were cozying up to one another, clearly in love and clearly drunk. Down the bar a ways, a middle-aged man chatted, his words coming out quickly, with two friends who looked eerily similar to him, all of them dressed in slacks and ironed shirts with ties, having just come from work by the looks of it.

"May I buy you a drink?" From behind her, the offer came from a far too masculine voice.

She turned her head over her shoulder, coming eye to eye with a handsome man in his early twenties. "That's very sweet," she said, offering a polite smile, "but I'm okay with just this one. Thank you."

"Maybe I could get your number?" With a voice as smooth as velvet, he'd have no trouble getting a date if he barked up the right tree, Alex thought. As it was, she shook her head gently.

"I'm afraid you're not quite my type," she admitted, her words precise and slow. She was still navigating the South and wasn't sure if there was danger in outing herself so early.

"Wrong team," the bartender said to the young man with a curt nod.

"Oh," the man said, drawing out the sound far too long. "I'm…I'm sorry," he said, backing away slowly as if she was a wild animal about to pounce.

"No harm, no foul," she said, turning away from him and returning her attention to where the bartender had set her drink.

"Just thought I'd help you out," he said, laughing with ease. "I'm Grant, by the way. I don't think we've been properly introduced." She reached to shake his extended hand, but stopped midair as Lennon marched over in their direction, catching Alex's eye but not stopping until she'd reached the shelf she was looking for. Expertly she climbed the ladder that hung along the wall and grabbed a top-shelf whiskey. Alex couldn't help but stare at the way her leather pants clung in all the right spots. Scurrying down the ladder, Lennon looked from Grant to Alex and smiled.

"Making another friend, I see," she noted and turned to fulfill her mission of making the drink that had been ordered.

"Alex," she said after catching her breath, taking Grant's hand and giving it a quick shake.

"Nice to meet you," he said, his good-natured smile growing. "How do you like your tequila?"

She stared at her still untouched drink and scrunched up her nose. "I haven't had a chance..." Her words were cut off by someone signaling for Grant's attention.

"I'll be back," he said, turning and walking over to the group of three businessmen.

From the far end of the bar, Lennon's laugh rang through the air. Alex couldn't pull her eyes away as she poured drinks, mingled with patrons, and flitted gracefully around like some kind of magical booze fairy. Her long, curly hair added to the magic, and when she loosened up enough to sing along to the radio, Alex's breath caught in her throat and goose bumps formed on her arms. She wrapped them around herself, hoping no one would notice the shudder that had run through her body.

Lennon's voice was deep and smoky, as she sang along with Ingrid Andress about being as ladylike as lipstick on cigarettes and drinking tequila straight. Alex closed her eyes and let the words wash over her. She'd only known the woman for twenty-four hours, but Lennon was all that and so much more. And as the song suggested, Lennon did indeed hold the power to bring someone straight to their knees.

Alex looked down and rubbed her finger over the place that had once proudly displayed a ring and shook her head. She *was* free to do as she pleased now, but it wasn't advisable.

She had wanted to come here and have a celebratory drink, but now that seemed foolish. Downing the tequila in front of her and biting the orange slice after, as Grant had suggested, she laid enough cash on the bar top to cover the drink and tip, grabbed her purse, and strode for the door.

"I told you she didn't come here for me," she overheard Lennon tell Grant as she passed the corner where they were working.

"Well, she didn't come for *me*," Grant said with a laugh.

She wanted to tell them both they were right. She hadn't come for either of them. She'd come for herself, but she didn't feel like dignifying their banter with a response. Instead, she turned down the sidewalk and headed for the grocery store. Maybe there she'd find a fresh start that wasn't ripe for more mistakes and heartache.

CHAPTER THREE

Even at eight o'clock in the morning, the sun was hot and the air was heavy. The thin, orange tank top Lennon was wearing was soaked through. Her lungs burned as she passed the four-mile mark in her run, but instead of stopping as she normally did, she pressed forward.

She sucked in a ragged breath, intent on pushing her body until it hurt as badly as her brain and heart did. Pumping her arms faster, she focused her eyes ahead on the tree line of the park, hoping to forget her fitful night.

When the images came flooding back, regardless how hard she fought, she stopped, leaning over and grabbing her ankles to stretch. She'd dreamt of the days not so long ago when she still believed in love, back when things were good.

Good. Lennon shook her head. Good didn't even scratch the surface. Things with Leigh had been transcendent, at least right up until they weren't.

That was the best it was going to get, and she'd blown it. She stood, stretching her arms overhead, fending off the insistent, repetitive negative thoughts.

"You're better than this," she whispered with a sharp exhale. She had to get her propensity to constantly overthink and dwell on the past under control. Her heart raced, less from the run and more from the voices in her head. She wished she had access to one of those fancy *Men in Black* devices that wiped memories clean. Maybe that would take away the hole that had formed in her gut.

Nausea rose in the back of her throat as she remembered the cries that had ripped through her less than a couple of months ago, seeming to come from someone—something—animalistic. She wasn't human in those days, existing on nothing but self-loathing and heartache, never sleeping. She reached up, running her fingers over collarbones that still jutted out far more than they ever had. She exhaled hard and straightened up. Dwelling on the past wouldn't make the future any better.

Glancing down at her Apple Watch, she turned and headed back toward her house. Her extra half-mile had taken its toll on her morning routine. Given the full day she had planned, she wanted to make sure she was ready in time.

* * *

Alone in the bar, which was lit at the moment only by the Edison bulbs strung behind the glassware and liquor bottles that lined the shelves, Lennon hummed to herself. She walked over to the windows and threw open the shades, letting natural light spring into the dim room. Standing back and looking up at the massive, sprawling shelves of liquor, she felt overwhelmed. Normally, she was totally on top of her game. This was her haven, the sanctuary of her own creation. She ran her fingers along the row of bottles, lingering in the wine section as she glanced from label to label. This place always brought her joy. It was truly her passion, the place where she felt she made a difference in the world.

Sure, it was *just* a bar to some—a scene for hookups, a place to blow off steam, or the perfect spot to find a little trouble. But to her, the charming old building that had come on the market at just the right time to bring her dream to fruition was a place of possibility. The place where her cocktails delighted taste buds, where people could sample the finer things in life, where quality mattered, and where her customers—many of whom comprised her chosen family—could enjoy a relaxing and fun environment. It was the place for celebrations, first kisses, broken hearts, and opportunity.

At least, that's what she normally saw. Today, her head was muddled. Despite her run, shower, and detox acai smoothie, nothing had worked to keep the night's demons at bay. Placing her fingers on her temples, she massaged them and took a deep breath, reminding herself she had work to do.

She tuned Pandora to the current hits station and set to work. All stations had to be cleaned and prepped before the bar opened, and there were boxes to unpack in the back. She glanced over her shoulder, wishing she'd had Grant set up today. Shaking her head, she took a deep breath. It would do her good to stay busy. She tried to sing along with the latest Ariana Grande hit coming over the speakers, but it was no use. She kept seeing the blue eyes she'd fallen into a million times. When she closed her eyes to drown out the memories, though, they were replaced by Alex's brown ones.

Pursing her lips, she let out a sharp breath. She unclenched her hands, forgetting that she'd been polishing a shaker. The sound of metal clanking against the floor brought her back to reality. There had been others since Leigh, and there were others still to come, she was sure.

She was rolling her shoulders to ease the tension there when in the back of the bar she heard the thud of a door being opened. She tensed up again and took two steps toward the noise, only to smile as Grant bounded through with a bag of muffins from Lillian's, a local bakery located between their house and the bar.

"What are you doing here so early?" Wrinkling her forehead, she wondered what she ever had done without him. "You didn't have to be here for another couple of hours."

"I know Brittany's out of town, so you were setting up alone," he said, pulling a muffin from the bag and shoving the rest in her direction. "I'm opening today anyway." He glanced around, noting the tasks she'd already completed. "Looks like you've got it handled, but I thought you could use some breakfast." He took a bite of the muffin.

"So you showed up three hours early just to bring me breakfast?"

"Mmm-hmm," he said, wiping the crumbs away from his lips.

"And?" Lennon smiled, knowing there was more to the story by the way his eyes lit up as he glanced down at the muffin.

"And..." he smiled broadly. "I wanted a chance to see that cute guy who works at Lillian's."

"Tell me more," she said, grabbing a muffin. She took a bite, grateful for a distraction.

"Well," he said, shifting his feet, "there's nothing to tell, I guess."

"Is he even gay?"

"Stop," Grant said, holding his hands up to silence her. "Don't ruin my fantasy. He *has* to be." He stared down at his muffin, the dreamy look in his eyes never wavering. "Anyway I'm pretty sure he is. He gave me my Americano for free, so that's got to mean something. Right?" He looked down at the coffee he'd set on the counter and narrowed his eyes, as if somehow the coffee held the answers he sought. "Isn't that what it means?"

Laughing, she placed a hand on his shoulder. If there was anyone who had been as unlucky in love as she had been, it was Grant. "Free coffee is definitely code for something," she said. "Honestly, free coffee is a pretty clear sign. Go back down there and ask him out."

"I will," Grant said, nodding and puffing out his chest. "Tomorrow," he added, exhaling as his confidence appeared to fade with the breath. "I'll get us breakfast there tomorrow."

Lennon laughed. "Good luck. You'll have to fill me in tomorrow evening."

"That's it?" he asked, throwing his hands up in surprise. "You're not going to pry or ask more questions?" He eyed her curiously. "What's going on with you?"

"Nothing," she lied. "I just have a handful of things to take care of before I take off."

"Take off?"

"I'm going to lunch with Aunt Bernadette," she said, hoisting one of the liquor boxes up to the shelf and arranging bottles as she spoke.

"I wish I'd known," he said, grabbing a box and following suit. "I miss Aunt Bern."

"You did know." She laughed. "We talked about it last week. That's why you're opening today."

"Oh, that's right." He grinned. "I'm just over here being the hero."

"That you are."

They shared a laugh and let their conversation come to a lull. As she stocked new bottles in each of the wells, she watched him out of the corner of her eye. She was happy to see that spark in his eyes, but she felt pangs of jealousy nipping at her heart as well. Being happy—*that* happy, anyway—seemed so naïve and blissfully oblivious to her now. How could you be so willing to jump headlong into something with the power to destroy you? She'd done it, of course. But that was just stupidity. *Never again*, she vowed.

They worked in silence, and as they finished up, she grabbed his arm. "Good luck with the muffin man, and thanks for your help this morning. I'm heading out."

"Tell my favorite aunt I miss her," he said, waving as he rounded the corner.

"Will do," she called back over her shoulder. "I'm sure she'll send love to her favorite nephew."

She laughed at the sincerity of the words. They might not have been related by blood, but thanks to their having grown up together, over the years family lines had blurred.

* * *

In almost an instant, it seemed, the sunshine had given way and rain fell in torrents from the sky. "Florida," Bernadette muttered as she fumbled with an umbrella and gathered her purse from her passenger seat. She smiled as she saw her niece's small pickup pull into the parking lot. Always punctual and always her favorite, Lennon jumped from her truck and rushed over to wrap her up in a tight hug.

"I've missed you," Lennon said, holding on to the hug for almost a full minute.

"I've missed you too," Bernadette said, smiling as she pulled back. "You're getting soaked, though. Let's go on inside."

"It used to be so easy to see you often," Bernadette added, shaking the rain from her umbrella and closing it as she stood under the awning of the gallery. "But then I moved an hour up the road, and some days you'd think it was a world away."

"I'm just glad you're here." Lennon smiled and leaned in for another hug. "How'd your appointment go, by the way?" Her eyes darkened with concern as she pulled back and looked her aunt up and down.

"It was a pap smear, honey." Bernadette shook her head and laughed. "I'm not *that* old. You don't have to worry about me every time I have a doctor's appointment, you know? Your mom is the old one. I'm still with it."

Lennon laughed and held the door open for her. "I didn't call you old," she said with a giggle. "Just making sure you're taking care of yourself. I don't want anything to happen to my favorite person."

"I take care of myself just fine," she said, stepping inside. "What about you?" She narrowed her eyes, turning her attention to Lennon and looking her over quizzically. "We'll eat lunch after a while," she added before Lennon could answer. "You look too thin."

"You sound like Granny when you say that."

"Yeah." Bernadette nodded. "She would have told you the same, and she'd have been right."

"Eh." Lennon looked down at her feet. "I'm fine, but I won't say 'no' to lunch. I'd love to hang out more."

"When do you have to be at work?"

"I'm the owner," Lennon said with a laugh. "I don't *have* to be there really at any specific time. I choose to be most of the time. It's my baby, so I like to keep a close eye on it."

"And you like to stay busy."

"Just like someone else I know," Lennon said, raising an eyebrow in Bernadette's direction.

"Exactly like someone else you know." Bernadette nodded as she made her way through the gallery. "Your mom was the laid-back Beatles fan without a care in the world, and I was always on the go. One of us found her happily ever after, even if it did turn her a bit uptight." She smiled at Lennon's laugh. The shift in her sister since settling down, getting married to a good old church boy, and naming her only daughter after her favorite singer was truly one of the most remarkable changes she'd ever observed in a person. She'd somehow gone from carefree, pot-smoking, music-loving hippie to a PTA-leading, strict mother in the blink of an eye.

"You're not unhappy, though."

She nodded. "That's a fair assessment. But, that's why you should listen to me. You and I are kindred spirits, so I know."

"What did you want to see here anyway?" Lennon asked, pointing to the walls covered in art, clearly changing the subject.

"One of my friends recently started a new series of paintings," she said, scanning the walls for the familiar signature. "He's one of their featured artists, so I thought I'd come check it out."

"A *friend*?" Lennon's eyes twinkled.

"A friend," she answered deadpan. "And just a friend." Lennon leaned forward as if she didn't believe it. "Trust me, I'm as disappointed as you are that I don't have any more salacious gossip or updates for you, but I don't."

"Yeah, same here," Lennon said, abruptly turning and looking at the art. "So what's this guy's name?"

"Not so fast," Bernadette said, eyeing her curiously. "Who is she?"

"There's really no one." Lennon looked like she might say more, but she scrunched up her forehead, looking lost in the task at hand.

"Dan Hayes," she answered, deciding to let it drop for now as Lennon set to work scanning the large gallery. While she didn't know the specifics, she knew Lennon had been through hell recently. Despite how much Lennon wanted to cover it up, her stubborn nature was no match for someone who had known her since she was born. Her niece clearly was struggling. It's part of why Bernadette had opted to take the day off and stick around town. She needed to see for herself that Lennon was okay. Calls and texts didn't always give the full picture. Now she stood eyeing her as covertly as possible, wondering if she'd ever get the full story of what happened between her and Leigh and what Lennon was doing now to pick up the pieces of her heart.

Her mind drifted back to the call, just a couple of months earlier, that still cut her in two. Lennon's tears, her gravelly voice, her heartache ringing through from the other end of the line. She'd driven down in a flash and held her, cooked her dinner, and stayed with her for a night. With the onslaught of tears had come the myriad of questions. "Why wasn't I enough?" "How was it so easy for Leigh to just walk away from what we built?" "Was any of it real?"

She didn't have answers to those questions any more now than she did then. And after that, Lennon had stubbornly insisted she was fine. She was moving past it. She was too busy with work. She didn't have time for long phone calls.

It was a tactic Bernadette recognized. She knew not to trust it. The hurt still simmered beneath the surface, she knew. And despite Lennon's best efforts at putting on a happy face, Bernadette had no doubts she wasn't dealing with things as she should be. It was like looking in a mirror twenty years ago. She shook her head and rounded the corner, following behind Lennon as she looked from piece to piece.

"I know this isn't what we're looking for," Lennon said, stopping in front of an abstract piece with brilliant silvers, pinks, reds, yellows, and blues. "But I think I might need it for the house anyway."

"You have good taste," Bernadette remarked, glancing at the price tag and beaming with pride that her niece, in her mid-thirties, could afford to scoop up a pricey piece of art on a whim. How she'd managed to set out with only a business degree, a dream, a small business loan, and the experience she'd made bartending throughout college to create her own little empire was nothing short of amazing.

Lennon grabbed the tag, turning back to smile at the piece.

"What does it make you feel?" Bernadette asked, turning to face the painting head on.

"Peace." Lennon's answer was simple, but the word held so much depth.

Bernadette bit her tongue. Lennon would talk when she was ready, she reminded herself. And, if nothing else, they would talk, shop, eat, and enjoy the same ease with which their relationship had always existed.

When she came upon the wall featuring Dan's work, she stepped back, eyes widening as she took it all in. He *was* so talented. She shook her head and drew in a sharp breath. Her heart swelled as she looked from piece to piece.

Beside her, Lennon tapped a finger on her lips and chuckled. She didn't speak the words and didn't pry, but Bernadette could tell she had been found out. "He's good," was all Lennon said as she too admired his work.

"He is," Bernadette agreed, as always enthralled by the work of a fine artist. She brought her hands up to her mouth as she caught sight of the painting in the corner. The brilliance of its colors caught her eye first, but she was drawn in most by the fact that she was looking in a mirror. Although the painting was abstract, the side profile in it was unmistakably hers.

"It's beautiful," Lennon remarked, cutting through her thoughts. "It takes quite a friend to capture that intimate beauty," she added when Bernadette didn't respond.

Bernadette felt the blood rush to her cheeks, and despite being a grown woman, she giggled nervously. She ran her fingers through her hair, knowing she had an opportunity to help her niece. As much as she wanted to stay mum on the subject, she was going to be the change she hoped to see in Lennon. Closing her eyes, she took a deep breath. Opening up wasn't supposed to be so hard, but given their family history of dysfunction, talking about feelings was like pulling teeth.

"I really care about him," she said, turning to face Lennon.

Lennon beamed as she threw her arm around Bernadette's shoulders. "I'm happy for you. You've always deserved someone who makes you smile that way."

"So do you," Bernadette said slowly.

"I'll find it one day," Lennon said, grabbing the tag to the painting. "My treat," she said, when Bernadette shook her head.

"Absolutely not, Lennon!" Her voice was stern but loving. "I won't take it."

"It's your early birthday present."

"My birthday isn't until February." Bernadette pulled out of the embrace, intent on snatching the tag from Lennon's grip, but Lennon strode away quickly.

She watched in awe of the one she'd loved since she first came into this world. She'd somehow found her place in the world enough to generously treat those she loved, but she still struggled to give herself the freedom to feel.

"Thank you," Bernadette managed as they walked out of the gallery, both holding new, prized possessions in hand. "You really shouldn't have done that."

"If I was in an art piece, it would be on my wall," she said, smiling. Momentarily she cast her eyes downward. Bernadette wanted to press but busied herself placing the painting carefully in her backseat.

"Let me buy you lunch to thank you."

"Deal," Lennon said, smiling as she hopped into Bernadette's passenger seat. "Where are you taking me?"

"Our spot."

Lennon smiled beside her, clearly having already known the answer. Since she was a kid, the two of them had always solved their problems—and the world's at large—over a towering plate of nachos from Salty's.

As they pulled into the restaurant, Bernadette grinned at the pirate ship to the left of the restaurant, remembering the days when Lennon would climb and play on it while they waited for their food. She thought about sharing the memory out loud but kept it to herself. There was no need to go down memory lane every time she had a fleeting burst of nostalgia. That was what old people did, and she wasn't *that* old yet, as she'd already reminded Lennon once this morning.

After they ordered, Lennon shared anecdotes about some of the unruly and hilarious customers at the bar, and Bernadette told her all about the latest in the wedding planning business.

"I'm so thankful I don't have to plan one of those," Lennon said, laughing as Bernadette finished a story about a bride whose cake toppled over prior to the reception.

"They're not so bad." Bernadette shrugged as she focused on building the perfect nacho with the right ratio of toppings. She turned her attention back to Lennon as she dangled her loaded chip over the plate. "I've had two myself and I've been at hundreds. But they're also not a benchmark for happiness."

Across from her, Lennon stiffened, only to shove a nacho into her mouth and nod.

"Are you back on the market and looking?" Bernadette asked gently. Had it been anyone else, she would have kept her mouth shut. She knew better than most that love wasn't needed for personal fulfillment, but she also knew Lennon longed to be with someone long term. She'd told her as much, and watching her struggle through heartache after heartache was painful.

The waitress walked up to the table, filling their glasses with sweet tea and giving Lennon an out. Once she walked off, Lennon looked out over the water. "I want a boat," she said, changing the subject.

"What kind of boat?" Bernadette snacked on a nacho and watched as Lennon looked out over the water.

"Honestly, I haven't looked that far into it." Lennon toyed with her straw. "Some days I just think it would be better to be far out there, rather than up here where all the people are."

"Sounds like an anti-Ariel sentiment if I've ever heard one." Bernadette's laugh rang through the air. "I want to be where the people *aren't*..."

"Precisely," Lennon said as she broke into her own fit of laughter.

"You should go for it, if you really want one," Bernadette said, keeping her tone light. "You've always gone for what you want. No reason to stop now."

Lennon pursed her lips and nodded. "You're right. Maybe I will."

"Good." Bernadette rested her chin on her hand, imagining the scene. "I'll have to come spend some time down here. We can indulge our nacho fix and then spend the day on the water, drinking beers and catching up."

"That alone would make the purchase worth it," Lennon said, looking out to the water wistfully.

"Speaking of drinking," Bernadette said, gesturing across the table to regain Lennon's attention. "What's new at work aside from the handful of crazy patrons? Anything fun you're working on?"

Lennon's eyes lit up as she regaled Bernadette with the latest updates at the bar, her newest creations, and her upcoming seasonal cocktail and tapas menu launch.

She leaned back in her chair. "You really are something special, Lennon," she said, shaking her head. "Sometimes I'm so damn proud, you'd think you were my own."

"And some days I sure wish I was," Lennon said. She laughed, but the smile didn't reach her eyes. They both knew the words held truth.

Lennon's phone buzzed and lit up. Bernadette watched as her eyes flitted down to the screen. A smile tugged at the corners of her lips, but she quickly hit Ignore and turned her eyes back to Bernadette.

Bernadette raised an eyebrow in silent questioning, and Lennon laughed. She cast her eyes downward for a moment and then bit her cheek. Grabbing a nacho, she took a bite and looked out to the water. "She's *just* a friend." Lennon echoed Bernadette's words from earlier back to her.

"Smartass." Bernadette laughed. "But really who is your friend?"

"I'm kidding," Lennon showed her screen and Grant's name popped up. "There really isn't anyone right now." She wiped her hands on the napkin. "There have been flings here and there since Leigh left, but nothing of substance."

"It takes time to heal."

"It does, and honestly I'm not sure I ever want to get into something like that again."

Bernadette furrowed her brow in concern. "Never's a long damn time, sweetheart."

"I know." Lennon pursed her lips and let out a long breath. "It's just…with Leigh…things were…" She bit her lip as she considered her words. "Things were so brilliant. It was a year of firsts." She looked down at the floor and blushed. "Not like that, of course. But after a string of bad breakups and casual dating, it was a breath of fresh air. We fell hard and fast. Or at least I did." She played with her cuticles, something Bernadette had seen her do out of nerves and uncertainty her entire life. "At this point, with how casually she was able to leave—leave me, leave town, and never call until weeks later—I don't know if I was dumb enough to be feeling all that on my own. But I felt it all. I thought she was the one. You know?"

Bernadette nodded. She waited for Lennon to continue.

"I'd been in love before her. You know that. This was different, though. It felt like, if it was the first time I was feeling all of this magic with someone who seemed to genuinely feel it too, it had to be right. It was like seeing colors I'd never seen before, tasting the delicacy of life in a way I'd never before tasted. And then the rug was pulled out from under me, as if it was all a dream." Lennon shook her head and grimaced. "I had a ring picked out and everything."

Bernadette reached across the table and grabbed Lennon's hand in a show of support. "I finally blocked her number, though. Now I can work to forget her, to forget how I was a fool," Lennon said, swallowing to no doubt keep the tears forming in her eyes from spilling down her face.

"You weren't," Bernadette interjected, but Lennon shook her head.

"I was. I fell too hard, way too fast. I saw things that weren't there." She let go of Bernadette's grasp, as if the contact was the straw that would break the camel's back. "Worst of all, I fell alone. Falling in love is the most painful thing in the world, especially when you're blissfully unaware that you're the only one on the trip. I'm never doing that again." She set her napkin on the table and took a gulp of her sweet tea. "I'm done being the fool."

"Some time alone to heal isn't a bad thing," Bernadette said, keeping her words soft and low. Lennon let out a ragged breath and nodded. "After a serious relationship, you probably need some time. I wish I could take the pain away or make it better."

"I'm okay," Lennon said, looking Bernadette in the eye again. Stubbornness shone through in the tears that glistened in her eyes. "I won't get hurt again. I think I've perfected the art over the past little while of staying on top of my emotions. I can have connections, but they don't get to go deep."

"What if you turn into the one who hurts someone who falls for you?" Bernadette asked the question before she thought better of it. Silently chiding herself, she bit her tongue.

"Well, I guess they get to play the fool then."

The answer was so quick, so succinct, so unlike Lennon.

"That's not who you are, honey." She opened her mouth, hoping to find something more to say, but Lennon cut her off.

"I'm not cold or mean. I'm just smarter than I used to be."

"Okay," Bernadette said, taking a moment to drink her tea and contemplate her response. "I just don't want you to hang on to the past so long that it changes who you are and clouds your view of the future." She scooped up a nacho and shoved it into her mouth before she could say anything else.

Lennon nodded. "Thanks, Aunt B. I'll be fine." Bernadette watched in silence as she looked out toward the horizon and seemed to chew on the words that Bernadette had said. She knew from personal experience how deep that stubborn streak ran. Kindred spirits, that's what everyone in the family had called the two of them since Lennon was a toddler, and they'd been right. She couldn't help but fear that her immense stubbornness would make things harder for Lennon. There was clearly more Lennon wanted to say, but she wouldn't.

Bernadette opened her mouth to change the subject, but Lennon's eyes were on her again. "Tell me more about your friend Dan," she said with a laugh.

Lead by example, she reminded herself as she regaled Lennon with a tale of embracing possibility after having been hurt.

CHAPTER FOUR

Natural light shone in through her open windows, and Alex leaned her head to the side, smiling as she took in the sound of a songbird making itself at home in the branches of the lemon tree outside. She was home. She looked around the simple one-bedroom, one-bathroom condo, dreaming of the life she was going to bring to this place.

"A thousand miles from the place I was born…"

The opening notes from one of her favorite Amos Lee songs played through her mind. She smiled and closed her eyes. Perdido Key, as stunning as it was, wasn't fully her home yet, she had to admit. But with the friendly faces, the bustling group of tourists who changed day to day, and the beach…it was growing on her. It was a beach she could grow old on, she was certain.

Determined not to dwell on the demands of planning long term, she picked up an apple from the fruit bowl on the counter and headed for the porch. As she ate her breakfast in the salty morning air, humming along with the birds, she mapped out her day.

It was time to start painting again. The time she'd taken off had been good for her soul, but she'd let too much time pass by without creating anything. There was too much beauty in the world to focus on just the negatives.

Tossing the apple core in the compost bin she'd started, she rose with newfound determination. In the dining area, she positioned a blank canvas on her easel and looked out the window, admiring the rise and fall of the waves.

That, she decided, was what she'd paint. The Emerald Coast, as she'd heard the locals call it, would make an ideal subject for her reemergence. It *was* a rebirth of sorts, she thought, even if it sounded all too theatrical.

She flipped through the radio stations on her phone, rotating her hips to loosen up her body and tapping her foot as she scrolled. The right mood for the day would be important, and her musical selection had to be on point. With a smile, she selected her favorite Stevie Nicks station and set it to play on her Bluetooth speaker. Moving her body to the soothing rhythm, she set out her paints and sang along as she let inspiration flow. She sketched and sang, creating the line work for the sand, the sea, and the sky. As Stevie sang of silver springs and broken love, a lump formed in the back of her throat.

Tears sprang in her eyes, and like a dark cloud the memories enveloped her. One minute she had been happily flipping through bridal magazines trying to pick out flowers and a dress and the next, horrors were unfolding before her eyes.

Her breathing escalated, and her heart hammered in her chest. She continued painting, stopped fighting the memories, and for the first time, let them flow without inhibition.

Relieved to be home after attending the gallery opening for one of her former classmates, she opened the front door. She tossed her high heels aside; her feet were killing her after standing around chatting and networking for several hours.

She stiffened, listening to the sounds coming from down the hallway.

Maybe it was a movie or a YouTube video, she thought, craning her neck in the direction of the noise. Making her way slowly down the hall, she stopped, curiosity growing by the second.

As she inched closer, she could tell the sounds were moans. Her body tensed at the thought of Olivia pleasuring herself. Wanting to join the action, she fluffed her hair and sauntered toward the bedroom door, which was slightly ajar. She quietly pushed it open. Her heart plummeted. Unable to move or speak, she watched wide-eyed as some strange woman moved inside her fiancée. Olivia threw her head back in pleasure, matching rhythm and thrusting in tandem with the woman, allowing her to penetrate deeper.

From somewhere deep inside her, she felt the rage and heartache collide, manifesting in a pained cry.

Just one single scream escaped. It was enough to make the scene in front of her stop. As they scrambled for their clothes, Olivia was talking quickly, her words spewing forth in a slew of unrecognizable syllables.

It was as if she was speaking a foreign language; none of it made sense. The nameless woman scurried past, careful not to bump into Alex, who was still standing in the doorway, as if in a trance.

No matter how many times Olivia offered empty apologies in the hours that followed, she expressed no remorse. The slamming of doors created a soundtrack to the heartache, as Alex packed her things and angrily drove away from the scene of the crime.

Alex wiped the tears from her eyes, staring at the canvas in front of her. What had started as a peaceful and scenic beach view had turned dark and stormy. It was fitting, though, and even cathartic.

"She will not win," Alex spoke the affirmation aloud, letting it resonate within her and bounce off the walls of the condo. She gritted her teeth and poured a dab of gray paint onto her palette. The hours passed into afternoon until finally she stood, staring at her handiwork. Pleased with it, she put the brush down.

She looked to the living room and gave the bare walls a half smile. The piece was more than a little dark but would still make the perfect first work of art for her new home.

Resurgence. That's what she'd call the piece, she decided, stepping back to admire it again. It told a strong story, even if she was the only one to fully get it. The fury, the passion, and the pain all combined in a setting that was once so vibrant and one day might be vibrant again, if only the sun decided to shine.

She looked outside. The sun *was* shining. It had just lost

some of its luster. She thought about sitting down to cry and sort through her feelings, but that wouldn't do any good. She didn't have time for that.

She bit her cheek. That was a lie, and she knew it.

Truth was, she thought, looking down at her paint-stained hands, all she had was time. But that wasn't going to stop her. She didn't want to dwell anymore. She'd poured her feelings into her work, and for now that was the best she could muster.

After a quick shower, she threw on a skirt and tank top and headed outside. A change of scenery would do her good. In her car, she rolled down the windows. The sunlight hit her skin and the salty wind flowed through her hair, reminding her again of her new surroundings. Waving her hand through the open window, she let the natural location ground her and keep her in this moment.

"Live in the moment," she chanted, repeating the mantra aloud before turning up the radio and letting the music take her thoughts from the morning's route of reflection and reconstruction.

She pulled her car into the parking lot by the nearby marina and walked to the pier to watch as boats glided gracefully over the water. This was paradise. She just had to figure out how her jagged edges fit into something so pristine.

Inside her pocket her phone vibrated. Fishing it free, she saw her sister's name on the screen and smiled. As a massive yacht streamed by, she took a deep breath, grabbed the wooden railing, and hit the button to accept the call.

"Hello," she answered, her voice sounding foreign even to her own ears.

"Hey," Lindsey said, her voice heavy with concern. "Where have you been? Better yet, where are you?"

Fuck. Alex had left without a word, partially on purpose, partially because she hadn't known where she might end up, but she hadn't meant to abandon everyone. "I…I moved," she said, tapping her foot on the deck. She dropped her arms and paced. "I meant to tell you."

"Moved? Where did you move?"

"I'm in Florida." The words felt strange on her tongue. *Florida*, she repeated mentally.

"*What?*"

She searched for an answer, but Lindsey didn't give her time.

"Why? I mean, I know things went badly, at least from what Olivia told me."

"You talked to *her*?" Alex hadn't meant for the words to come out as a hiss, but she couldn't retract them now.

"I had to!" Lindsey's voice was rising. "You didn't answer your phone. You weren't home. What the hell was I supposed to do?"

"I don't know," Alex snapped, "but you didn't need to involve her."

"What happened? She wouldn't tell me everything, but if you ran thousands of miles away, it must have been bad."

"I don't want to talk about it," Alex said, keeping her voice low as she walked past a family of five that was as sweetly enamored with the boats as she had been moments earlier. She sighed and straightened her shoulders. "I'll explain when I can, but I needed a fresh start."

"Florida? Why?" Lindsey circled back to her previous question.

"First of all, if you talk to Olivia again, don't mention where I'm at," Alex said, making sure her bases were covered, even though her sister was the one person she knew she could trust.

"I won't," Lindsey assured her. "I have no reason to talk to her if you're not with her. You know me better than that."

"I do," Alex conceded. "Anyway, I'm in Florida. I don't have any answer other than that it felt right, so here I am."

"When are you coming home?" Lindsey's voice was hollow, as if she realized her only sister had picked up and moved without so much as a goodbye.

"I got a place here." Alex's heart sank as she heard Lindsey's gasp. "I'll come visit before too long," she added quickly, hoping to avert causing too much damage to their relationship. "And you can come visit me. I'd love for you and Connor to see the beach down here. It's so different from home." She continued, describing the Gulf Coast, but Lindsey had already checked out, she could tell.

"I'm sorry," she said, pausing for a moment.

"I get it, I think," Lindsey said, her voice thick with emotion. Although she couldn't see them, Alex could hear the tears in her words.

"I wish I had taken the time to stop by and see you both before I left." She thought of Connor, her sweet nephew, and wished she could have stopped in there to give him a hug, but she knew why she hadn't.

"It was too hard to say goodbye when I already felt like I'd lost a huge chunk of my life. Telling you all that I was leaving would have made it real, made it so that she took even more from me, and I don't think I would have been able to bear the look in either of your faces." She spoke truths she hadn't even let herself broach yet. "I had to leave, but if I'd have seen the two of you, I would have stayed."

"We miss you." Lindsey's response was simple, but heartfelt.

Alex wiped a single tear from her cheek. "I miss you both," she said, stopping to lean on the railing for support. "Once I get settled, I'm flying you both down."

"You don't have to."

"I insist," she said. Lindsey started to argue, but Alex cut her off. "I'm working on meeting people here, but everyone else seems connected somehow. It's small enough that, while there are tourists, the people here know one another, and I'm an outsider. It's a bit lonely, but I think it's what I need."

"We'll talk about it and make a plan," Lindsey finally agreed. "But in the meantime, I'm just glad you're okay. You scared me," she chided, clearly unable to keep her older sister temper at bay. "At least let me know where you're going next, okay?"

"Okay," Alex agreed.

As the call wrapped up, she couldn't help but play Lindsey's questions back in her mind. What *was* she doing here, and why had she signed a twelve-month lease? This move was a gamble, but she'd been making a lot of those lately.

Straightening her skirt as she righted herself, she gave the boats one last glance before rounding the corner and heading back toward the beachfront gallery she'd been eyeing since she pulled into town.

If she was going to stick around, she had to start finding her place somehow, and work seemed to be the easiest, least confusing avenue by which to do that.

CHAPTER FIVE

The Florida sun beat down on her bare shoulders, and Lennon laughed as the cool waves tickled her feet. Lying in the sand, listening to the steady rise and crash of the waves, she wondered how anyone ever felt stress at the beach. This was, and always had been, her happy place, her escape.

Some people had a church or a building that made them feel a part of something bigger, and out here, she could almost understand it. This was where magic still existed.

"You look one hundred percent blissful." Grant's words interrupted her thoughts.

"Yet here you are, talking and ruining the moment," she teased, tossing a bottle of sunscreen playfully in his direction.

"Sorry," he said as she eyed him over the rim of her aviator sunglasses. At over six feet tall, he towered over her, creating a perfect shady spot as she propped herself up on her elbows. "I was just thinking that it might be nice if you took more days like this."

"So I'm not always telling you what to do at the bar?" she shot back with a grin.

"That," he said with an enthusiastic nod, "and so you actually get to enjoy some of the perks of being the owner. You don't have to tend the bar four to five days a week. You don't need the money. You can hire in more help."

When she narrowed her eyes at him, he held his hands up in mock surrender. "I'm just saying, I've seen the books, and you made bank last year. You could hire in someone else and enjoy more days on the beach."

"You want me to retire at thirty-three? What am I supposed to do? You want me to take up knitting and crosswords?"

"First off," he said, holding up his finger and shaking his head, "there are worse hobbies. Second of all, you deserve it. It's not retiring. It's enjoying what you've worked your ass off to achieve. You could be living the dream. That's all I'm saying."

"I thought you were already living the dream, Mr. Brewer," she said, sitting up and turning to face him as she bundled her sunscreen, Hydro Flask, and book into the beach bag beside her. "You live with me for starters. Then there's the fact that you work at the best bar in Florida, alongside the best boss. You get great pay, you have great hair, and you have your pick of men. What more could you want?"

"I want for nothing, my queen," he said, bowing to her in jest. "I'm just thankful to be in your presence."

"You know, it's a shame neither of us wants the parts the other has to offer, because that," she said, motioning her hand in a circle in his direction, "is all I've ever wanted in a partner."

They laughed as they gathered up the rest of their things. "Feeling is mutual, darlin'. Feeling is mutual."

"I wouldn't trade this for anything, though," she said, smiling up at him as he grabbed the bags and headed up toward the pier.

"Speaking of partners…" he started. She held up her hands to stop him.

"There's no one."

"Not true," he said, his voice rising in disbelief. "There have been a couple of someones since…well, since you've been single." He looked down at the sand. "You seem to forget we share a house."

"That doesn't make them a partner." She wrinkled her nose, choosing to ignore his near slipup. "You know that as well as I do."

"What about that girl last week who showed up at the bar afterward the next day? Have you talked to her since?"

"Nope." Lennon shook her head. "I haven't talked to any of them."

"What about..."

"I swear to you that if you say her fucking name again, I'll cut you." She spun to face him. "There's no one special. I'm not running. I'm not in pain. I'm not heartbroken. I'm fine, and I'm not dating anyone. Understood?"

She threw her arms up in the air in frustration. She narrowed her eyes, knowing if they were at home, he might have challenged her further, but in public, he wouldn't make a scene.

"Got it," he said. She saw him roll his eyes but she chose to ignore that too.

She stifled a sigh. Maybe he was right about her needing to take off more time, but he wasn't right about the rest. She was fine, and she was better than ever since her breakup with Leigh. *Closure.* The word bounced around in her head like a ball in a pinball machine. Everyone had told her that was what she needed, but she was pretty sure it didn't exist.

She had enough closure when Leigh packed her things and left town in search of a new beginning somewhere. Lennon racked her brain, but once again she was sure she'd never got an answer as to where that new beginning was even taking place. If Leigh had been unhappy, she hadn't shown it. Either way, she'd still chosen the unknown over the life they had been building together. For what had to be the hundredth time, she wondered if there had been someone else all along—someone in another city who'd lit Leigh's world on fire in the same way Leigh had done for her.

Her thoughts ran rampant, and her heart rate accelerated. Closure wasn't possible, and none of Leigh's rationalizing would make any difference. The one phone call they'd had since she left had proven as much. There was no remorse, no explanation, nothing but a hollow apology. All of her friends had seen what an utter disaster Lennon was in the aftermath. To say she'd made a scene or two was an understatement. It was no wonder they all were so concerned with the state of her heart, but since she was at least holding it together publicly these days, she wished they'd drop it.

"Tacos?" he asked, breaking the silence and nodding in the direction of one of their favorite restaurants. It was little more than a small wooden hut with a tented roof, but they served the best tacos in the county there.

"Obviously."

As she strolled up the boardwalk, she stopped in her tracks. As if on cue, on the far side of the restaurant, sat Alex.

"Well fuck me," she muttered under her breath. She turned to leave, ready to forfeit tacos for the inferior burger stand, but Grant didn't catch the clue and was already barreling into the restaurant closely behind her. When she turned, she struck him in the stomach, causing him to fall backward, drop their bags onto the floor, and pull her down with him.

"Damn! You two know how to make an entrance," Jake, the regular afternoon bartender and waiter, called out to them as he made his way around the bar and over to them.

Just as Lennon had feared, Alex had already caught sight of the commotion and had half stood. Probably trying to decide whether or not to offer help or how to make a speedy exit, Lennon guessed. Not giving her the chance to choose, Lennon jumped up and dusted the sand off her legs.

"Two margs and two taco plates, half beef, half veggie?" Jake asked. "That should help cure the fall, right?"

Grant laughed and nodded. "Sounds good, man. Thanks!"

Lennon wanted to protest, but she knew her jackassery had already gotten them this far into the situation. Not to be rude, she nodded a greeting in Alex's direction.

"Hey," she said, waving and taking her normal seat at the midway point of the bar.

"Hi," Alex said before returning her attention to the plate in front of her.

"Why don't you come over here and join the fun?" Jake asked, waving Alex over. "You said you were new to town, so you might as well make some friends."

Lennon opened her mouth to tell him they'd already met but bit her tongue. She looked at Jake and then over at Alex. "He's right, you know?" She offered a smile, despite her erratic heartbeat and the alarm bells ringing in her head. "Come over and join the gang."

Alex gave a slight laugh, rubbed her neck, and picked up her plate. Lennon couldn't tell if she was doing so out of a headstrong nature or to go along with the flow. She thought for a second while Alex situated herself on the barstool next to her. She couldn't decide her reason for doubling down on the invitation either.

"Are you getting settled in?" Lennon asked, working to keep her tone neutral.

Alex flashed a warm smile, and Lennon's heart beat even faster. "I am." She took a sip of her fruity drink and looked at Lennon over the rim. "These aren't quite as complex as the drinks at your place," she noted, keeping her voice low so she didn't insult Jake.

"Thank you for the compliment." Lennon nodded. "You can come back sometime and have another drink." Even as she extended the comment, she regretted it. Sure, she'd afterward served drinks to several of the women she'd slept with and kept it casual, but there was something different in Alex's eyes. Maybe it was the fact that she just moved here and didn't know anyone, or maybe it was the way she could so completely undo Lennon with a single touch. Whatever it was, Lennon knew she was playing with fire.

"I just might," Alex said, smiling as she picked up one of the tacos on her plate. She brought it to her mouth but stopped before taking a bite. Lennon's breath hitched as she watched Alex gently bite her lip and raise her eyes to meet Lennon's stare. "Thanks for the offer," she added, before biting into the soft tortilla.

Lennon struggled to pull her eyes away, remembering how those thick lips had felt on her own, on every inch of her body. Grant elbowed her, and she jerked her eyes forward to where Jake was setting plates in front of them.

"Thanks." Her voice faltered, but she took a swig of her margarita to mask the sound.

"What do you do?" Grant asked, leaning over Lennon to face Alex.

Lennon wanted to elbow him this time, but she knew it would draw too much attention.

"I'm an artist."

The answer was simple, yet complex. Lennon had so many questions. What medium? What subjects? Where did she sell her work? She bit the inside of her cheek, keeping her words at bay. It would only complicate the matter at hand to show the extent of her interest.

"Very cool!" Grant had taken over now, so she took the opportunity to eat. "What type of artist?" He was doing the heavy lifting to ease her curiosity. For that, she was grateful, even if he was prone to acting like the nosy big brother she'd never wanted.

Lennon watched Alex out of the corner of her eye. Alex's eyes brightened and her smile grew. Her face lit up, and she leaned in, at once looking more comfortable in her new surroundings. "I paint mostly," she said, playing with the corner of the bar napkin in front of her. "I draw and dabble a bit with jewelry making, but that's just for fun. I'm fortunate enough to be able to make a living off my paintings."

"Damn!" Grant whistled through his teeth. "That's impressive. Are you, like, famous?"

"Hardly." Alex laughed. "But I make a decent living and don't have to be chained to an office all day."

"Same," he nodded, laughing as he cast a glance toward Lennon. "And I have a delightful boss," he added with a wink to Alex before rolling his eyes.

"You're an ass," Lennon shot back, laughing.

"An ass who's going to be late to work," he said, pointing at the neon clock behind Jake's head. "I hate to run. Great seeing you again, Alex. Bye, Jake." He looked at Lennon and tapped her on the shoulder. "See you tonight."

"See you later," Lennon answered, wishing she'd paid more attention to the time.

"What's that like?" she asked, turning her attention toward Alex, without a buffer now that Grant had left and Jake had busied himself cleaning the kitchen.

"What do you mean?"

"Just creating art all day," she said, tilting her body toward Alex. "How often do you have to work?"

"That all depends on how much I need to survive," Alex said. She glanced out toward the water and leaned back in her chair. "How much I make is directly related to how often I work." She bit her lip, as if contemplating her answer. "I generally spend most of my early mornings and nights working on my projects. In the daytime, I like to explore, especially when I'm in a new place." She opened her mouth to add something but shut it abruptly as if she had revealed too much.

"How much of the new place have you seen?" Lennon asked, crumpling her napkin and pushing her nearly untouched plate to the side. "I know you've been to the best bar and best taco stand"—she laughed and faked a tip of the hat at Jake who gave a playful bow to accept the compliment—"but have you seen much else?"

"I've explored a bit." Alex looked out to the water wistfully. "There's still a lot I haven't seen. I've been drawn in by this." She motioned out toward the emerald waters, where a kid on a stand-up paddleboard moved by in the distance. "I've been painting a lot lately, so between that and decorating my place, I haven't been out and about too much."

"Do you have to work tonight?" Lennon couldn't stop the words from escaping her mouth.

Alex leaned back, a grin starting to form. "Are you asking me out?"

"N-no," Lennon stammered, shaking her head. "I was asking if you wanted to take a tequila shot with me."

Alex laughed. "In that case, I don't *have* to work, and even if I did, I could paint while a little tipsed."

"Tipsed?"

"It's like tipsy, but a little looser and more relaxed. Like when you're tipsy, you're ready to party. When you're tipsed, you're ready to enjoy wherever the flow of the day takes you."

"I like it," Lennon said, laughing as she repeated the phrase again. "Okay, Jake," she said, shifting in her seat. "Line 'em up."

As Jake turned to pour the shots, Lennon watched Alex. She pegged her for late twenties, early thirties. She knew she could have asked, but she hadn't and wouldn't. It hadn't mattered the other night, and it didn't now.

Jake set the shots down in front of the women, and Lennon tapped her glass against Alex's. "Cheers to new *friendships*"—Lennon made sure to stress the word to make her intentions clear—"and to your new beginning," she toasted before downing the shot.

Alex followed suit, wincing as she set the glass back on the table.

"You okay?" Lennon eyed her cautiously.

"Yeah," Alex said slowly. "I should probably take a bit of a walk, though. I've been sitting out here in the sun, and that was my second drink."

"What would you say to me giving you the tour of Perdido Key?" Lennon offered. "We'll get a water to go, and I'll show you around to give you a dose of Southern hospitality."

"Is that actually a thing?" Alex asked, narrowing her eyes in question.

"It is around here." Lennon nodded. "At least if you go to the right people. There are still assholes, same as anywhere, though."

"Fair enough." Alex hopped off her barstool. "I'll agree to the tour. I wouldn't mind getting acquainted with a few more spots."

* * *

Lennon looked around, assessing the ambiance of the water crashing into the shore next to their table and the brightly colored umbrellas dotting the driftwood deck and hoping she had chosen well for Alex's first stop of the afternoon.

Lennon watched Alex from afar as she returned from her trip to the restroom. The artist was shifting in her seat, seemingly struggling to get comfortable, a move that looked so out of place with how confident she appeared at other times. Alex was playing with the straw in her drink, while her eyes darted to and from items on the menu. She was shaking her head and didn't look overly pleased.

Damage in the house, she thought. But truth be told, it took damage to recognize damage. She sighed, shoving her hands into her pockets and strolling back to her spot. Alex Daniels was a walking contradiction, a beautiful conundrum, and despite everything, Lennon wanted to figure out what made her tick.

CHAPTER SIX

The heavy air seemed to hold an aura of mystical potential. Alex closed her eyes, paying attention to the sounds of music from the band onstage as they mixed with the rhythmic crash of the nearby waves.

"You know, it kind of feels like paradise here," she said after a moment.

"It really does," Lennon said, smiling as she stood. "I was born and raised here, and the fact that it's so serene is part of why I never left."

"What do you like most about living here?" Their conversation had been easy, and once they settled into their booth at a dive bar a few blocks down from Lennon's bar, all traces of awkwardness had dissipated.

"I love so many things," Lennon said. "The beach is incredible. I love the mix of locals and tourists who drink at my bar every night and allow me to do what I enjoy. I have a chosen family full of great people." She laughed. "I have real family here too, but they're not so much in my day-to-day. Overall, it's just a fun, laidback place to live." She smiled at Alex, wondering if her answer summed up everything Alex wanted to know. She glanced toward the water. "The real question in determining whether or not you'll like it here is you. Aside from drinking"—Lennon nodded at the cocktail in Alex's hand—"what do you like to do?"

"I like a lot of things," Alex said, brushing her long hair out of her face. Lennon stared at her as though she was hanging on every word. "I like being outdoors, dancing, singing karaoke, being on the water."

"And painting women like one of your French girls, right?" Lennon waggled her eyebrows in jest, referencing the iconic line from *Titanic*. She laughed, and Alex joined in with her. When she stopped laughing, she settled into a smile. "You'll like it here," she assured Alex.

Sipping her fruity drink, Alex arched her back, releasing some of the tension she didn't realize she'd been holding on to. She'd mostly been sipping water throughout the day, but the alcohol was taking effect, and Lennon's blue eyes were like beacons of light in the darkness. She scooted back in the booth so she could pull her feet up under her and face Lennon. "I know you feel it too," she said, toying with her straw. "The fact that we're playing a dangerous game."

"We don't have to." Lennon took a long drink of her whiskey and ginger before pushing it back. She ran her tongue along her lip and looked off into the distance before leveling her gaze with Alex. "The way I see it, as long as we're clear on where we stand, we'll be okay."

Alex clasped her hands, considering the statement. Beside her Lennon shifted her weight and leaned forward.

"I'll let you in on a secret," she continued. "This town is small, and even though there seems to be an inordinate number of lesbians for the small population, it *is* small. That means we're going to run into each other a lot. We can either decide to be friends or it can be awkward for the rest of your time here."

"It has been awkward," Alex said, nodding. "So damn awkward."

"It doesn't have to be." Lennon smiled and signaled to the bartender to bring another round of drinks. "And since we're here on a night out, I don't see any reason we have to pretend we aren't attracted to each other."

"I'm not looking for anything," Alex said, gripping the glass in her hand tighter. "I don't want to get serious."

"I don't do serious, not right now," Lennon answered, not giving Alex a chance to take it any further.

"What do you mean 'not right now'?"

Lennon tapped her foot against the table rapidly and downed her drink. "I think it's clear you got out of something recently, and, not going into any details, so did I. I think we're in the clear for thinking now's not a good time for anything serious. In fact, I don't think I'm looking for anything at any point in the foreseeable future."

"I know the feeling," Alex said. She cast her eyes downward, warding off the memories.

"The thing is," Lennon said, "my heart's pretty fucked up. What's your damage?"

Alex leaned back, both in awe and grateful for the boldness of the question. "You sure you're ready for that?" she asked.

"Yeah," Lennon nodded. "Might as well lay it all out there. We've established we're just having a good time. No need to put that best foot forward, right?"

"I'll spare you the details as well." Alex looked down at her drink. Was she sparing Lennon? Or herself? "But long story short, I was supposed to be getting married in a couple of months, and now…I'm not."

"Damage, indeed," Lennon said, wincing. "How long have you been un-engaged?"

"Since a couple of weeks before I ran into you. And you?"

"I didn't have a ring." Lennon clenched her jaws, then continued. "It was serious, though, and it really sucked when it ended. I've been doing my own thing for a couple of months." Her expression was unreadable as she cleared her throat, slapped her knees, and stood. "Want to dance?"

Alex leaned back in hesitation. It seemed to be a request from out of left field. Lennon smirked and stretched her hand toward Alex. Like a moth to a flame, Alex stood and took her hand, smiling at how easily it fit within her own. The soft skin of Lennon's fingers ran over her palm, and she shivered, remembering the skill they possessed.

They hit the floor as a classic beach tune ended and, as if by some sick and twisted master design, the band started to play a slow song about lovers in the night. Without missing a beat, Lennon tangled her fingers through Alex's and spun her around, drawing her back into a respectable but intimate embrace.

"Smooth." Alex smiled despite her best efforts to keep a game face.

"I try." Lennon took the lead in moving them around the floor, and Alex couldn't help but notice the way she wasn't trying to hide her smile any longer. Gone was the cool and aloof Lennon she had come to know and in her place was a woman lost in the power and poetry of their bodies moving together.

With every brush of their bodies against one another, Alex tensed. Her heart pounded as Lennon pulled her just inches from her face. Alex almost leaned down for a kiss, but as the music came to a close, Lennon spun her back around once more.

When the song transitioned to a faster one, Lennon took advantage of the momentarily quieter music. "I should warn you, I'm not much of a dancer to this"—she motioned to the amps—"but I'll give it my best effort."

"I think you'll manage just fine," Alex said, and as the beat intensified, she showed no hesitation intensifying her own moves. Lennon watched, her jaw dropping, as Alex moved her hips in perfect beat to the music and ran her fingers up and down Lennon's arms, teasing her with gentle touches.

Lennon leaned her head back, her lust-filled smile stretching as she leaned in for a kiss. Passionate and slow, she moved her hips into Alex's.

"You're actually a pretty damn good dancer," Alex said breathlessly, pulling away from the kiss.

"If this is dancing, then I was wrong," Lennon said, laughing. "I love dancing."

Alex smiled as Lennon's lips trailed down to her neck. Her body quivered, and she fought the urge to moan as wetness collected between her legs.

As the song faded, Lennon took her hand and they walked back toward the table. Thankful for a moment to catch her breath and readjust the dress that now clung to her body in the dense humidity, she grabbed her water glass and chugged its contents.

"August is our hottest month," Lennon said, letting go of Alex's hand in order to grab her own water.

The phrase held multiple meanings, and it wasn't lost on Alex. "What is it we're doing?" she asked, having caught her breath. She wasn't some schoolgirl in love who was going to get swept off her feet by a smooth-talking woman who asked her to dance.

"I think I'm dancing with a pretty woman and having a good time." Lennon shrugged, grabbing her whiskey and ginger and taking a seat in the booth. "We already established boundaries, so there's no reason we can't have a little fun."

Alex nodded, taking in the words as she sat. "I'm new in town. I might have a bit of fun with more than just you."

"I hope you do," Lennon said, holding eye contact as she raised her glass in the air in a playful toast. "To fun with whoever you want, whenever you want. That," she said, taking a sip and tilting her head upward to savor the flavor, "is the essence of freedom."

"To freedom," Alex said, raising her glass in the air in response.

Emboldened and with independence coursing through her veins, Alex leaned over and kissed Lennon. Running her fingers through her curls, she deepened the kiss before pulling back smiling.

"Freedom tastes pretty sweet sometimes," Lennon said, leaning back into the booth and laughing.

"That it does." Alex looked her up and down. With her broad shoulders, full breasts, and muscular arms, Lennon looked as if she might have been an athlete at some point. Running her tongue along the back of her teeth, she savored the sight. She took a deep breath before blurting, "I'd like to paint you."

"That could possibly be arranged." Lennon cast her a sidelong glance, but nodded. "I'd like a cigar," she said, standing and pointing at Alex to see if she wanted anything.

"Get your cigar," Alex said, fishing through her purse and pulling out a pack of menthol cigarettes. "I have my own bad habits to stick to."

Lennon laughed and left Alex alone for a moment with her cigarettes and her thoughts. The lines had been drawn, and that was supposed to mean she was safe—safe to explore, to laugh, to enjoy, to fuck, and to fuck others. She liked the possibilities, almost as much as she enjoyed Lennon's company.

A friend with benefits. She'd seen it done. She'd even done it successfully. Besides, she was far too raw for it to cross any other lines. Thankfully Lennon seemed to be in the same boat.

She used the silver ashtray in front of her as a mirror and reapplied her lipstick. She heard Lennon approach before she saw her. She turned her attention upward, her body tightening as Lennon leaned down and grasped her hand, ushering her out of the building.

Out on the patio, Alex lit her cigarette and handed her lighter over to Lennon for her cigar. Taking a drag, she leaned into the wooden bench.

"What's the next stop on the tour de Perdido?" she asked, looking down to where Lennon sat sprawled on the floor of the deck.

"I think it's your turn to take me home," Lennon said, making a smoke ring as she exhaled.

"I could do that." She smiled devilishly, glancing down at Lennon. The moment felt like one of pure rebellion, even though she had no one to rebel against. Flicking her cigarette into the ashtray, she stared toward the Gulf. The rise and fall of the waves there reminded her of how small and insignificant her problems really were, and with each drag of the cigarette and each stroke of Lennon's hand on her leg, the troubles seemed further and further away.

* * *

"I've always loved these," Lennon said, admiring the outside of Alex's condo. Its bright blue paint contrasted so beautifully with the pink of the one next door and the green of the one beyond that. It was such an iconic housing unit, set right on the beach, that it often appeared on postcards for the area.

"Yeah, something about the bright beach vibe caught my eye that first day, and I couldn't imagine living anywhere else," Alex said as she unlocked the door. She swung her arms out in front of her as if she was laying down a welcome mat. "After you," she said.

Lennon stepped inside and took a deep breath. The scents of patchouli and rose lingered faintly in the air, and she closed her eyes to breathe them in, wondering if they came from a candle, incense, or maybe perfume. Wherever the origin, they were out of place in her world but were so perfectly fitting for Alex. The space was bright and airy and simply decorated, although Lennon figured that had more to do with Alex being new in town than anything else.

"Is this your work?" Lennon asked, walking over to the single painting on the wall, a silhouette of a woman kneeling on the shore of an angry sea. The grays, blacks, and deep blues evoked sadness from somewhere deep within Lennon's heart.

Behind her, Alex lit a candle and draped a tapestry throw over the small blue loveseat in the center of the room. "It is," she said, busying herself in the living room, never glancing in the painting's direction.

"It's stunning," Lennon said, staring at it. "Truly."

"Thank you," Alex said, coming up behind her and turning Lennon to face her. "Come here," she beckoned, grabbing the lapels of Lennon's shirt and pulling her backward until they tumbled on top of one another on the loveseat.

As Lennon straddled Alex, she glanced into the kitchen, where she saw a handful of simple items—a bottle of wine, a stack of tarot cards, a journal, and an array of pencils. All seemed harmless enough, but this mysterious artist whose fingers were now pumping inside Lennon seemed so out of place in this town.

Inhaling the earthy scents and relishing the aphrodisiac powers they held, she let go of her inhibitions. Grinding her hips into Alex, she quickened the pace and let out a moan. Reaching forward greedily, she tore at Alex's shirt and pulled it over her head, freeing her beautiful, perky breasts so she could feel the smooth skin beneath her fingers, eliciting a gasp from Alex's lips. As Alex moved inside her, ecstasy blurred her vision, and Lennon decided this delicious mystery was one she'd delight in solving.

CHAPTER SEVEN

The soft jazz music playing in the background and the candlelight in the dimly lit restaurant were clearly intended to create a romantic setting. But the only thing romantic about this place were the feelings Lennon had for her steak. Polishing off the meal, she wiped her mouth with her napkin and pushed her plate back.

Glancing up, she watched as her friends Natalie and Mike engaged in a small show of PDA across the table. She thought about clearing her throat but leaned over to Grant instead.

"Are you going to cuddle me like that?" she whispered, laughing quietly so as not to disturb the happy couple.

"Me?" he asked, amusement dancing in his dark eyes. "Why don't you ask your newfound out-of-town lover?"

"Did someone say 'lover?'" Natalie piped up from across the table. Her grin and raised eyebrow spelled trouble, and Lennon shook her head, elbowing Grant in the gut at the same time.

"Not at all," she answered with a smile.

"Oh, come on," Natalie said, her voice getting higher with each passing second. "Don't hold out on me. Now that I'm settled down"— she cast a sideways glance in Mike's direction— "I never get to hear any good gossip about the dating circle."

"There's nothing to tell, at least from me," Lennon said, crumpling her napkin and dropping it onto her plate.

She could feel Grant's eyes boring into her skull from the side. Instead of giving him the satisfaction, she focused her attention on the glass of red wine in front of her. Taking her time, she pulled it close, swirled the contents, and savored a sip.

"If you're not going to tell them, I will," Grant teased. She shot him a no-nonsense look, hardening her gaze with each second until he threw his hands up in mock surrender. "Never mind," he muttered.

Natalie cleared her throat, bringing the attention back to her across the table. She leaned forward until her chest was almost resting in what was left of her chicken parmesan. "Now you have to tell us," she said, keeping her voice low. "Or maybe Grant has some tales of his own to regale us with."

Lennon laughed as Natalie turned her attention toward Grant, who looked up at the ceiling coyly. "Well, I'm never one to Grindr and tell, but…" He smiled and gave an exaggerated shrug. "I have my fun here and there. Unfortunately, the love of my life, the muffin man, seems to have changed his shifts, so our paths never cross these days. It's truly a tragic tale."

"Damn." Natalie shook her head. "That is tragic. Speaking of tragic…" She grabbed her glass of white wine and leaned back. "Work is a nightmare. Some days I wish I'd found my niche like the two of you have." She sipped her wine and looked into the glass, as if it were a fountain for wishes. "Aside from the finances and the business side of things, your work doesn't follow you home too often, does it?"

"Sometimes you take it home. Or sometimes it takes you home and you disappear for…" Grant dramatically drummed his fingers on the table, grinning as he brought the conversation full circle, "four nights in a row, leaving your roommate to think you died or that you finally just U-hauled and started a new life with your new love."

Lennon rolled her eyes but laughed despite herself. "Sometimes there's some spillover from bar life to home…or… bedroom life," she admitted with a glance to the floor. "But that was weeks ago, and just because it was a few nights doesn't mean it's any more life-altering than your time with your Grindr men."

"So no U-haul and secret marriage, I guess?" Mike asked.

"Unfortunately no, although that is the dream," she shot back, taking a drink of her wine.

Natalie leaned closer, doing her best to position her body so that she blocked the view of Mike and Grant. "I hope it's the hot sex you deserve," she whispered, raising an eyebrow.

Lennon laughed and looked down at the ground. "I'll tell you about it later," she mouthed, soliciting a huge grin from Natalie. From college on, they'd shared too many details, and that wasn't going to stop now.

"In the meantime, I'm going to the restroom," she said, standing and pushing in her chair.

As she applied a fresh coat of lipstick in the bathroom mirror, her mind wandered. Where was Alex, and how was she doing? Lennon fished through her purse, pulling out her cell phone. She opened up the last text message from Alex and thought about reaching out. Her fingers hovered over the keyboard, and she looked up, staring at her reflection in the mirror.

Not today. She locked her phone screen and put it back in her purse. Taking a deep breath, she practiced the meditation she had been studying. Looking into the mirror, she analyzed the features she appreciated most. Her eyes were a rare color of blue, one that shone and sparkled as if she were a mythical creature. She smiled and felt her breathing return to normal. Aunt Bernie had always said her dimples, along with her bright white smile, held the power to light up a room. Gripping the sink, she reminded herself she didn't need someone by her side. Flipping her curls back, she smiled at her reflection and headed back to the table.

"I took care of it," Grant said, rising when she returned to the table. "Just to make up for all the hell I've given you." He smiled and held out his arm for her. As they rounded the corner to exit the restaurant, he pulled her in closer. "Sorry for telling them about your girlfriend."

"Thanks for dinner, and I'm sorry for making you spill about the muffin man."

"It's still fresh," he said, feigning tears.

"I know," she joked, patting his arm. "We'll find you a new pastry maker."

"Where are we headed?" she called out to Mike and Natalie, who were steps ahead of them, in an active effort to ignore Grant's antics.

"Flora-Bama," Mike said, turning around and offering her a smile. "We figured we all needed a night to let loose a little, maybe dance if we feel like it and drink away the worries of the week."

She raised an eyebrow, laughing at him as he walked backward, attempting to do his best dance moves while still walking hand in hand with Natalie. "Don't you two lovebirds have work tomorrow?"

"You're only in your twenties once," he said, laughing as he turned back around to watch where he was going. *Twenties.* That ship had sailed for her. She shook her head. Since she'd changed her major three times—from psychology to culinary arts and then finally to business—and worked her way through school, she'd ended up a few years older than Natalie and the rest of her graduating classmates.

"Yeah, and it all hurts a bit more by those early thirties," she said, but she didn't make an effort to stop.

"What are you worried about?" Grant asked, careful to keep his voice low. He looked down in her direction with his forehead knit together in concern. "You're never opposed to an evening of fun."

"I'm not worried," she said, scrunching her face up to make him laugh. "It's just been a weird week, and I wanted to make sure they knew what they were in for. I'm off tomorrow, and I know you don't have to go in until six. I just didn't want them to feel like hell tomorrow and blame us."

"Never party with the bartender unless you can play in the big leagues," he said nudging her. "They know the rules."

"Fair enough."

In front of them, Natalie stopped and turned around. "Lennon, come up here and walk with me. The guys can do their thing while we catch up."

"What's up?" Lennon asked, coming up beside her as she and Mike traded places.

"Nothing really." Natalie hesitated. "I just wanted to spend a little time with you. I figured I'd let the guys be guys back there so you and I could hang out. It seems like we haven't done that in forever."

Lennon cast a look over her shoulder. "You're right. It seems like we've always got these two tagging along." She laughed. "Seriously, it's like we're on some sort of weird type of double date."

"You two do make a cute couple," Natalie said, making a joke of how often they were told just that.

"My parents are still on that track," Lennon said, shaking her head.

"One day he's going to find his Prince Charming, or you're going to find the queen you deserve, or your parents will just wake up from their homophobic dream and they'll let it go."

"God, I hope so." Lennon laughed.

"In the meantime, I meant what I said at the table." Natalie nudged her and smiled. "I hope it's the best sex of your life."

Lennon laughed, keeping her voice low. "It's in the running," she whispered. "I'll fill you in at some point."

"Deal."

"For now, let's focus on the most important decision of the night," Lennon said with a wry smile.

"Which is?"

"Obviously, we have to answer the age-old question."

Natalie shook her head, looked up as if trying to remember what Lennon was referencing.

"Vodka or tequila." Lennon laughed. "You're killing me here. What are we drinking?"

"Tequila," they said almost in unison, then smiled.

"I'm glad we agree," Lennon said, holding the door open for Natalie as they reached the bar.

She watched as Mike walked up to Natalie and kissed her as though he'd been away from her for days instead of a mere five minutes. She slipped through the crowd while they caught up. Sidling up to the bar, she made eye contact with the bartender. He nodded in her direction.

"Double 1800 silver on the rocks with a splash of lime," she said, rattling off the order.

As he set to work making her drink, she glanced down to the end of the bar. She laughed and shook her head. Grant and the others had made their way to a table on the other side of the bar. Grabbing her drink and handing over the cash, she tapped the bar top with her free hand, weighing her options. She waved at their table, getting Grant's attention and holding up a finger to signal she'd be over in a minute. Then she walked over to the only occupied seat at the bar and climbed onto the barstool beside the woman sitting there.

"Hey," she said, leaning her elbow on the bar, hoping she looked as casual as she was trying to appear.

Alex jumped and turned around slowly, making eye contact before breaking into a smile. "Hey." The word came across as almost a laugh. She shook her head, questions dancing in her eyes. "What are you doing here?"

"Weird coincidence, I guess." She shifted her weight, lacking anything more substantial to say. She took a sip of her drink and gestured to the table in the corner. "I'm with a group of friends. This is one of our go-to spots when we're out on the town." Alex nodded and looked down. She traced the outline of her straw with her finger and swirled it around in her drink, seemingly choosing her words every bit as carefully as Lennon was trying to do.

"I was going to text you to see how you were doing," Lennon said when Alex didn't respond.

"No, you weren't." Alex smiled. Her response held no edge, just truth.

Lennon looked down. She lifted her hand, opening her mouth in preparation to speak, but dropped it just as quickly. With a sigh, she nodded. "You're right," she admitted. Folding her hands together in her lap, she offered a sheepish grin. "But I did think about it, if that counts for anything."

"No worries," Alex said, taking a sip of her drink. Lennon watched as her lips closed around the small cocktail straw and remembered the feeling of her kiss. Exhaling hard, she tried to ignore the shivers that went through her. "All is good, though. I've finished a couple of paintings, and I sold one I did of the Gulf right after I arrived."

"Congratulations." Lennon beamed as she raised her glass in the air. "Cheers."

"Cheers." Alex tapped her glass with Lennon's. After taking a drink, she turned her chair to face Lennon's. "You know you don't have to make excuses for things like not texting. We agreed to as much."

"I know." Lennon took a minute to gather her thoughts. "I felt a pang of guilt and wasn't sure what else to say. But I did think about reaching out. I just wasn't sure if it was in either of our best interests."

"Probably not." Alex shook her head as she downed the rest of her drink. "But I'm not sure anything we've done so far was in our best interest."

"Come on. You're kidding, right?" Lennon leaned in closer so only Alex could hear. "We had mind-blowing sex. How is that not in our best interests?"

Alex smiled and bit her lip. She took a deep breath and nodded. "It was mind-blowing, wasn't it?"

Lennon tensed at the thought of the passion they'd shared. She nodded her head and raised an eyebrow. "It sure was."

"Hey…" She heard Grant's voice approaching. "There you are." His voice trailed off as he looked from Lennon to Alex. "Nice to see *you* again," he said, smiling and recovering quickly from his confusion.

"Nice to see you as well," she said. Turning back to Lennon, she nodded to her drink. "I'll let you get back to your evening with your friends. I'm just having some drinks and then I'm going to call it a night."

"I…" She started to protest, but with Grant standing there, it felt much more awkward than it had only seconds before. She turned her attention to Grant. "I'll be right over. Just going to order another drink."

He nodded and grinned before turning away.

"Are you going to stick around, or are you going to dart off and never come back?" she asked Alex, hoping for the first.

Alex toyed with the bar napkin and looked up, as if contemplating her options. "I'll stick around for a bit," she said after a moment.

Her sweet voice and gentle mannerisms were driving Lennon crazy—in all the right ways. She smiled and signaled the bartender. She ordered two drinks, one for her and one for Alex. "Care to join me at the table?"

"Maybe later," Alex said, giving the group a sideways glance. "For now, I'll hang out here and listen to the band. You go. I'm a big girl. I can take care of myself."

"I know you can," Lennon said, taking her drink. She slid off the barstool and slid Alex's drink closer to her. When she did, her hand brushed against Alex's and she thought she might explode from the sheer electricity she felt running between them. "I'll see you in a bit," she added, breathlessly turning to walk away. With each step she took, her heart warred between staying where her body wanted to be and going where her mind knew was the safer option.

"Just a girl you met in a bar?" Natalie snickered as Lennon took her seat at the table again.

"Strangely enough, yes," Lennon said, no longer up for their little games. "Multiple times at that. I've met her multiple times in a bar by random coincidence."

"You know what they say about fate," Natalie said with a wide smile before taking a long drink of her margarita. "But enough of that for now."

The others went back to their conversation about an upcoming party, but Lennon's mind wasn't at the table. Chewing on the inside of her lip, she wondered if she should get some input from those who knew her best. What she felt when she saw Alex was making her blur the line between the physical and the emotional every time. She felt like she knew nothing about the woman, but at the same time like she had known her forever. It was mind-boggling, and as much as she'd tried to sort it out, she was falling short.

"Get a grip," she whispered to herself.

"What?" Grant asked, snapping his head in her direction.

"I didn't say anything," she protested, but she knew that she had expressed her thoughts verbally.

"You're acting so weird tonight," he said, laughing as he pushed her glass of tequila closer to her. "Drink up, and get out of your head."

Pressing her lips together, she nodded. "Sorry." She wished she had a hectic workweek or something to blame, but Grant would see right through that, given that they shared a workspace.

"Want to go with me to order another round?" Grant asked, breaking into her thoughts with a nudge in the arm.

She looked at him confused and pointed to her still-full glass. He smiled and shook his head, pointing to the empty glasses of everyone else at the table. "I'll need extra hands to help me carry it."

"Right," she said, nodding. Standing, she followed him.

Once they were out of earshot, but not quite to the bar, he turned toward her. "Go for it," he said, keeping his tone gentle. "We're not going to judge you for it. I think they remember what single life was like." He glanced back over to where their friends were snuggled up in the corner. "Maybe they don't," he said, laughing, "but I do. Go have some fun."

"I think I might," she said, looking over to where Alex sat. When she turned back to tell him "bye," he had already turned and walked away, headed for the bathroom, leaving her standing there. Turning back to look at Alex, Lennon saw the way she sat, poised with her shoulders back, her head held high, and one leg crossed elegantly over the other. Even from the back view atop a barstool, she was a sight to behold.

She took a deep breath and walked back to Natalie and Mike. "Thanks for a great evening," she said, giving each of them a hug. "I'm going to take care of something, and I'll be in touch so we can grab a drink soon."

"Call me soon," Natalie said, squeezing her hand. "Promise?"

"Promise," she said, flashing an exaggerated smile before she made her way back to the bar.

"I'm back," she said, the smile on her face making her voice higher.

Alex turned around in her barstool, her smile gleaming. "I knew you would be," she said, letting out a low laugh. "So what is it you want to do, Lennon? You want to sit here and down drinks until we lower our inhibitions enough to fuck, or do you want to go ahead and get out of here?"

Lennon shook her head. "You are so blunt." She laughed. "But I appreciate that. It's different."

"What'll it be?" Alex's confidence shone through her challenge.

"Let's get out of here," Lennon said, setting her full drink on the bar top as she considered her options. "But let's go grab a beer somewhere quieter. I'll take you to my favorite beer joint up the road. It's just a short walk down the street, and we can have a good conversation over there."

"I may be blunt," Alex said, handing the bartender her card to close out her tab, "but you've always got surprises."

Lennon feigned surprise. "Sometimes I shock myself too," she said, smiling as Alex slid down from her barstool. Looping her arm through Alex's, she tried to still her quickened heart rate. As they strolled down the streets, she couldn't discern exactly what she felt. Excitement, fear, uncertainty, curiosity and lust swirled around inside her, crafting a cocktail potent enough to knock even the most seasoned vet off her stool.

CHAPTER EIGHT

A slight ocean breeze swept through the air, bringing with it a brief chill Alex hadn't expected. Her bare arms prickled in the wind, and she shivered. Wordlessly, Lennon wrapped her arm around her waist and pulled her closer, offering her body as a comfort.

The move was touching and unnerving all at once, a combination that threatened to play tricks on Alex's mind. She closed her eyes, warding off an emotional onslaught as she realized this was the first physical contact she'd had with another person since her last encounter with Lennon.

Like flashing lights, the warning signs dinged in her head, telling her to steer clear of the dangers of dependence. But as Lennon opened up the lines of communication, she was helpless to stop herself from investing her attention.

"How do you like it here so far?" Lennon asked.

"You've asked me that in a variety of ways multiple times," Alex answered slowly, carefully choosing her words. She smiled. "I do like it here, though. I've always lived close to the water, so I definitely appreciate that, even if this is a totally different atmosphere than I'm used to. And the people are nicer. There's something to be said for that Southern charm you hear everyone talking about. That said, I'm not sure I'm what the South had in mind for a good ol' Southern gal."

Lennon stopped walking and turned to face her. "What do you mean by that? Has someone been rude to you or made you feel as though you don't belong?" Her tone was serious and protective.

Alex laughed and shook her head. "No." She knitted her brow. "No one has been rude or suggested I don't belong here. Things just seem a little more conservative than where I'm from."

"More conservative than California?" Lennon raised an eyebrow. "I'd say that's a given, but hopefully you encounter more of that Southern charm than you do of the handful of assholes who live around here. And if anyone does mess with you, you know where to find me."

"Thanks," Alex said. They'd agreed to a hookup scenario, but somehow Lennon whisking her out of the bar for a night of quiet conversation and offering protection against the town idiots felt more intimate. She eyed Lennon curiously, silently questioning her motives.

Lennon nodded and continued walking, blissfully unaware of the war raging within Alex's mind. "Where are we going?" Alex asked after a moment.

"A little hole in the wall spot. I think you'll like it." Lennon smiled, then stopped walking again. "You do like beer, don't you?"

Alex crinkled her nose. "I haven't drunk much of it to tell you the truth, so I'm not sure."

Lennon's mouth fell open. Alex laughed at her reaction, noting that Lennon couldn't maintain a poker face if she tried.

"I'd love to try it," Alex said before Lennon could respond. "I'm sure it's better than the PBR and Keystone I was offered at high school parties." She looked Lennon up and down. "It seems like you have good taste in alcohol," she said with a smile.

"You think?" Lennon asked, laughing. "You can smell boozehound from that far away, can you?"

Alex shook her head. "Let's keep going," she said.

"Right," Lennon said, picking up the pace. "I'm sorry. I forgot you were getting chilled." She ran her fingers over the thin material of Alex's tank top. Alex's breath caught in her throat. "I can't imagine why." She pointed to Alex's attire. "But let's get you inside."

They rounded the corner, and Lennon held open the door, letting Alex walk inside first.

"What do you recommend?" Alex said, scanning the list of craft beers written on a chalkboard menu behind the bar.

Lennon looked at Alex, looked at the menu, and then looked back to Alex, peering into her eyes as if she was staring into her soul. "For a first timer, I'd recommend something light, maybe a blonde."

"Blondes usually aren't my thing," Alex said with a laugh, "but I'll give it a go."

Shaking her head and giving her a goofy smile, Lennon stepped up to the counter and placed her order. "I'll have a Wicked Rooster IPA and a Scallywag Blonde."

Alex laughed hearing the comical words roll off Lennon's tongue with ease.

"Thank you," she mouthed, accepting the drink when Lennon handed it over to her.

"Over there." Lennon pointed to a table in the corner.

Once seated, Alex took a sip of her beer. Across from her, Lennon watched, amusement and anticipation evident in her expressions. Tapping her foot, she waited until Alex swallowed the drink. "What do you think?"

"It's surprisingly not bad," Alex said, nodding as she wiped foam from her lips. "Considering the last beer I had was almost a decade ago at a house party, I'm assuming this is probably a little better quality."

"The things they deprive you of out there in California," Lennon said, laughing as she took a drink of her own beer. With her glass still in midair, she stopped. "I want to know more about you," she said, abruptly changing the tide of the conversation. "I want to know what you like and what you don't, where you come from, what your story is."

"Ah," Alex let out a deep breath and clasped her hands together. Tapping her foot, she considered her response. "Why the sudden interest?" she blurted out instead.

"You're different," Lennon said. She set her drink on the table. "That came out wrong, but you're not like anyone I've ever encountered. You're raw and honest, somehow confident but unsure all at the same time, and you're kind. You go out of your way to make sure you're not intruding on someone's time or space, and that type of awareness is rare. I just want to know what makes you tick."

"I'm the unicorn. Is that it?" Alex kept her tone even, wanting to keep Lennon on her toes, without giving away her own amusement.

"Fuck," Lennon muttered. "I sound like a jackass, don't I?"

Unable to fight it, Alex gave in to her laughter. "Not at all," she said after a moment. "I'm actually honored to hear you think of me that way, as some kind of complexity. I'm just teasing you."

Lennon playfully threw her hands up in the air. "I've been getting that a lot lately. No one seems willing to cut a girl some slack."

"My bad," Alex said, smiling to ease the blow to Lennon's ego even though they were bantering. "But to answer your many, many questions, I'll just give you an overview. I'm twenty-nine. Born and raised in northern California—not So-Cal. I like many things, but my favorites are art, books, camping, being outdoors in general, dogs, good wine, and enjoying conversations about real shit."

She rattled off the words like a laundry list, unsure of what it was Lennon wanted to know. She eyed her cautiously and leaned back to sip her beer.

"Real shit?" Lennon moved her head to the side and leaned in closer. "Tell me more."

"I'm not good at small talk," Alex said, drawing a circle in the frost on the beer glass. "I never have been. Don't get me wrong. I can put on a good face and talk with people in the grocery store and whatnot. I'm not rude or unpleasant, but I'm not good at the meaningless conversations. I like talking about issues or situations that have depth, rather than providing a list of my likes and dislikes."

"This..." Lennon said, extending her hand palm up across the table in a gesture to Alex, "this is why I wanted to talk more in-depth. Tell me what it is that's on your mind, and we'll skip the small talk."

"I have several things rolling around in my mind right now."

"Shoot," Lennon said, leaning back and crossing her legs.

Alex took a deep breath and gulped down another mouthful of beer. Clearing her throat, she leaned back and crossed her legs as well, in an effort to settle into a more comfortable spot. "I'm curious," she said, after a moment. "About you. About this place. About everything that lies ahead. I'm in a brand-new town, without my usual comforts or support system."

She stopped and looked off to the wall. Taking another deep breath, she shook her head. She turned her attention back to Lennon and propped her head on her hand. "For that matter, I'm questioning how solid a support system I had in the first place if only one person from back home has even reached out to see how I'm doing. I keep replaying the debacle that took place right before I fled California and wondering if my tendency to wreak destruction on everything that's going well played a part in what happened. I'm in the midst of dealing with a bit of depression, and while I know I should be doing normal human things like eating and sleeping, I'm failing at that. Also, on a lighter note, I'm wondering if I'm going to like it here and what role you play in this whole mix."

Lennon nodded, sipping her beer. Her eyes darkened as she appeared to mull over the words Alex had thrown out.

"I'm sorry to hear your support system wasn't better," she said. "Depression is a bitch, isn't it?" She nodded, silently answering her own question. "Been there, done that. I get it, and I'm glad you're open to talking about it. It's always a bit easier to manage when you put it into words."

She paused to sip her beer. "As for me, I don't want to muddle or confuse anything. I know you're in a tough place, and I am too. I just want to get to know you. I feel like you're far too interesting and kind to be ignored as though you didn't affect me, when clearly you have."

"I affected *you*?" Alex raised an eyebrow and gave Lennon a sideways smile.

"I'm sitting here, aren't I?" Lennon shrugged. "Anyway, I like it—the 'real shit' you speak of," she said, adding air quotes for emphasis. "It's genuine. So in honor of talking about real shit, I have to ask the most important question of the night."

Alex placed her beer glass on the table and leveled her gaze at Lennon. "Okay," she said, drawing out her response. "I think I'm ready."

"Good." Lennon took a deep breath. "Sasquatch, aliens, and ghosts. Do you believe or not?"

Alex shook her head, laughing. "You're something else, you know?"

"Well, are you going to answer or not?" Lennon's eyes widened in anticipation. "I'm very interested in your answers."

"Okay." Alex bit her lip. "Sasquatch…" She winced. "Nope. Aliens, for sure. Ghosts, I've seen them."

"Hold on a minute." Lennon raised her hand to motion for a full stop. "We'll circle back to the rest of it. But why such a quick no to Sasquatch?"

"*That's* the thing you're holding on to?" Alex laughed. "You don't care that I've seen ghosts, but it's all about a Yeti?"

"Yeah." Lennon took a sip of her beer. "That Yeti matters."

"Okay then, what about you?"

Lennon put her beer on the table and leaned forward. "One hundred percent believe in Sasquatch. I'm a bit iffy on aliens, but could probably be convinced, and I believe in ghosts or spirits or…something."

"I could feign just as much shock that you're iffy on aliens," Alex said, playfully putting her hands on her hips, "but I'll respect your beliefs."

"I just find it hard to believe that someone who loves camping and the outdoors doesn't think that there's something more lurking in the woods," Lennon challenged with a good-natured grin.

"All right," Alex said with a laugh. "My turn for a 'real shit' question. What's your favorite song to belt out at the top of your lungs?"

"Of all time? Or current favorite?"

"I'll take either answer," Alex said, her smile growing as she tried to figure out what made Lennon tick.

"I'd have to say Joni Mitchell's 'A Case of You,' although it's far too high and varied in pitch for me to do anything but butcher it." Lennon's deep laugh rang through the air, and Alex raised an eyebrow, wondering what her throaty voice would sound like as she sang the song. "What about you?"

"I'd go with 'What's Up' by 4 Non Blondes. Hands down, my favorite." She smiled, reaching across the table and running her fingers across Lennon's palm. The move was risky, but she couldn't resist. "Can I have one more question?"

"Shoot."

"I want to know what you're thinking. No holding back either. I don't want anything sugar-coated."

Lennon straightened her shoulders. She looked into Alex's eyes, and Alex could see her weighing her options. She nodded, took a deep breath, and grabbed the edge of the table.

"I like talking with you," Lennon said after a moment. "I like not holding back on the weirdness or the deep stuff. It's kind of nice." She furrowed her brow and looked up, making eye contact before diverting it. "It feels weird to throw it all out there with someone I've slept with," she added, taking a long drink.

"It's all good," Alex said, raising her near-empty glass in the air. "Cheers to a little transparency, something it seems our generation is getting better at. What do you say we have another one? I've got this round," she added, standing up and walking over to the bar when Lennon nodded.

As she waited on their drinks to be poured, she watched Lennon out of the corner of her eye. Her confusion evident, she was opening and closing her mouth as though she were replaying their conversation mentally. Alex smiled and shook her head. Together they made one strange connection, but it was a raw connection, and that was something—a solid foundation for a friendship, no matter how messy.

She bit the inside of her cheek and straightened her shoulders, wanting to make a good impression instead of just being that weird girl from out of town. Lost in her thoughts, she jumped when the bartender cleared his throat, gesturing at the beers that were ready for her. She thanked him and grabbed them, scurrying back over to the table.

"Thank you," Lennon said, her drawl coming in thicker after a beer. "I appreciate it."

"Of course." Alex slid back into her seat and propped her elbows up on the table, framing her face with her hands. She dropped her hands to the table and clasped them together, opting to forgo the cutesy effort. "Where were we?"

"Just getting into the details of who we are, I suppose." Lennon looked down at her hands, as if trying to decide whether or not to add to her statement. "Will you answer a question for me?" she asked, looking back up to meet Alex's gaze.

"Absolutely. After all, we're baring our souls here," she said.

"Do you want to let go of the stupid restrictions we put into place?"

Alex stiffened in her chair, waiting for further explanation.

Lennon cleared her throat, shook her head, and then gulped a large drink of her beer. Putting her palms down on the table, she leaned back in her chair.

"We set all these parameters on what we should and shouldn't do, without really saying as much. So much so that it felt as if one of us should feel awkward for being in the same bar as the other. So much so that even when I wanted to text you to check in, I didn't because I didn't feel like it was appropriate. What do you say we say 'screw appropriate' and just live?"

"And what does that just living entail?" Alex smiled, both scared and excited at the possibility of blurring the lines and breaking the rules. Her heart longed for freedom without rules. She gulped, though. What risk did it hold?

"It means if we want to hang out, we do." Lennon took in a deep breath. A smile fell over her face. "It means if we enjoy each other's company, especially while you're just getting settled and don't want to feel all alone in a new place and while I'm enjoying being around you as much as I do, let's cut through the bullshit and stop placing so many limits—spoken or unspoken—on what we can and can't do."

"I like it." Alex nodded slowly, considering the proposal. "But still nothing serious, right?"

"Of course not," Lennon smiled. Her shoulders relaxed as she grabbed her beer glass. "That wouldn't be a good deal for either of us right now."

"Then I think it sounds like a good plan," Alex said, unclenching her jaws and relieving some of the tension she held. "Where does that plan lead us after we finish these beers?" She smiled seductively, hoping she already knew the answer.

"Your place or mine, as long as you're game." Lennon winked.

Alex let out a heavy breath and nodded. One of these days, she'd find a way to tell Lennon how that wink undid everything in the fibers of her resolve. For now, she'd drink her beer and follow wherever the night may lead her.

Focusing her attention on her beer, she took a sip and let the tastes mingle on her tongue. She looked up and saw Lennon's stunning blue eyes staring into hers. "What is it?"

"You looked like you were savoring every drop," Lennon noted. "I was just watching you."

Alex's cheeks burned, and she knew they were showing redness. "It's tasty," she said, grinning. "I really think I might like it more than I anticipated." Under Lennon's stare, her lust built. She wanted nothing more than to feel Lennon's lips against hers.

Throwing caution to the wind, she leaned across the table and kissed Lennon deeply. When she leaned back, Lennon's hand grabbed hers, and their fingers intertwined.

"That's what just living looks like, right?" Alex asked, running her finger across her bottom lip, confident that wherever this path led, it would be a journey worth taking.

CHAPTER NINE

Sinatra was blaring throughout the house accompanied by the smells of the shrimp diavolo simmering in the kitchen. Grant sang along, toasting himself with his glass of champagne. He tried to drown out Lennon's little giggles and the sound of her typing on her phone and embrace the fact that his dinner party for two had practically turned into a dinner party for one, since she'd long since stopped listening to a word he said. Sitting across from him, she was engaged in what appeared to be a very in-depth texting conversation ever since she'd offered to help out with the cooking.

"Put that thing down," he finally snapped, his impatience getting the best of him.

"Sorry." She grinned sheepishly and set her phone down on the table. "I was just…"

"You were texting Alex," he said, shaking his head. "Don't bother coming up with an excuse."

"I…" she started, but he held up the tongs in his hand and snapped them in front of her.

"Don't worry about it. It's fine," he said, setting down the tongs and reaching for the glass of champagne he'd poured for her. Handing it to her, he smiled. "I'm happy to see you happy. I just also want to hang out with you."

"I know," she said, nodding too quickly. He could tell she was frazzled, but he knew better than to push the subject. If he asked too many questions, she would shut down entirely and he would be left eating dinner in silence as she sulked.

"Have I told you lately that…" he started, and she shook her head, a laugh bubbling up from deep inside of her.

"I'm your hero?" she asked playfully.

He nodded. "It's true. Now get in here and help me chop this salad. I need my sous chef."

She rolled her eyes but smiled in his direction and set to work chopping the vegetables and the mozzarella.

"How's that going by the way?" he asked in the silence between songs.

"It's good," she answered, but her words came out too quickly, too pointed.

"What is it?" He stepped closer, lowering his gaze to make eye contact.

She opened her mouth and shut it, then reached for her champagne. "Nothing new to report," she said, downing the glass and handing it back to him for a refill.

"The lies you tell," he teased. "There's some kind of report in there, but on another note, let's change the subject. Let's talk about me."

She laughed and nodded. "Yes, let's. That's something we haven't touched on in a while," she said.

"You know it's my favorite subject," he said, keeping his voice deadpan. "But anyway, I was thinking that maybe you and I could go out on Saturday after we get off. I checked the schedule and we're both working afternoon shifts. We should be done by nine, unless it gets crazy. After that, let's hit the town, and you can play wingman for me."

"Why can't we play wingman for each other?"

He slid in between her and the vegetables and placed his hands on his hips, staring at her with curiosity.

"You know that's dangerous when I have a knife in my hand," she said, shaking her head.

"It was worth the risk," he said. "Why on earth would *you* need a wingman?"

"I told you this was nothing serious." She glanced into the salad bowl, avoiding eye contact. "We don't have a label. We're not exclusive. She's free to do as she pleases, and so am I."

He nodded and slid back down the counter. Wiping his hands on the dishtowel, he stared at her. Paying him no mind, she continued chopping, and he shook his head. Denial was strong. Normally, he'd call her out on it, but she seemed intent on keeping up the charade.

"So are you in or not?" he asked after a moment of silence.

"Saturday sounds good," she said, casually looking over her shoulder and offering a smile. "I'm in."

"Good," he said, plating the pasta as he talked. "After dinner, do you want to watch the new Superman flick?"

"Actually..." She drew the word out too long, and he already knew what was coming next. Before the words were out of her mouth, he reminded himself to keep his expressions neutral. "Alex is going to come over later tonight."

His expressions betrayed him, and he smirked. Forgoing neutrality, he poked her in the rib. Jumping, she cast him a serious look. "You know I'm ticklish."

"I know you are, just as much as you know I'm right about you and Alex," he said, mocking her serious face. "I don't know what it is with you lesbians, pairing up so damn quickly and then denying it. It's only been a few weeks."

Lennon raised her hand in the air, knife still in tow, and cut him off. "A little over a month," she corrected.

His smile grew, and he shook his head. "Whatever." He laughed. "So it's been a month—only a month—but y'all spend practically every night together." He waited for her response. When she gave none, he shook his head, setting the plates on the table. "You two are a cat adoption and a matching flannel photo shoot away from being a statistic."

Despite the faux anger in her eyes, she laughed. "I'm allergic to cats," was the only retort she offered.

"Let's eat," he said, pointing to the plates.

Her sass-filled stare was replaced with wide-eyed wonder as she looked at the pasta in front of her. "This looks amazing," she said, smiling up at him. "Thank you."

"You're welcome," he said, taking his seat. "But you're not off the hook. If the nightly lesbian slumber party is going to take place in this space we share and if this woman is going to take away my enjoyment of your post-breakup hang-out time, I want to know more."

Lennon unsuccessfully stifled a sigh and nodded. "You've been down in the trenches with me, and you've helped me through a lot of bullshit, so what is it you want to know?"

"What makes this one so special?"

In lieu of an answer, Lennon stuffed a large bite of pasta and shrimp into her mouth. Knowing she was just buying herself time, Grant spread out a napkin on his lap and waited. Wanting to push her buttons just a bit more, he laid his hands on the table. "Does she have nipples that taste like bacon?" Lennon coughed, almost choking on her shrimp, and scowled at him. "I mean, what is it?" he continued. "What flipped the switch in your head and said this one was worth breaking your rules?"

"You're an ass," she said as she swallowed. "It's not like I made any decision other than to see her more than once. And when I did, the world didn't end. I'm having fun. She's having fun. There's no harm. It is what it is."

"That's a poor excuse for an answer," he said, narrowing his eyes. He picked up his fork. "But anyway, we were going to talk about me."

"And you're the one who keeps changing the subject," she quipped. "Want to fill me in on the life and times of one Mr. Grant Brewer?"

"I'd love to," he said, his response mock-serious in tone. "In the life of Grant, not much is new, aside from the fact that I booked tickets today and I'm finally getting out of this town next month."

"Did you bite the bullet and decide it was time for your New York trip?"

He nodded proudly, his smile growing with each passing second. "I need to get away. As for Saturday, I need a little outing to get back in the game before I travel alone."

"Good," she said. "It'll be fun." She smiled, but it didn't quite reach her eyes. Instead, concern deepened their color, giving her away. But he didn't question it. Whatever was going on with her was far too complex for him to get involved with. He'd step in and be her shoulder to cry on if and when she needed him. For now, it was best to keep it lighthearted.

"What do you think of the shrimp diavolo?" he asked, pointing to her plate.

"It's so good I'm thinking about my options of marrying a food product," she said, this time giving him a genuine smile. "Thanks for keeping me fed."

"Someone has to," he teased. "The way you flit in and out of here, off to work, off to play, off to do..." he paused, deciding to let the worn-out joke fade into the evening, "other things."

Taking his cue to brush their banter under the rug, she smiled and continued eating. As she cleaned the kitchen later, he thought about asking her what time to expect Alex. His thoughts were interrupted by a knock on the door.

"I'll be in the living room," he said, making a beeline for the couch to get out of the way. Whatever was happening between them—lasting or not—he didn't want to be a hindrance.

"You can have a drink with us, if you'd like," Lennon said, drying her hands quickly on the dishtowel and stopping in front of the dining room mirror for a second to fluff her hair and apply a rose lipstick before heading to answer the door.

He waited to answer, watching her mouth fall open when she eyed Alex standing in the doorway. Dressed in a fitted black miniskirt and gold sleeveless blouse, complete with black stilettos, she looked ready to hit the town. Lennon looked down at her attire, jeans and a fitted baseball tee. Looking back at Alex, she glanced up and down, smiling.

Alex cleared her throat, and Lennon blushed. "Sorry," she said, catching her breath. "Come inside. I...uh...you look good."

"Thank you," Alex said, stepping beside her to enter.

"Do you want to go out?" Lennon asked, looking down again. "I can go change."

"No," Alex said, kissing her before stepping inside. "We can stick around here."

Grant waved from the living room, watching the scene unfold.

"Oh, hi," Alex called, returning his wave.

"Since we're staying in, how about we all have a drink?" Lennon asked, looking from Grant to Alex. Grant waited in silence, wanting to see how Alex would respond.

For someone who looked so sexed up and ready to party, it surprised him when she smiled good-naturedly. "I'd love that," she said, laying her purse on the dining room table.

He'd be the first to admit he'd had his reservations about this woman, but she glided around the room effortlessly as if she'd always belonged there. The thought made him stiffen. It was too much, too soon, even if Lennon didn't seem fazed by it.

As he mixed a batch of whiskey sours, he thought back to just a while back when Lennon wouldn't eat, couldn't sleep, and became a shell of who she was. Looking at her now, he could see that she still hadn't fully recovered.

Yet, as Alex fell in step beside Lennon, drying the dishes she washed, he watched with curiosity. He had to wonder how they even tried to pretend they weren't coupling up. As much as Lennon would deny it, her stubborn nature couldn't hide the inexplicable way that they were drawn to one another.

He shook his head, taking a sip of his drink to taste test, thankful that they seemed to have forgotten he was there. He wanted Lennon to be happy. He just hoped this was it, because he'd seen the crash and the fall before, and no one was ready for that storm.

CHAPTER TEN

Awakening to a gentle caress on her neck, followed by Alex's arms encircling her body, Lennon offered a lazy smile before she even opened her eyes. With Alex's naked flesh pressing against her own, she leaned back into the embrace. Alex ran her fingers through Lennon's hair, and although Lennon could hear her talking about how nice it was to touch the curls without reprimand for once, she kept her eyes closed, hoping to wait for conversation until she'd had coffee.

She couldn't count how many mornings had started this way since they'd made the decision a few weeks prior to remove the unspoken restrictions between them. But she wasn't about to complain. Slowly rolling over to face Alex, she smiled up at her, now propped up on one elbow, her brown eyes sparkling in the early morning light.

"Good morning," Lennon said, her voice still thick with sleep.

"Good morning to you," Alex said, trailing her fingers up and down Lennon's arm as she inched closer for a kiss.

Lennon welcomed the kiss, and as their lips met she couldn't ignore the tension mounting again in her body, but alongside it, the longing to feel Alex's hand in hers, Alex's body in her bed, Alex's laugh throughout her day.

She pulled back. "I think it's time for coffee."

"Are you sure it's time *right* now?" Alex pulled back the covers, displaying her naked body and biting her lip.

"Mmm-hmmm." Lennon nodded. They'd spent their share of days tangled up in the sheets already, but she wasn't going to get caught up in that today, not when her emotions seemed to be challenging their agreement. "Didn't you say you wanted to go to the beach today and rent kayaks?"

Alex sat up, her smile an obvious attempt to appear not fazed by Lennon's quick rebuff. She glanced toward the window and pointed her thumb in the direction of the yard. "You might want to take a look outside before we commit to that."

Before Lennon could respond, a clap of thunder boomed, shaking the house. "I guess we need to make other plans?" she asked with a laugh.

"Looks like it."

"Actually…" Lennon looked around the room, mentally taking note of all she *needed* to do. "I have a bunch of things that I should take care of if I'm not going to be off gallivanting and having a good time."

"Who says we can't gallivant *and* get things done?" Alex's playful smile elicited a laugh from Lennon, and she shook her head.

"Quite the problem solver, aren't you?"

Rising from the bed, Alex sauntered over to her side and stood in front of her. "Whatever you have to do, I'm happy to help," she said, her voice husky with desire, as she leaned in for a slow and lingering kiss. "And then, maybe we can have some fun indoors afterward."

Lennon moaned, pulling Alex in for another kiss. "I just can't fucking resist you," she whispered through a ragged breath, ignoring Alex's proposal completely. Clenching her teeth, she called upon on the few remaining strands of her willpower in order to stand, never letting go of her hold on Alex's soft hands.

"So I take it you're in?" Alex asked, shimmying her shoulders.

"I'm in." Lennon slipped into a pair of jeans and an Alibis tee and grabbed a blue and gray flannel to throw over it to complete the ensemble. Pulling her hair into a messy pile of curls on top of her head, she nodded to Alex. "Ready when you are."

Donning the skirt and tank she'd been wearing the night before, Alex glanced in the mirror briefly and nodded.

"Hold on," Lennon said, holding up a finger and rummaging through her closet. "Here." She tossed a hoodie in Alex's direction. "It's a little chilly."

Alex laughed as she pulled the garment over her head. "When I was a teenager, giving your hoodie to someone meant something," she said, popping her head through the top with a grin.

"Oh, it still does," Lennon said, nodding. "It means it's cold and I don't want you to freeze." She waited a second and stepped in for another kiss. "It's also my favorite hoodie, so it means I'm trusting you not to run off with it."

The weight of the unspoken insinuation hung in the air between them. Lennon waited, biting her tongue, waiting for Alex to speak. When she didn't, Lennon's heart beat faster. Had she stepped over a line? Whose line was it, anyway? Was she making the rules, or was Alex? She opened her mouth to speak, but Alex closed the distance, drawing her into a kiss.

"Let's get breakfast first," Alex said when she pulled away. She glided out the bedroom door, leaving Lennon speechless. She took a deep breath, pulling herself together before following.

After a stop at the bakery for bear claws and coffee, Lennon opened the back door of Alibis and ushered Alex inside. Outside the thunder roared and rain poured down in torrents, but as she turned on the lights and brought the bar to life, she silently rejoiced. This place was always a welcome hideout on days like today. While she wasn't behind the bar tonight, she still had some tweaks to make to the new menu and the inventory list.

She perused the menu she'd left on the counter, grabbing a pen and crossing out items that hadn't arrived in their shipment for the week. With a smile, she nodded as she read through the new drink list. Sweater Weather was going to be their biggest hit of the seasonal drinks, she was sure, although the Lotta Sap—which contained maple syrup and got its name from *Christmas Vacation*, her favorite Christmas movie—was sure to get a lot of orders for the sheer comedic value.

Finally adding some light snacks to the menu was going to be an undertaking, so she'd kept it easy with a hummus and veggie tray, roasted nuts, and a charcuterie board. Making a couple of notes for their marketing manager, she put the list back in its place.

"What can I do to help?" Alex asked, breaking the silence after a few minutes.

"First of all, pick some music if you'd like," Lennon said, handing Alex the tablet connected to their speaker system. "Then come join me in the back."

Alex raised an eyebrow, and Lennon laughed, despite the fact that the simple movement sent her mind into a flurry of fantasies about taking Alex right there in the place she'd worked so hard to build, a celebration of her successes. She shook her head, thankful Alex had turned her attention to the tablet in her hand, and walked back toward the storeroom.

Unsure of when her raging teenage hormones had returned, she shoved her hands in her pockets and looked around the room. She had bigger problems to focus on, like the fact that whoever had been here when the last shipment had arrived had done absolutely nothing to organize the product. Unopened cardboard boxes of liquor were stacked about the room in a haphazard manner, and nothing had been sorted, let alone counted to allow for an overview of what all was needed for the new concoctions they planned to start serving in just a week's time.

Wasting no time, she took off her flannel, draping it over the chair in the corner, walked over to the pile, and grabbed a box. Poison blared from the speakers overhead, and Alex walked into the room, stopping in the doorway to look Lennon up and down.

She let out a low whistle. "Look at those arms," she called, moving her left arm into a flex. "The guns are out today," she added, waggling her eyebrows playfully.

"You are so cheesy," Lennon said, even though she couldn't stifle her laughter.

"You like it." Alex walked over to pick up a box and bring it over to where Lennon had set a similar one.

"I do," she admitted. "If you want to sort them all by spirit and bring them over here, that would be amazing," she said, pointing to the rows she had outlined on a chart along the back wall.

"Anything for the biggest fan of my comedy." Alex chuckled as she set to work. She sang along to each of the classic rock songs that played, and in between unboxing and checking items off the list, Lennon watched her out of the corner of her eye. Somehow she fit into this world as easily as she fit in with old beach hippies, the polished art critics, and the tourists at the local galleries they'd visited together. She seemed to be at ease and put others around her at ease, but with Lennon, she did far more than that. She brought peace, but also beauty, uncertainty, and so much life.

"You're something else," Lennon said, shaking her head in awe.

"This old thing?" Alex said, pointing playfully to herself with her head tilted to the side.

"Stop," Lennon said, standing from where she sat and placing the clipboard in her hand on the desk. "I guess I'm just trying to thank you. I know you had your heart set on a beach day, and now you're helping me work."

"I'm having a good time," she said, leaning against the wall. "I'm just hanging out with you, and getting a little weight lifting in so maybe one day I can have guns like those." She cast her glance back to Lennon's arms, and Lennon basked in the compliment for a moment. Years of hard work in the gym followed by years of heavy lifting around here had left her with a toned physique, and her arms were her favorite attribute.

"Really, though," Lennon said. "Thank you. Not just for this, but for making the last couple of months as fun as they've been."

"It's been fun for me too," Alex said, walking by just close enough to grab Lennon's ass. "Really, you don't have to thank me. I was going to hang out with you either way, and I'm enjoying your occasional laughter at my dad jokes." She turned and walked toward the last remaining box. "After all, once we finish up here, I've got plans for us for the rest of the day."

"Oh yeah?"

"Yeah!" Alex's smile beamed. "You've showed me your world—well, the parts of it that are behind the scenes, and, honestly, the not-behind-the-scenes parts of a bar are so much cooler. But I digress. You've showed me your process, and I'm going to show you mine."

"I like it." Lennon stood. "But if I'm really going to show you the behind-the-scenes bit, I have to take just a little more of your time."

"For what?"

"You'll see once we go back in there," Lennon said, pointing to the bar top. "Take a seat."

"Do I have to go back to the other side? Doesn't that negate the point of the behind-the-scenes bit?" Rather than waiting for an answer, Alex pulled out a chair tucked below the bar and sat down. Shimmying in her seat, she giggled as though she'd gotten away with something.

"Make yourself at home." Turning toward the fridge, Lennon studied the ingredients, suddenly wanting nothing more than to add a little excitement to Alex's day. She'd have to do it the only way she knew how—by combining a handful of ingredients to make a taste so memorable it held the power to transform an ordinary day.

Selecting a handful of items from the fridge, she set them on the counter and perused the shelves of liquor in front of her. Homing in on her pick, she slid the ladder along the wall and climbed up until she reached the top shelf. As she climbed down, she glanced over to Alex, who was watching with her brow crinkled.

"Is that a beet?" she asked, pointing to the pile of ingredients Lennon had left on the counter.

"Beets are the unsung heroes of the kitchen, and I think you'll like it."

"I love beets," Alex said, shaking her head. "I just thought this was…you know…a bar?" Her voice rose sweetly in bemusement.

"It may be just a beet, but it'll still pack a punch."

"Oh, and I'm the only one with dad jokes?" Alex laughed. "Well, hit me with your best shot."

"Make it stop," Lennon said, laughing as she set to work, first creating a cold pressed juice, then melding the flavors of the ginger, beet juice, lemon, bitters and whiskey. When she finished, she presented the cocktail to Alex, whose eyes grew as she took in the sight.

"It's a work of art," Alex said, leaning back to admire it better before placing it to her lips and taking a sip. "Wow! It actually is really good too."

"You sound surprised," Lennon said, feigning offense.

"I'm not," she said. Setting the drink down, she stood and pulled Lennon into an embrace. She wrapped her arms around Lennon's waist and inched her closer. "I'm just impressed. You took a motley bunch of ingredients and created a masterpiece."

"That's the process," Lennon said, scraping her teeth gently across Alex's neck and trailing kisses along her soft skin as she ventured back toward her mouth. "I can't wait to see yours."

Behind them, the back door slammed closed, and Lennon jumped back as if she'd been caught red-handed.

"At ease," Grant called out, laughter ringing through his voice. "I'm just grabbing my phone charger. I left it here last night."

Alex's lips twisted into a half grin, and she handed her glass to Lennon, as if she sensed Lennon's discomfort. She took a sip, nodded, and handed it back. "Thanks. Finish that up, and we'll head out."

As she cleaned up the materials she'd used, Lennon's thoughts ran rampant. What was Grant going to say about this whole ordeal? He'd already been giving her hell about how much time they'd been spending together, and her responses were starting to sound like excuses, even to herself.

She sighed and glanced up to the spot above the sink where she'd stashed a sticky note a while back. *Be in the moment.* She took a deep breath, trying to ground herself, and dried her hands on a towel. She grabbed Alex's hand and her things and waved a quick goodbye to Grant on the way out.

* * *

"So what's the game plan?" Lennon asked, carrying an armful of grocery bags into Alex's condo. "We've got the snacks and the wine, but what sneak peek do I get?" She set the bags on the counter and turned to face Alex.

"I hope you're not insinuating anything." Alex's laugh filled the air, and she looped her fingers through Lennon's belt loops, pulling her close. "I've already given you a pretty good peek or two, I think."

"I'd say you have." Lennon put her arms around Alex's waist and couldn't stop a smile from spreading across her face. "But if it's not *that*, what could it be? Do I get to see the master at work?"

Alex nodded and smiled. "I was thinking paint and wine day at home. I have a canvas for you too."

"Oh." Lennon cast her eyes to the ground and shuffled her feet. "I'm not so great at that. I'm really good at wine, but I don't know anything about art."

"You don't have to." Alex placed a finger to Lennon's lips and slipped out of the embrace. Walking over to the large freestanding cabinet in the corner, she threw open the doors, displaying a myriad of paints, pencils, easels, books, and canvasses. Lennon's eyes widened as she took in the sight. She knew Alex would have to have a pretty impressive setup to paint professionally, but this was an incredible picture of organized chaos. "You can paint whatever you want, and we can erase the canvas if you want."

"Erase it?" Lennon stepped forward, dutifully taking the blank canvas handed to her, even though she wasn't sure she wanted it. She held it out in front of her, staring at it as if it was an unidentified foreign object. "But it's paint," she said, shaking her head in confusion.

"I'll show you," Alex said, nonchalantly waving her hand. "While it's wet, there's nothing a little water won't fix."

"Are you like my personal Bob Ross, guiding me through my happy little accidents?"

"Something like that. But I've seen you in action. You're poised and put together and so creative. Whatever you make is going to be perfectly yours." She gathered supplies from the closet and set them on the table. "Come on. Let's pop the cork on one of those bottles and get set up."

"Ah, the wine," Lennon said, laying her canvas on the table and almost running toward the kitchen. "I'm on that. That's my specialty." Thankful that Alex had a corkscrew already out on the counter, she busied herself pouring two glasses of cabernet and serving them with faux grandeur at the table. She connected her phone to Alex's Bluetooth speakers and cued up a rainy day playlist.

After setting up a tabletop easel for Lennon and a freestanding one next to it for herself and pouring paint for each of them, Alex took her place next to the table and gestured for Lennon to take a seat and begin.

"Go ahead. Blank canvas. Fresh start. Make it whatever you want."

"God," Lennon said, looking down at the canvas with a grimace. "There's so much pressure." She took a sip of her wine, as a familiar old story popped into her memory. "I feel like Beezus in *Beezus and Ramona* when she wanted so hard to find creativity in art class, but kept painting ordinary things." They shared a laugh, and Lennon hovered her brush over the palette.

"Take a deep breath." Alex laughed and shook her head. "Relax. It's supposed to be fun."

"What are you drawing…er…painting?"

"Home," Alex said wistfully, staring at the canvas as if it held some secret.

Mesmerized, Lennon looked at her and darted her eyes back to her own canvas. "I had kind of just decided on a cow," Lennon said sheepishly. "Now that seems pretty lame. Back to the drawing board."

"Please paint a cow," Alex said, leaning over to kiss Lennon on the top of her head. "Whatever you do, it'll be great. Because you made it."

"And you'll help me fix it if I screw it up?"

"You can't screw it up."

"But I will."

"We'll talk about it if it comes to that." Alex reached her left hand over and gave Lennon's hand a squeeze. "I believe in you." She added a winning smile for good measure.

"Got it," Lennon said, downing the rest of her wine and refilling her glass before dipping her brush into blue to start a background.

As she rhythmically moved the brush back and forth, trying to use the right amount of paint, but somehow glomming it onto the canvas, she decided that Alex was undoubtedly wrong about not being able to ruin the painting.

Nonetheless she had to admit, she was having fun. Throwing caution to the wind, she moved on to the grass. By the time she was on her third glass of wine and starting the outline of the cow, she stopped to watch Alex out of the corner of her eye. The playlist switched songs, and as if perfectly timed, Patty Griffin's voice came through the speakers singing of a "Heavenly Day." Lennon bit her lip and smiled. This was heavenly indeed.

As Alex swept her brush across the canvas, making a vibrant mountain stream come to life, Lennon's breath caught in her throat. Alex's eyes shone with possibility, and she seemed to have been transformed to this otherworldly goddess, as though the act of creation completed some previously unseen part of her. The corners of her mouth were lifted ever so slightly and her teeth grazed along her bottom lip as she concentrated, humming along to the song the whole time. Cognizant that she was losing control of her emotions and that she was also powerless to stop, Lennon knew she'd do just about anything to have moments like these as often as possible.

By the time Alex finished her painting, Lennon had given up on her cow and leaned back in her chair, content to watch Alex make magic. She wanted to be a part of that magic, to feel Alex as she got lost in the beauty of the world. She let out a light sigh, part desire, part gratitude.

"What do you want to do now?" Alex said, turning from her easel and coming closer, breaking Lennon free from her thoughts.

"Actually," Lennon said, biting her lip and knowing she couldn't wait much longer. "I have a surprise for you."

"A surprise?" Alex raised an eyebrow. "For me?"

Lennon nodded and smiled mischievously at Alex. "I think you'll like it."

Alex narrowed her eyes, her smile widening. "When your voice darkens with lust like that, I almost always like it." She put a hand on her hip and walked over to Lennon, standing over her for a second before throwing her leg over and straddling her. "Is this the surprise?" she asked, running her hands alongside Lennon's inner thigh.

Lennon's breath caught in her throat. "I'd say you've already unwrapped that present a time or twenty." She laughed and kissed Alex's neck. "Hold that thought, though." Grabbing her by the waist, she pulled Alex up and stood. "I have to go to my truck. I'll be right back."

Her hands shook with an equal mix of excitement and nervousness as she reached for the shopping bag in the backseat of her truck. She reached into the bag and felt the smooth material of the brief harness in between her hands. Her body tensed as she imagined the possibilities.

Once back inside the house, she felt the heat rise on her cheeks. Was it too soon? Would she go for it? They'd talked about it in passing, and Alex's curious smile had prompted the purchase. But now she glanced back into the bag, wondering if it would have been better as a joint purchase. Alex was perched on the chair, cross-legged, with a questioning smile.

"What do you have there?" she asked, her voice dripping with desire.

"Here you go," she said, holding the bag out. As Alex reached for it, she pulled it back slightly. "If you hate it, don't stress. No pressure."

Alex crinkled her nose and grabbed the bag. She looked inside and raised her eyebrow. Reaching inside the bag, she smiled and met Lennon's gaze. "I don't hate it," she said, her eyes darkening with lust. "Come here, and put it on for me."

Closing the distance between them, Lennon took Alex's head in her hands, pulling her in for a long, passionate kiss. In a tumble, she pushed her backward toward the living room and onto the couch. Alex tore at her clothes, hungrily deepening each kiss. Her teeth scraped across Lennon's shoulder, and as they moved, skin on skin, Alex leaned back. "Put it on. I'm ready." Lennon's gut tightened with Alex's wink. She lay back, her legs spread and waiting.

As quickly as Lennon could manage, she slid the harness on, put the dildo in place, and lubed up the tip. Reaching down, she felt Alex's wetness and smiled. "You certainly are ready," she said, positioning herself between Alex's legs. Watching Alex's eyes widen, then close, as she slid inside slowly, she let out a moan.

Alex threw her head back, elevating her hips and inviting Lennon in deeper. "Yes," she moaned softly as Lennon thrust in and out in long, slow strokes. As she sped up the pace, Alex's moans grew louder and deeper until she clawed down Lennon's back and cried out in bliss.

"Fuck," she whispered, as Lennon stayed inside her unmoving. "I'd say you're full of good surprises."

"The fun is just beginning," Lennon said, smirking as she pulled the harness off. "Are you ready for another surprise?"

Alex nodded and reached down to feel Lennon. Her mouth fell open. "You're *so* wet."

"That's not the surprise," Lennon said, her smile growing. "This is," she added, climbing up and straddling Alex's face. She ground against Alex's tongue, moaning with pleasure. As she came, she couldn't remember a time she'd felt freer.

CHAPTER ELEVEN

Fast-paced dance music played throughout her condo, and Alex danced through her morning routine, smiling again as she held out the envelope that had come in the mail yesterday.

She opened it again, looking at her Florida driver's license and registration. She ran her fingers over the photo on her California ID and shook her head. The youthful and naïve smile on that face seemed to her now to have belonged to another woman entirely.

Gripping the mascara tube in her hand, she steeled herself against the jaded thoughts. Things were falling into place. As she put on her mascara, fresh excitement flooded her veins. In her new home, with her newly purchased furniture, she was poised to fully take back her life and start over. Her thoughts drifted to Lennon and her smile grew. To add beauty to the entire package, she had someone to share it with—and not just any someone, but someone whose laughter could change anyone's sour mood and whose wit and charm were equally powerful.

She drifted into thought, lost at sea when it came to Lennon. Lennon was striking. There was no doubt about that, but matters of the heart were dicey. Alex let out a deep breath and shook her head, once again killing her own buzz.

Considering the emotional rollercoaster she had been on, it would serve her well to stay levelheaded. But when confronted with the blazing passion that embodied Lennon, she was helpless to stop. She was being reckless, she knew, but she couldn't pull away, even if she wanted to.

As she applied her eyeliner, she smirked at her reflection. Chaos or not, she liked it, and she wasn't going to pull away—not willingly anyway.

Her phone ringing brought her out of her daydream.

"Up so soon?" Alex asked, laughing as she recollected how late she'd kept Lennon up last night. She hadn't expected her to be up for hours. She'd call her back in a minute, she thought, adding the final touches to her makeup.

Biting her lip, she recalled the way Lennon's body came alive beneath her touch, the way they drew passion out of each other unlike any she'd ever experienced. Closing her eyes, she saw Lennon sprawled out on the bed, hungrily begging Alex to join her. Like a slideshow, it came back in images vibrant enough to make her blush. Sighing, she realized she'd turned herself on just by the thought of being in bed with Lennon again.

When the phone rang again, she shook her head, snapping herself out of the fantasy. She walked over to the dresser and picked up her phone. Wide-eyed, she saw Olivia's name flash across the screen and dropped the phone, jerking backward as though she'd touched a hot stove. Clasping her hands together to try to stop them from shaking, she brought them up to her face. Her heartbeat accelerated, and her breath caught in her throat.

Hot tears stung the corners of her eyes, and she vehemently shook her head. When the phone finally stopped ringing, she picked it up and stared at the simple phrase: "Missed Call – Olivia."

Her heart hammered in her chest, and she paced back and forth along the carpeted floor of her bedroom. When the phone dinged with a voice mail, she almost dropped it again. Steadying herself, she took a seat on the edge of the bed, trying to calm her rampant breathing. When that didn't work, she stood and paced again.

Glancing at the phone once more, she realized fifteen minutes had passed and if she wasn't careful, she was going to spend her entire day brooding. That wasn't an option when she was planning to meet with a gallery owner. Determined not to dwell, she scooped up her purse and portfolio, turned off the lights and ran to her car, still distractedly clutching her phone.

During the drive, she used just one hand to steer; the other was holding onto her phone with a death grip. At the first stoplight, she pulled the phone closer and hit the Voice mail button. Just as quickly as she'd made the decision, she hit End and set the phone down in the passenger seat.

There was no need to listen to it—at least not right now.

"*Run away. It's what you're good at.*" She heard the words that had been hurled at her time and time again in the past echo in her mind. Placing both hands on her steering wheel, she shook her head, refusing to allow that type of negativity to penetrate her thoughts on a morning when she had felt so confident and happy.

Turning the radio to a local pop station, she cranked up the volume. Lady Gaga streamed through the speakers. As Gaga sang about giving her one reason to stay, she angrily hit the Seek button, looking for anything that wasn't about a breakup.

"Every Rose Has Its Thorn" was on the classic rock station, and she gave up. With a sigh, she hit the Off button, letting silence fill her car. She thought about calling someone, *anyone*, but thought better of it. This was her dark hole to climb into and out of alone.

By the time she pulled into the parking lot of Wistful Dealings—a popular and exclusive gallery in town—she was finding it difficult to breathe. Thanks to her speedy driving, she had managed to make it there in record time. Gripping the steering wheel, she closed her eyes. It would be better to rip off the Band-Aid than to wonder all day what Olivia had to say.

Gritting her teeth, she grabbed her cell phone and, after hitting the Speaker button, played the voice mail before she could chicken out.

"Hey, it's me," Olivia said on the recording. Alex's stomach lurched. Laying her head on the steering wheel, she felt as if the world was spinning too quickly. "I just called to see how you were doing. I know you probably don't want to talk to me." Olivia laughed. Alex hit the console between the seats.

"How dare you laugh!" she seethed.

"Well, I know you don't want to talk to me or you would have answered. Anyway, I know we had a bad time last time we spoke, and things probably aren't any different now. But I just wanted you to know I was thinking about you, and I hope you're doing well."

As the voice mail ended, Alex let out a scream, picking up her phone and throwing it to the passenger-side floorboard. Flipping down the overhead visor, she fixed her mascara smudges with her finger and took a deep breath. As she grabbed her things, she thought about leaving her phone in the car, but picked it up anyway. Anger coursing through her veins, she pulled up Olivia's call and blocked her number. No more would her intrusions dampen otherwise perfectly good days.

She flipped down the mirror again and studied her reflection. Her eyes were red and her face pinched. She deepened her breathing and unclenched her jaws. Fishing through her purse, she pulled out eye drops and used them to alleviate some of the redness.

Closing the mirror, she grabbed the portfolio from the passenger seat. She was on a mission, and she wasn't about to sacrifice even more of herself to the woman who'd nearly destroyed her world. She got out of the car and strode up to the gallery. She took a minute to examine the storefront up close, even though she'd driven by it several times. It was a quaint remodeled house that had clearly been there for decades, and the vibrant mural on its exterior beckoned her closer. She opened the door and was greeted by a familiar ding.

"Welcome," an old Southern voice called.

"Hello," Alex answered, taking a look around but not seeing where the voice had come from.

"What can I help you find?" A woman's head popped around one of the corner shelves. "I'm just fixing this case," she said, her laugh cracking, the result of what Alex guessed was years of heavy smoking.

"Take your time," Alex said, waving a hand through the air. "I'll look around for now, but I would love to talk to you when you have a moment."

The woman's leathery face crinkled up as she stepped from behind the shelf and into plain view. Her white hair was streaked with purple and seemed to stand in every direction, pairing perfectly with her leopard print framed glasses. "Are you selling something?"

"Yes and no," Alex answered, choosing her words carefully. "I'm an artist."

"Oh thank God," the short, older woman said, wiping her hands on her jeans and stepping forward. "I've had the Jehovah's Witnesses, the Mormons, and a vacuum salesman all this week. The only people I want knocking on my door are customers, clients, and maybe some Girl Scouts selling cookies."

Alex laughed. "I agree, and I'm happy I fall into one of the acceptable categories." She shifted her portfolio to her left hand and reached out her right. "I'm Alex, by the way."

"Patsy," she said, nodding curtly and accepting the handshake. "Step into my office," she said, gesturing to the counter and laughing again. "What kind of work do you do?"

"I paint," Alex said. "Acrylic mainly, but I dabble in other forms."

Patsy nodded and fumbled with a handful of papers behind the counter. Shaking her head, she furrowed her brow and continued her search. "Go on," she said.

"I paint a variety of topics. Some political, some personal, some landscape, some social commentary, some romantic." She offered a polite smile as Patsy finally made eye contact again.

"Let's see them." Patsy's voice was no-nonsense and her expression was neutral.

Alex handed over the portfolio, thankful her hands didn't shake despite her feelings of unrest. This woman was hard to read. Patsy took the folder and flipped through the images. Her eyes lit up as she homed in on one featuring the silhouette of two women in an intimate embrace.

"This one," she said, raising an eyebrow in Alex's direction. "I like it."

"Thank you," Alex said. She shifted her weight from one foot to the other and tried to feel out where Patsy was coming from. Was she a lesbian, or did she simply enjoy the provocative nature of something out of the norm for this small town?

"You really weren't wasting my time," Patsy said, her eyes widening as she flipped through the pages. "You're good." She flipped the book shut and pointed at Alex. "I'd like to sell some of your work here."

"I was hoping you'd say that." Alex beamed as she accepted the book back from Patsy.

"Unfortunately, I'm not sure too many of the Sapphic prints will sell here, but I'd like to keep one of those up if you have one to spare."

"I have several." Alex laughed. "And I could always make more."

"Personal experience?" Patsy narrowed her eyes in Alex's direction, looking her up and down.

"Are you asking if I date women?"

"I didn't say anything about dating." Patsy laughed again and pushed her glasses back up on her nose. "I dabbled back in my day, but ended up married to a man named Robert." She shook her head. "Best and worst decision of my life. What about you, dear? Anyone special?"

"She's special all right." Alex's smile deepened as she thought of Lennon. "I don't know that she's mine or that she should be, but she's special."

"The illusive muse is always a bit more inspiring than the one that sticks around anyway," Pasty said. "Oh, I think I'm going to enjoy having you around."

"You might be onto something there."

"I always am." Patsy gestured to the walls around her. "That's what made this place what it is. How about you come back early next week and bring in…let's say five pieces, and we'll set you up over there?" She pointed over to the area where she'd been doing repairs. "Does that work for you?"

"Thank you so much. That will be perfect."

With renewed passion, Alex set out to continue blazing her path to success. After her visit with Patsy, where she had managed to secure a place for her art at her first-choice gallery, she made a successful visit to a second one down the road. Despite feeling nauseous since seeing Olivia's name on her phone, she choked down half a banana for lunch and busied herself by selecting paints at the art supply store. By the time evening rolled around, though, she had run out of the energy needed for running from her feelings. Not knowing where to go or what to do to find a shred of comfort, she drove to the nearby park and let the tears come.

She cried for all that she had lost but also for all that she had once had, remembering how it had felt when Olivia touched her hand with tender reassurance, the times in which they'd held on to each other for dear life through good and bad, always working as a team, and the sweet kisses she used to give.

She thought about their home and for that matter, home in general. She missed the California sunsets, the fast-paced city life, the world she'd always known, and her family. God, how she missed her family.

She straightened in her seat. Clearing her throat, she reminded herself why she had left—why she had no other choice. Calling upon every reserve of strength she'd ever had, she imagined herself picking up shattered shards of glass and using them to create a mosaic, a metaphor she felt perfectly encapsulated her current situation.

"Now is just the time to make the brokenness into something beautiful." She spoke the words aloud, letting them have power. "But first, a drink and a little time to forget."

She got back in her car, backed out of her space, and sped off, leaving her demons behind for a night of rebirth. With nowhere in particular calling to her, she drove to a restaurant off the main dock that Lennon had said was noted for its expansive wine selection, taking only a couple of minutes in the car to redo her makeup after her crying episode.

She narrowed her eyes at her reflection, noting the newly developed fine lines around them. Her brown eyes had been darkened by her mood, it seemed. She was fine with that. There was no need to feign joy when she did not feel it.

Inside the restaurant, dimly lit booths and tables made her feel welcomed, made her feel as if she didn't have to be the picture of perfection and that there might be some sort of anonymity here. Taking a deep breath, she chose one of the far seats at the bar, as far away as she could get from the three other patrons who were already seated there.

"Good afternoon." A friendly man in his thirties approached her, his perfectly trimmed beard in stark contrast to his bald head. On a normal day, his genuine smile would have solicited the same from her. Instead, she nodded a greeting, unable to muster up words. "Would you like a menu?"

Swallowing, she shook her head. "No thanks," she managed. "Can I just grab a glass of your house cab?"

"House cab coming up," he said, his smile never breaking despite her moodiness. "Just so you know, that's going to be Wallen Farms, a rich red with hints of cherry and tobacco," he added.

She mirrored his nod and tried to smile, but she knew the effort fell short of being convincing. Dropping her head, she was grateful when he walked away to pour her glass. She loved wine and would have usually been interested in knowing all about it, but today she didn't care. She didn't want fancy or over-the-top. She just wanted to cry into a glass of wine and forget.

She took a sip when it was set down in front of her. The bartender lingered for a second, seeming to wait on her response. She kept her gaze on her glass. "It's good," she said quietly.

He took the hint and walked back to check on his other customers. Grateful for a moment of peace, she sipped her wine, trying to find anything else to fill the spaces of her mind.

When her phone dinged, she tensed, then reminded herself she'd blocked Olivia. Her head pounded as she reached for her phone.

I hope you're having a good day!

Lennon's text was accompanied by a smiley face that seemed so out of place in the day Alex was having.

Her fingers hovered over the keyboard as she contemplated how to best respond. Glancing down, she saw her wineglass and a tired smile crept up on her face. If nothing else, it had been sweet of Lennon to check in, even if her timing was horrible.

Snapping a quick picture of the half-empty glass, Alex hit Send.

Better now. Thanks for checking. I hope yours is good too.

She thought about adding an emoji but decided against it. She didn't have the capacity for unnecessary niceties. She set her phone down and picked up her wineglass. She drank the rest while people watching, then made eye contact with the bartender and raised her empty glass.

He nodded in her direction. She wanted to tell him to just bring the entire bottle. Knowing that wouldn't be socially acceptable for a party of one, she smiled and thanked him when he refilled her glass.

Her phone dinged again.

It's good. Thanks. I'm on my break, but hopefully I can see you tomorrow. I know me getting off at two in the morning sucks, but maybe we can do lunch tomorrow?

Alex pressed her lips together, contemplated the idea, then…

I still might be up when you get off work. Just text me to see. If not, lunch would be great.

She typed the reply, hit Send, and set her phone down, knowing Lennon would have to go back to work soon. And it was a good thing. She needed time to sort out her thoughts before they spoke again.

By the time she had gulped down two more glasses of wine, the place had filled up. An older man was sitting next to her now. His overdone cologne was enough to make her gag, but combine that with the creepy way he looked at every woman who passed and he was definitely ruining her experience. She grimaced as he inched closer and turned his attention to her.

"Hey," he said, smiling and looking her up and down openly.

"Hi," she said, looking up to catch the bartender's attention to get her tab.

The bartender looked her way and nodded to her glass. She shook her head and mouthed "check."

"You're not leaving so soon, are you?" His tone was condescending. She narrowed her eyes and him but offered a tightlipped smile.

"I've been here a while, but I hope you and your friends have a good evening," she said, gesturing down the bar to the troop of men he'd come in with.

"It would be better if you stayed," he urged, wiggling his eyebrows.

She fought to keep her expressions neutral and shook her head. "Thanks for the offer, but I've got to get going."

Feeling thankful for good timing, she watched as the bartender ran her card and handed her the receipt to sign. "Have a good night," she said, sliding off her stool. She wobbled, but righted herself quickly. It was too late. The older man had noticed.

Rising from his own seat, he reached for her arm. She pulled back instinctively.

"Let me help you," he offered.

"No thanks," she said, quickening her pace as she exited.

She heard him mutter something as she escaped, but she didn't care to stick around to hear it more clearly.

Out in the fresh air, she looked around. There really wasn't much else she wanted to do, but she knew she didn't want to go home where the quiet would engulf her and echo her most depressing thoughts. She looked left and saw only beach-themed shops. Shaking her head, she headed to her right.

At the next intersection, she weighed her options. She could go down to Alibis and enjoy the banter that came with fucking the bartender or she could go somewhere new and risk a run-in similar to the one she'd just had with the creep at the restaurant.

She assessed her condition and smiled. Her level of intoxication had made the emotional pain fade. Head held high, she let liquid courage take the reins and rounded the corner, heading for Alibis.

The bar was bustling. That much was clear before she even entered the door. The cacophony of drunken debauchery sounded out into the street. She put her hands into her pockets, reconsidering if she was up for it. With a shrug, she continued making her way inside.

"There's no stopping the train once it gets going," she muttered to herself, weaving through the crowd until she saw one single seat available shining like a beacon at the end of the bar. She made a beeline for it, not wanting to sit in a booth and deal with the bumbling idiots she had just passed by.

"Well, if it isn't Miss California." Grant's voice boomed over the noise created by the music and the chatter of the other customers. "And sitting in my section," he said, walking over to her, his smile growing. "How are you doing?" he asked, leaning against the bar top.

"Eh," she said. "Next question."

"That good a day, huh?"

"It's been quite the day," she agreed, scrunching up her face. "That's for sure."

"Well, if you wanted to make it better with great cocktails and a little eye candy, you came to the right place." He shimmied and did a twirl behind the bar.

"By sitting in my section, you chose the most attractive bartender we have on staff." His laugh met hers, and she couldn't help but feel more at home in his presence. She looked down the bar and made eye contact with Lennon. Mid-shake of a cocktail, Lennon flashed her a smile and mouthed something unreadable. Grant slid in between the two of them before she could respond. "She's pretty too," he said, placing his hands on his hips, "but I think I smell better."

"You're both lookers," Alex said after a moment of laughter. "And you both make a mean cocktail."

A smirk spread across his lips and Alex shook her head. "Don't make a cocktail joke," she warned, and he threw his hands in the air.

"It's too easy anyway," he said, moving out of the way so she could see the selection behind him. "What can I get you tonight?"

"Something that packs a punch."

His eyes lit up and he looked every bit the part of an impish child, despite his towering stature and beard. "Have you ever had a Viking Funeral?"

"No, but I'll take one if that's what you recommend." From the way his smile grew, she thought she should probably decline, but now was not the time to stop the party.

"Viking Funeral for Miss California," Grant hollered down the bar, soliciting a cheer from Lennon. She stopped what she was doing, slid down the bar, and rang the giant bell off to the side.

"Skol!" Everyone shouted at once as Alex watched, dumbfounded.

"This place is weird," she said, still laughing when Lennon walked down to greet her.

"You have no idea," she said, looking from customer to customer. When she turned her attention back to Alex, Alex's heart raced. There was just something about those intense eyes that made her question everything. She looked down, watching as Lennon's lips twisted into a smile and thought about how sweetly Lennon had let her taste those luscious lips so soon after knowing her. Her body tensed, but she shook it off, trying to pay attention to what Lennon was saying.

"Some day I'll tell you stories that'll make your mind spin. For now, I'll whip you up a funeral." Lennon turned toward the liquor, selecting a couple of items before turning back to face Alex. Her right eyebrow was raised and she looked her up and down. "Before I make you this, have you eaten today?"

"You sound like a mom," Alex retorted, straightening her shoulders.

"Not a mom, just a seasoned bartender," Lennon said, measuring the liquors into her jigger. "I'll take your sass as an answer, though," she added with a smile. "So if you drink this, I'm driving you home tonight. I'm also going to bring you a charcuterie board—on the house."

Alex clasped her hands in her lap and considered the offer. "Deal," she said after a moment, even though every fiber of her body wanted to resist. As Lennon shook the drink, Alex frowned. "What were you going to do with that drink if I didn't agree?"

"Drink it myself, sell it to someone else," Lennon said with a shrug. "I'd find it a good home and make sure it was well loved."

Alex tried to scowl but broke into a smile anyway. "Well, bring it here, and I'll give it an adoption day celebration." When Lennon set down the glass in front of her, Alex's eyes widened. The golden, frothed liquid looked and smelled delightful. Alex cast her attention back to Lennon. "Maybe you and I can celebrate later," she added.

"Maybe," Lennon said, giving her a sideways grin. "But my guess is that, after you drink that, combined with whatever you've already had, you won't really be in a place for celebrations." Lennon looked down the bar and nodded to a customer at the end. "I've got to go for a bit, but I'll be back. Bottoms up," she added, raising an eyebrow as she walked away.

Alex watched her as she walked, admiring every movement. Her body tingled as she envisioned the things she wanted to do with Lennon. The things she wanted to whisper in Lennon's ear. She was too far away to do that now, but… Alex fished her phone out of her purse. She typed what she'd wanted to whisper and hit Send before putting her phone back in her purse.

I want to fuck you on the bar.

Smiling coyly, she waited for the moment Lennon would open the message, thankful to know she'd still be in the bar and be privy to watching her expression change to lust.

CHAPTER TWELVE

The crowd was rowdy tonight. Eyeing the second spilled drink of the shift, Lennon tried to get Grant's attention, a feat that proved impossible over the loud music and twenty-odd conversations that were happening at once.

With a sigh, she decided to deal with the spill herself. After wiping the bar clean, she refilled a water glass for a now cut-off patron and assured him he had indeed had enough.

Glancing down the bar, she checked on Alex. Still drunk and still chatting Grant's ear off about God knows what, she noted. Even in her drunken stupor, the woman was unbelievably beautiful and at the same time somehow designedly disheveled—like a work of art. Lennon wasn't sophisticated enough to cite its exact style, but it had definitely captivated her. "Never one to walk away from a good time," she muttered, quietly scolding herself for taking her attention off work.

By the time she had cleared everyone aside from Grant and Alex out the door at two, she felt like a zombie. Her head throbbed and her feet were aching. Limping, she rounded the corner and draped her arm over Alex's shoulder.

"What do you say I take you home?" she asked, bracing herself for the fight she knew was coming.

"I'm not ready yet," Alex whined. "I still have half a drink."

"That's water." Lennon laughed. "We have some of that at home."

"Hmm," Alex said, regarding her skeptically. "Fine, we'll go back to your house, but that's not *my* home."

Lennon shook her head as she slid her arm under Alex's underarms. "No, it's not," she agreed. "But it is where I'd like you to stay so I can keep an eye on you tonight."

"You're not in charge of me," Alex slurred.

Lennon stiffened. "I never claimed to be," she said, careful to keep her voice gentle. "I just want to make sure you're okay. This was part of our deal when I mixed you that drink, which, from your speech, your behavior when you came in, and the text you sent me, I know wasn't your first drink of the evening."

"Nope," Alex said. "Sure wasn't."

"Okay, then let's get you to the car."

"Do you need help?" Grant offered behind her.

"If you can close up, I'll see you later at home," Lennon said. "I've got this covered."

"No, *I've* got this," Alex said, pulling her arm from Lennon's grasp and promptly falling to the ground.

"Let me help you, please?" Lennon asked, reaching down to grab Alex's hand.

"Fine," Alex said, her face set into a pout.

Normally Lennon's patience would be wearing thin, but she hadn't just accepted the role of taking care of Alex. She wanted and needed to make sure she was okay. And she was going to see it through. The last thing she wanted was to see Alex get into trouble when things were going so well and she was getting settled in town.

We've all been drunk and unruly at some point, and we've all let bad days take us lower than we needed to go, Lennon silently reminded herself, helping Alex into the car. On the ride back to her house, she rolled down the windows. Alex's face looked pale, and more than once, Lennon had seen her stomach lurch.

Thankful when they finally arrived, she helped Alex through the front door. Alex looked around, clumsily reaching to the wall for support.

"Let's get you to the bathroom," Lennon said, placing her arm around Alex's waist. But it was too late. Before they could take another step, Alex doubled over and vomited.

Lennon closed her eyes and breathed through her mouth. "It's okay," she said, keeping her voice steady, looking away to avoid becoming a sympathetic vomiter. "I'll clean it up. Come on," she said, gently maneuvering Alex toward the bathroom. Once she had her set up to vomit in the toilet, Lennon headed back to the living room. Her stomach lurched itself as she cleaned up the floor, but with her teeth gritted, she pressed through.

"I need to tell you something," Alex called from the bathroom.

Lennon let out a deep breath, tossing the soiled rag into the laundry basket.

"What is it?" she asked when she was back in the bathroom. Careful not to look at Alex in fear that she might yet heave as well, she leaned against the counter and waited.

"My ex called me today," Alex said before throwing up a third time. Wiping her mouth, she looked up in Lennon's direction. "And it made me wonder if I'm just doing what I'm doing because I'm using you as a replacement."

Lennon felt as though the air had been knocked out of her. Keeping a level tone, she turned to face Alex, puke and all. "If that's the case, you need to sort that out and let me know. Either way, that's up to you to figure out," she said, exhaling the surprise stab of pain she felt instead of giving voice to it like she wanted to. "But for now, you probably need to drink some water and get some rest."

"It's such a mess," Alex said, sobs coming in between heaves.

"I cleaned up the mess," Lennon assured her, stepping closer to hold back Alex's hair. "There is no mess anymore."

"Not this," Alex said, her tone suddenly clear in contrast to her sobs only seconds earlier. "Me. I'm the mess."

The words hit Lennon in the gut. *I'm the mess.* How many times had that truth resonated within her in the past few months? Some other time she'd tell Alex about the mess she'd been just a couple of weeks before Alex met her, blacking out in bars like a college kid, walking into the wall of her bedroom, waking up in strange places in clothes she'd never seen. As Alex's body convulsed into another round of throwing up, Lennon's heart broke. She'd been here very recently.

Lennon wanted to hold her, but she resisted the urge. This… whatever it was…wasn't anything. Alex had said it herself. They were each using the other to fill a void.

"Come on," Lennon said, helping Alex to her feet once she was certain she was done throwing up. She laid out a washcloth and waited while Alex attempted to clean herself up and then helped her to the bedroom.

"You can put these on," she said, tossing a pair of sweatpants and T-shirt in Alex's direction. Alex let the clothes drop to the ground, and Lennon looked up at the ceiling, trying but failing to stifle her sigh. "Or you can sleep in what you have on."

Alex didn't budge. Lennon walked over to her and looked up, attempting to make eye contact. Alex turned her head away in defiance.

"Come to the bed, please," she asked. "Come and get some rest."

Alex shook her head and slid down the closed bedroom door. "I want to be down here," she said, covering her face and sobbing again.

What had started as mild annoyance had now transformed into a full-blown headache. Rubbing her temples and drawing on the last shreds of patience she had left, Lennon sat down on the floor next to Alex. Wrapping her arm around her, she let Alex's head fall onto her chest.

"It's going to be okay," Lennon said, running her fingers through Alex's long hair. She spoke the words in Alex's direction, but also to herself. *Is it going to be okay?* She wasn't so sure, but she'd been lying to herself thus far and didn't see a point in stopping now.

"This," Alex said, looking up at her, anger flashing in her eyes as she waved her arm in front of herself, "isn't okay. This is fucked up, and I don't even know why you're still here. You should leave."

"I live here," Lennon said, unable to hold the words back.

"Right," Alex said, wiping the tears from her eyes and smearing mascara across her face. "Well, I don't know why I'm here."

"Because I asked you to be."

"You don't want to be with me." The words were barely above a whisper, but they hit their mark. Lennon stiffened and pulled back. "Maybe you're just using me too," Alex added, leaning up against the wall.

"You know, I didn't ask for this," Lennon said, unable to keep her growing annoyance at bay. Rising from her place on the floor, she strode over to the bed and turned out the lights. She hadn't wanted this. This was chaos—the exact stuff she'd been trying to avoid. *Worse actually*, she thought. This was chaos unlike anything she'd ever encountered, with its ups and downs and lack of clear boundaries. She closed her eyes, but Alex's mascara-smeared face was seared into her mind. As capricious and enchanting as a wildfire, she was just as dangerous and unpredictable.

* * *

Sunlight streamed into the room through a gap in Lennon's soft black curtains. Stretching, she reached for the other side of the bed and found it empty. As if reliving a bad dream, she closed her eyes. Last night's events flooded her memory. With a yawn, she rolled over to look at where Alex had sat slumped over last night, only to find the space empty too. Shaking her head, she rose to take care of whatever might still need cleaning.

Out of the corner of her eye, she caught sight of a piece of paper on her nightstand.

I'm truly sorry for last night and incredibly embarrassed. Thanks for your help. I tried to clean up but didn't know where you kept cleaning supplies. Call me if you still want to talk to me.

-Alex

Lennon read the words twice, sitting on the edge of the bed, trying to make sense of it all. She held the note for a second and then let it drop to her lap. Resting her elbows on her knees, she dropped her head into her hands. If she wanted it, she had an easy out. All she had to do was speak the words—say that she couldn't deal with this level of chaos, with pushing away help out of sheer stubbornness.

Picking up the note, she crumpled it. "Another one bites the dust." She tossed the balled-up piece of paper toward her open closet. She tried to feign anger, but instead she felt the sting of rejection.

Balling her fists, she stood. She took a ragged breath. She had sworn she wasn't going to fall again and that she wasn't going to be weakened. That was her original plan, a good plan, and she was sticking to it.

With a scowl on her face, she threw open her bedroom door and strolled to the kitchen. She could opt not to call, or she could have a chat face-to-face. Either way, she certainly didn't have to decide before breakfast.

"Good morning," Grant called out from the kitchen. "I figured last night might have been a bit rough, so I took the liberty of making you a decent breakfast to start today out better than yesterday ended."

"Thank you," she said, wanting nothing more than to collapse into his arms and let his tall frame support her for a moment. Instead, she walked to the coffeepot, pouring a cup of determination.

"My pleasure," he said, flipping a pancake with the spatula in his hand. "By the way"—he turned to face her—"what did happen when you got her here?"

"You don't want to know," she said, taking a sip of her coffee. "Trust me." She shuddered. "I don't even want to know what happened in there, and I lived most of it."

"Most of it?"

She let out a sad laugh. "I fell asleep somewhere in the mix of it all. She was gone when I woke up."

"I heard her leave this morning around six," he said. He set a plate down at the table. "Forget about it, and eat for now."

As she stuck her fork into the stack of pancakes, she smiled at him. "Thank you," she said again. "This is just what I needed."

He laughed. "Disaster relief should always include pancakes." He poured himself a glass of orange juice and took a long drink before coming to sit at the table with her. "And by the way, just because your lord and savior Lady Gaga sings about a bad romance, it doesn't mean you have to live one. Remember that."

He took a bite of pancake. After he swallowed, he leveled his gaze at her. "But that's also coming from a bitter old queen who's still single. So take it with a grain of salt. Above all, you take care of you. I don't want you getting hurt while trying to take care of someone else."

"I won't," she assured him, but as she ate she couldn't be sure she was telling the truth. The words Alex spoke the night before—drunken or not—still stung. When she finished eating, she stood up from the table and took both their plates to the sink.

"Big plans for the day?" she asked, hoping to change the subject.

"Not too much going on," he said, turning his attention to a magazine on the table. "I plan to get in a workout at the gym and then do a little shopping for my upcoming trip."

"I'm jealous," she said, washing the dishes as she made small talk. "I'd love to get away from all this right now."

"Like I said, don't stick around if things are bad." He rose from the table and continued talking as he walked away. "If she's worth it, stick it out, but if she's not, you know how to walk away a winner." As he rounded the corner into his bedroom, she could hear him singing the old Kathy Mattea song, unable to resist belting out the lyrics he'd spoken.

Shaking her head and muttering under her breath, she grabbed the Clorox wipes from under the sink and headed back to clean up more of the tangible remnants of her rocky night. The rest would have to wait until later.

After ensuring the place was clean, she showered, dressed, and headed out to run errands. Throughout the day, she kept her efforts and attention focused on tasks at hand, giving little thought to the emotional conundrum she'd somehow gotten herself into. Only once did she check her phone, relieved to see she didn't have any text messages or calls.

Her visit to the farmers' market served to take her mind away from the situation for a while. As she searched through fresh, locally sourced produce, she checked items off her list for the winter menu with all local ingredients and mostly local spirits. After dropping her purchases off at the bar, she felt more herself than she had at the start of the day. Her confidence renewed, she reminded herself as sunset neared that she wasn't a coward.

Taking a deep breath, she pulled her phone from her bag and opened up her text messages.

Let's meet up tonight to talk.

She sent the message to Alex and then reread it. Damn. She sounded as if she was a nagging wife reaching out to a spouse of eighteen years instead of a fling reaching out to reexamine boundaries and smooth over the rough edges of a booze-fueled fight. She sighed, waiting as the bubbles on the screen told her Alex was typing a reply.

Sounds good. I'll be home in ten minutes, if you want to come over now.

Lennon chewed on her thumbnail, considering the offer.

She would have preferred neutral territory, but she wanted desperately to stay away from her house, where the demons of the previous night still lingered, so she agreed.

When she got to her car, she thought about touching up her makeup but decided against it. That would only feed her petty need to show Alex what a prize she was walking away from with her hurtful, albeit potentially true, words. White-knuckling the steering wheel, she stared at her reflection in the visor mirror. The hardened person she saw staring back at her wasn't who she was raised to be or who she'd fought to become so many years ago, but it was the person who circumstances and failed romances had turned her into over the years.

Relaxing her grip, she took deep breaths and allowed herself to think back over all the times she had given and given of herself until there was nothing left, only to be left heartbroken and alone. People took. That's just the way it was. Alex was different. She hadn't asked. She hadn't taken any more than was readily hers. But somehow, Lennon still ended up feeling dumbfounded and hurt.

Preparing a speech in her head, she drove across town. When she arrived, she waited in her car a moment to make sure she was making the right decision. Her thoughts were interrupted by Alex poking her head out the door. Lennon waited a moment longer to remember her like this. Unsure, but poised, her long hair blowing in the evening breeze, she stood in the doorway offering an apologetic grin.

Lennon pressed her lips together, her thoughts just as muddled as they were when she had awoken this morning. She opened her car door.

"You can come inside if you'd like," Alex offered.

Lennon nodded, stepping from the car. Before she even made it to the front door, she saw Alex's shoulders droop.

"I really am so sorry about last night," she said, bracing herself in the doorframe. "I feel like an ass, and I know I said some things. I know it was a disaster, and I know I wasn't easy to deal with. But I wanted to thank you."

Lennon gulped. Even in shame, Alex's sincerity rang through crystal clear. "I'm glad you're feeling better," she said quietly as her frustration subsided. She was not sure what else to say.

"I am, but I'm not at the same time." Alex crossed her arms over her chest. "You didn't deserve to deal with that, and I'm sure that's part of what you want to talk about."

Lennon nodded, and Alex moved out of the doorway, extending her arm to wave Lennon inside the small condo. "Have a seat if you'd like." She offered Lennon a spot on the couch. "I picked up a bottle of wine for you. I'm not drinking any, but if you'd like a glass, I'll pour you one."

Considering the offer, Lennon nodded. "That would be nice," she said, swallowing hard. "Thank you."

Presenting the glass of wine as a peace offering, Alex carefully took the seat next to Lennon. She clasped her hands together and sat poised, as if waiting for the unleashing of a verbal lashing. Her chin jutted to the side slightly, signaling to Lennon that she was ready for whatever might come from this. Something in her eyes suggested the "we're done" speech was something she'd sat through a few times before. Lennon glanced down at Alex's slender hands and looked back up to her deep eyes, trying to find the right words.

"The new décor looks good," Lennon blurted out, pointing to a tapestry that hung along the far wall of the living room.

"Thank you." She shifted her weight to the side in a nonverbal question.

Lennon took a drink and rested the wineglass on her thigh before clearing her throat. "I did want to talk about last night," she started. She let out a long sigh. "I came over here to tell you I can't deal with that kind of chaos, but as I'm sitting here, I know that's not who you are at the core."

Alex shook her head. "It's not, and I don't know how you can see that clearly after all the evidence I've shown you to the contrary. But I'm going to work on keeping my outbursts to myself."

Lennon pressed her palm against her forehead, nodding slowly. "I'm not sure what there really is to say." She took another drink of wine, trying to make sense of the colossal sweep of emotions she was feeling.

"It's okay," Alex whispered. "I know I tried to push you away, and more often than not, I succeed at that."

"Except somehow you're not succeeding with me, and I don't know what to do with that," Lennon admitted. She exhaled, and it felt like the wind leaving her sails. "I'm still here, and as I look at you, I don't want to leave. I didn't want to when you first told me to go—even though we were in my house." Lennon raised an eyebrow and let out a small laugh.

"Yeah." Alex drew the word out. She winced. "Sorry about that."

Lennon gave in to the laughter. "First few months in town, and you're already acting like Columbus. You discovered a new world, and you're ready to claim it as your own, other people's houses included."

"Can I make it up to you?"

Lennon narrowed her eyes. "What did you have in mind?"

"Dinner, sex, or both." Alex shrugged, her smile timid and seductive at the same time. Lennon stared at her, bewitched at how the tables had been turned.

She took a deep breath. "Let's start with dinner. I'm not sure about the rest yet, but dinner will be a good place to begin."

"Fair enough," Alex said, rising from her spot on the couch and heading to the kitchen. "I don't have a lot of things yet, but I have one trusty pan, a wooden spoon, and some groceries. I can whip you up something if you'd like." From the kitchen, she turned and smiled.

Lennon felt her breathing ease and the tension she had been harboring dissipated at the sight of the pure and genuine smile. "That sounds great. Would you like some help?"

"You took care of me last night," Alex said. "I'd like to take care of you for once. If that's okay."

Lennon pulled her mouth to the side, thinking it through. She held her breath for a second, never having been one to take from or to owe someone something.

"It's just dinner," Alex said, her smile broadening. "I'm not asking to be your caretaker or wait on you hand and foot. I'm just offering a home-cooked meal."

Lennon tried to catch her breath. It was as if Alex had just read her mind. "Okay."

She sipped her wine while Alex cooked, but Lennon's thoughts ran rampant. She could have bolted. Why hadn't she? For some reason she still couldn't define, she had chosen to stay. Time and again, she had chosen to be by Alex's side, despite the red flags Alex raised, despite her own hang-ups, despite her mind urging her to run away.

Shaking her head, she stood. Walking toward the kitchen and leaning up against the countertop to watch Alex chop vegetables, she decided the reason didn't matter.

Humming to herself, Alex was precise in each of her movements. Every effort was strategic. Lennon couldn't remember the last time she watched someone so carefully orchestrate a meal, as if it were a work of art.

She wanted to go to her side, wrap her arms around Alex's waist, and pull her in for a kiss. In a perfect world, she'd grab a bite of the bell pepper Alex was slicing and banter with her while she cooked. She shook her head. That's not why she was here.

"Before dinner," Lennon said, shifting her attention to the more pressing matters at hand and hopping up to sit on the counter beside Alex's work station, "I need to know something… about last night."

Alex's brow creased in anticipation and she nodded. "Ask away." Her words came out quietly. Her tone was pained and her body was tensed, but she stood tall.

"You said that you were using me as a replacement and that you thought I was doing the same." Lennon ignored the way the repeated words drove a knife through her just as much the second time they were spoken aloud as they had the first. She gripped the counter beneath her, trying to keep her expression neutral. "Is that how you feel?"

Alex shook her head. She opened her mouth, but Lennon held up her hands to stop her.

"If it is," she said, "I just need to know. I stand by what I said last night. If that's how you feel, that's okay. We were never supposed to be anything serious anyway. We're *not* serious," she added, knowing her statement was intended as a reminder to herself as much as it was to Alex. "And if we need to stop seeing one another, it's okay. I just need to know."

Alex's hands shook as she reached for a spoon and she let out a ragged breath. "Moment of truth time?" she asked, sounding anything but certain.

Lennon braced herself, unsure whether she felt hurt or offended. "Moment of truth time," she agreed.

CHAPTER THIRTEEN

Alex tried to take a steadying breath. Failing, she turned to Lennon. Closing the distance between them, she put her hands on the counter on either side of her legs and stared into Lennon's eyes. The enchanting blue eyes that stared back at her were shrouded with guardedness. She gulped, regretting having done anything to raise the defenses in Lennon's heart any higher than they already had been.

She cleared her throat, realizing she was losing more ground with Lennon with every passing second.

"It's not like that," she croaked after a moment. "I was drunk and I misspoke."

"It's not that simple." Lennon clasped her hands together. "I wish it were that easy to pretend you didn't say the things you said, but you did. I'm going to need a little more of an explanation." She rubbed her temples.

"Fuck!" she exclaimed a moment later as if suddenly remembering something. "I don't need an explanation. You don't owe me that. We're not a couple. There's no need for that."

Alex's heart pounded so rapidly she knew Lennon had to hear it hammering in her chest.

"I do owe you an explanation," she said, continuing despite the fact that Lennon was fervently shaking her head. "I meant it in a way, and let me explain that."

She looked to the floor, desperate to choose the words that would make sense. Lennon was stubborn and after all, they had gone into this with the notion that it was fleeting. She straightened her shoulders, hoping her sincerity would shine through the words she was no doubt going to butcher.

"I just came from something I thought was going to last forever. You also just came out of a serious relationship. With that in mind, it's easy to see that both of us have expectations of what a relationship *should* be. I think I'm putting too much pressure on you to be those things. And I think I failed yesterday to see them as two separate things. I think, in the state I was in, I saw myself as weak and saw myself using you as a quick-fix solution to get over my heartache, as though you were a placeholder."

Lennon shook her head, anger flashing in her eyes. "What you're saying makes sense logically, but from where I stand, you're saying you see me the same as her. I don't really have any value to you if that's the case. But it doesn't matter. This isn't serious."

Alex put her hands on her hips, chiding herself for not getting it right. "No. Please let me finish." She gripped the counter as she worked to steady her thoughts. "I'm saying that because she called yesterday and fucked up my psyche I misplaced my anger. I'm not angry at *you*. And I'm not angry at myself for getting involved with you." She paused. They were stomping all over that line they'd agreed upon that day over beers—a line that wasn't all that clear to start with.

"I don't know what we're doing. We've crossed over these lines. I know we're not serious. We're not a couple. But I'm not angry about whatever this is," she said. "I'm angry at *her* and only her. And you are nothing like her.

"Furthermore, I thought about it a great deal today. I think I was right to check myself. I probably shouldn't have verbalized it to you last night, but I'm a mess right now. And I don't honestly know when I won't be a mess. You have your chance if you want to run away from this train wreck, but if you want to stick around and keep doing whatever we're doing, just know I'm working on myself."

"I'm confused," Lennon said. "You were right to check yourself to see if you have been using me. If you've thought about it, are you?"

"I'm not," Alex said, bending a bit to maintain eye contact. "I needed to make sure that I wasn't exploiting this situation. To make sure you weren't caught in the crossfire of my actions."

"You don't have to worry about me," Lennon said stiffly. She leaned back, widening the distance between her and Alex. "I won't be hurt." Darkness flashed in her eyes and she set her jaw. Alex shuddered at the icy tone of her voice.

"I want to be with you." Alex blurted the words out, fear mixing with heartache at the thought of somehow not seeing Lennon again. "It's you I want," she added, looking up to meet Lennon's gaze. "I know it's been crazy, but I'm happy to be here with you in this moment."

Lennon placed a hand over her face as if to find a moment to process Alex's confession. Alex wanted desperately to know what was going on inside her mind, but she was too afraid to ask.

"I don't think I'm what you want," Lennon said, finally breaking the silence, her tone devoid of emotion. "I'm not the marrying type, and I don't think I'll ever be. Right now, I'm not even the dating kind."

Alex stepped back, bracing herself on the counter as she replayed the words in her head.

"Who said anything about marriage?"

"I did," Lennon said, her voice still monotone, "because that's what you came from. That's the void you told me you were trying to fill last night. Even if that's not what you meant, it's what you said. And beyond that, we're already in too deep. This is far more serious already than either of us envisioned."

"I'm not asking for that," Alex said. "I'm not asking for anything more from you." She ran through all she'd said, wondering when their conversation had flown off the rails.

"I'm just asking for another shot at keeping your company and doing…whatever it is that this is." She grabbed Lennon's hand, wincing mentally at how stiff and unresponsive it was. "What *is* this, by the way?"

"I don't know," Lennon answered, her voice barely above a whisper.

Before Alex could respond, a worrying sizzle snapped her attention back to the stove. "Shit," she said, scurrying over to a sauté pan that was beginning to give off smoke. "I guess I should have been paying attention," she said, filling the silence awkwardly as she worked to save their dinner.

"My bad for distracting you," Lennon said.

Alex glanced over her shoulder, but she couldn't read Lennon's expression. Was she mad, hurt, or just ambivalent about what was happening? Sighing, she turned back to tend to the stir-fry in the pan.

"Dinner's ready," she said after a few minutes, though she was no longer sure if Lennon thought eating together was a good idea. She dished the food onto two plates and held one out. Lennon hesitated briefly before hopping down from the counter, but accepted the plate and headed for the table. Taking a seat across from her, Alex picked up a fork, then cleared her throat and set it down. She wasn't going to eat until she finished saying what she needed to say.

"I'm sorry if my words were offensive or clumsy or if I broke some unwritten rule and said things that I wasn't supposed to say. I realize that I'm bad at this. I'm just bad at it all. I say too much, or I feel too much, or I *am* too much. But I'm trying. And I didn't mean to hurt you."

"You didn't hurt me." Lennon grabbed her fork and cast a look in Alex's direction, defiance shining in her eyes. "It's fine. And you're not too much."

Alex started to protest, then sucked in a deep breath. Exhaling, she nodded. "Be that as it may, I didn't intend to say hurtful things. I especially didn't mean to do or say anything that would threaten me getting to spend time with you. I enjoy your company. Very much."

For a second, she thought Lennon might retort angrily. Alex watched instead as her frown softened. "I enjoy yours too," Lennon admitted quietly.

"Good," Alex said. She picked up her fork, then set it back on the table again. "One more thing," she said, clearing her throat. "Can we please figure out whatever this is or is not, so we don't sit here in the future batting the boundaries back and forth?"

"What do you want?" Lennon asked, looking as if Alex was the only one with a say in the matter.

"I think there's more to it than that."

"Like what?" Lennon asked, taking a bite of the stir-fry.

"Do you want to continue spending time together?"

"This is good," Lennon said after a moment. She brought her napkin to her mouth, dabbing, and kept her eyes glued on her plate.

"Thanks."

Alex clenched her fist under the table in frustration. Lennon was obstinate when she wanted to be. She opened her mouth to speak, but Lennon cut her off.

"What type of seasoning did you use?"

"Fuck, Lennon!" Alex said, slapping her palm against her forehead. "I don't give a damn about dinner right now."

Lennon scowled.

"Play the tough guy all you want, but if we're going to get somewhere we have to actually talk about this."

"I don't know what I feel," Lennon admitted, staring at a spot on the far wall.

"I'm not asking you to get deep and introspective." Alex placed her hands on the table, leaning into Lennon's line of sight. "I'm asking if you want to continue spending time together."

Lennon looked into Alex's eyes, but she never wavered in her detachment. After what felt like an eternity, she responded. "I do."

"Good," Alex said, feeling as though she was pulling teeth just to get Lennon to be present. *That should be a red flag, shouldn't it?* She exhaled, removing the negative thought from her head. "I want that too. Do you want to keep it like it is, or would you like to date exclusively? Nothing serious, just so we know we're actually dating."

Lennon twisted her napkin in her hand as she considered the question. After a long pause, she nodded. "I don't have any interest in seeing other people at the moment, if that's what you're asking," she said.

Alex tried to smile, despite feeling a bit like she was receiving a consolation prize. She swallowed hard. "Okay," she said slowly. "Do you want to give this thing a shot, and we'll take it slow?"

"Slow?" Lennon laughed, showing real emotion for the first time. "I don't think we've done anything slowly."

"Fair enough," Alex answered. "But for this, let's see where it goes?"

"I'm in," Lennon said, grabbing her wineglass. She tipped it up, emptying it of its contents.

The uncertainty that lurked in her eyes echoed what Alex felt in her heart. The ground beneath them wasn't steady, but what in life was?

She picked up her fork once more and took a bite, as confused as she'd ever been, yet grateful for getting another chance.

CHAPTER FOURTEEN

Lennon stretched her legs on the couch and leaned back into the overstuffed cushions as a cheesy romantic comedy played on the television in the background.

"It feels good to relax," she commented, enjoying the ease and comfort of being in the home of one of her oldest friends.

Natalie lay on the couch beside her, nodding in agreement. "I'm so glad we decided to stay in instead of going out," she said. "Unless we could find somewhere we could go in sweatpants."

"Let's start our own business, one where sweatpants are not only allowed, but required."

"You already own a business," Natalie said. "You could implement Sweatpants Mondays or something." She leaned over, propping her head up on a pillow so she was looking up at Lennon. "I'm glad you came over."

"Me too." Lennon reached for a Red Vine from the package on the coffee table. "I know I've been a little hard to hang out with lately."

"Life is busy." Natalie shrugged, taking it in stride. "I understand that."

"This new…" Lennon paused. She'd been keeping things under wraps, but this was her best friend. "This new relationship has been keeping me pretty busy."

She watched as avid curiosity colored Natalie's face. Ignoring it, she rushed on. "That and trying to keep up with work, launching our new winter menu, and helping Grant with some DIY projects for the house has made it so I don't really feel like I have much free time. With him gone this week, though, I have a little more time to focus on other things in my life."

"Relationship?" Natalie asked, finally getting a word in edgewise. Crossing her legs, she turned to face Lennon. She placed her elbows on her knees and rested her face in her hands in anticipation. "When did this happen?"

"Recently," Lennon said, chewing on the candy to buy herself time. "It's not a big deal," she added after a moment. "I'm still trying to figure things out. But I like her and I respect her. I enjoy the time we spend together, and I'm happy for the moment."

"You sound like such a cynic," Natalie said. "Why not just embrace it?"

"It's different with her," Lennon said, forgoing her usual approach of keeping details limited. Natalie was someone she trusted.

"Actually, maybe you can help me sort through some of the things I'm feeling," she said.

"I can try," Natalie said, offering a genuine and tender smile. "God knows you've been there for me when I've been in the throes of relationship drama."

Grabbing a throw pillow and clutching it in her lap, Lennon looked up to the ceiling. "I like her," she said. "That's the problem. I wasn't supposed to. She was a one-night stand. We both knew we were just hooking up. And somehow we just kept hooking up. I wasn't ready to get into something, and now I'm in the thick of it. We're spending almost every evening together. We've decided that we're not seeing other people."

"Why is that a problem?" Natalie's blank expression was full of innocence.

Lennon wanted to scream. *Why couldn't anyone keep up with why this was problematic?*

"I just got out of something," she said, holding her hands up to make the point. "You remember Leigh? You were there for it all. You watched my heart get tossed around like a beach ball, only to get popped in midair. You watched me cry and helped me get through it. And while I'm mostly over it, I'm pretty sure I'm not ready to give my heart away again. And I'm pretty sure that getting into this relationship, no matter how much I enjoy it, wasn't a good call timing-wise. You should know that best, since you were there for all of the drama."

"Easy," Natalie said. "Of course I remember. That was also a few months ago. You are so hard on yourself. We all deal with heartache how we need to in the moment, but you emerged out the other side. And, despite all this stubborn bullshit you put out there, you met someone—someone who I think is kind of amazing from what I've seen."

"You've only met her once and at a distance," Lennon protested, letting the rest of her friend's comments slide without dispute.

"So you're saying she's not amazing?"

"I didn't say that." Lennon reached for another Red Vine. "She is..." She paused and smiled. "She's really amazing and somehow as enchanting as she is terrifying, but...that's not the point I'm making."

Natalie laughed. "I can tell how amazing she is in the fact that she won you over. You're not exactly the easiest person to convince to let your guard down. But continue, please. I'm sorry to cut you off." She shook her head. "Wait, before you continue, why is she terrifying?"

"I never know what to expect." Lennon smiled, then frowned. "I really don't. She's unpredictable, and it catches me off guard. I'm used to understanding where people are coming from. But she's complex. I'd say mysterious, but she's not really. She spells out what she's thinking and feeling for me, but even so, it's never something I'm expecting. She keeps me on my toes, and that's a little unnerving sometimes."

"Anyway," she said, drawing her friend's attention back to the subject of the hour, "as I was saying, I wasn't ready to start dating again. In fact, I know I wasn't. The timing is all wrong. There's also the issue of this being harder than normal."

"How so?"

"With Leigh, there wasn't conflict like there already is with Alex," Lennon said, running her fingers over the ridges in the candy she held. The words sounded petty even to her. "I'm not trying to compare the two," she said quickly. That's exactly what she was doing, though, she admitted to herself. She bit at a fingernail, her nerves mounting. "I'm just saying that there have already been issues, and I'm working harder to stay in something than I've had to in the past. And I don't even know if I wanted a relationship that I had to fight for."

Natalie's brow furrowed. She opened her mouth—and then reached for a Red Vine. Chewing on it, she eyed Lennon.

"When it's real, it takes work," she said. "I know that's not what you want to hear, but it's the truth. Maybe this thing is real"—she raised an eyebrow—"and maybe it's not. Time will tell, but I can tell you that you need to stop living in the past. Leigh is gone. She's not coming back, and whatever you had with her was what it was. Sure, it was easy, but it didn't last. You can't dwell on that and place your expectations from that relationship onto this new one or your past will ruin the present—and potentially your future."

"I'm *not* dwelling on the past," Lennon protested, then sighed. There was no use arguing with Natalie.

"Not everything fits in a perfect little box," Natalie said. "I know you want life to go according to plan and you want it to be neat, but it doesn't work like that."

"Some semblance of order is all I ask for. It's not supposed to be *this* messy."

"Some of the best things are," Natalie said.

"I like order."

"You like control," Natalie corrected gently.

"No." Lennon pressed, even though she knew there was no use.

"You always have wanted things to work exactly as you planned, or you overthink them." Natalie placed a reassuring hand on Lennon's shoulder. "And that's okay, but it also takes away from just living in the moment and going with the flow."

Lennon opened her mouth to argue, but Natalie grinned, stopping her in her tracks. "So... Tell me more about Alex," she said, leaning back onto the couch cushion, smugly as though she had just won an argument.

Lennon huffed. She wanted to get defensive, but the mark of a good friend was that they'd be there to call you out on your bullshit as quickly as they'd be there to celebrate you. She shook her head, and, following suit, leaned back into the plush cushions behind her.

Natalie motioned for her to go on with the explanation, and even though she wanted to fight it, the words came easily.

"She has this depth about her, making it so that I never know what's coming next. It's exhilarating and sometimes unnerving. She's brilliant, with an eye for beauty that's unmatched. She makes me see the world in a new way. She's weird...maybe quirky is a better word."

Lennon paused, chewing on a Red Vine and mulling over her thoughts.

"She's kind, and she's easy to talk to. She's honest—sometimes a little *too* honest—but it's refreshing. She's stubborn and fierce and untamed—almost like a hurricane. I don't really know how to describe her, other than she's a force of nature, and some days I just feel as though I'm along for the ride."

"That," Natalie said after a moment, pointing at Lennon, "is why I would make the case that she's worth the fight, even though I don't really know her."

"What do you mean?" Lennon asked, tilting her head.

"I haven't seen you smile when describing someone or talking about someone like that in all the years I've known you." She laughed. "Your face gives you away, even if your pride doesn't want to admit it. You beam when you talk about her, and the fact that she isn't easy to figure out is a good thing."

When Lennon didn't respond, Natalie leaned closer. "Just because she isn't easy to pinpoint or describe, just because she's unlike the others you've known or loved, and just because she doesn't follow your plan perfectly doesn't make her someone you should run away from. A little work is necessary for anything that's going to last, and I think you owe it to her and to yourself to take a chance."

"I'm already taking the chance."

"Not really," Natalie said, handing Lennon an unopened bag of gummy bears as a peace offering. "You're in the relationship, but you're holding back because of preconceived notions about what it should or shouldn't be. You can't live like that, and even though I know you'll tell me it's too early to even mention, you certainly can't love like that. You have to give the relationship and Alex—*and yourself*—a little bit of slack. No one is perfect. Nor is any relationship. Take a close look anytime you have two people together. You'll see just how imperfect even the best couple can be."

Lennon pondered her words. Letting out a deep breath, she finally nodded. "I'll take that into consideration," she said, although she wasn't going to give Natalie the satisfaction of completely agreeing with her. She ripped open the bag of gummy bears, popped a handful into her mouth, and turned her attention back to the television.

"You deserve a happy ending, you know?" Natalie's tone was soft, and the words alone threatened to undo Lennon's resolve.

A knot formed in her throat as the issue at the heart of the matter came crashing forward. "I don't know that I do," she admitted. "And it's not like I'd recognize it if it came knocking. I always fuck it up first."

"Be kinder to yourself," Natalie scolded gently. "You *do* deserve it."

She bit her tongue. It wasn't cute to argue in the name of self-pity, even if she would have been telling the truth when saying that she really didn't think she deserved something like that. "Thanks," she muttered, choosing to gloss over anything deeper.

"Anytime." Natalie reached over and put her arm around Lennon's shoulders, pulling her in for a hug, before rising from the couch.

"Regardless of how you may feel about your new relationship, I know how you feel about champagne," she said, her eyes twinkling. "I have a bottle in the fridge, and I'd like to drink a toast to your new relationship. You can drink to your love of champagne if you'd rather."

"Can't I drink to both?" Lennon asked, laughing and standing to join her friend in the kitchen, thankful for the abrupt change of pace.

"There's my girl," Natalie said, pulling her in for a real hug this time. "I knew that smile was lurking somewhere under all that angst." She grabbed the bottle, popped the cork, and giggled as she poured two glasses and handed one to Lennon. "Cheers," she said, holding out her glass. "Here's to new beginnings, regardless of where they may take us, and to you finding your smile again."

"Cheers," Lennon responded, clinking her glass against Natalie's. "To all of that, to us, and to champagne for being the steadfast buddy it always is."

Laughing, they each took a sip of their champagne. Setting her glass on the counter, Lennon smiled at her friend. "Thank you," she said. "You know I don't want to admit it, but you're usually right about these things. I just feel so much pressure."

"Why?" Natalie's nose crinkled as she considered the subject. "I don't understand what could be so full of pressure. It's a new relationship. The possibilities are endless, but at that time there's also no expectations."

Lennon stared at the bubbles in her glass, watching how they scurried to the top mirroring how her thoughts seemed to bubble up and take flight to the worst possible conclusion. Taking another sip of champagne, she leaned against the counter. "I just don't want to screw things up—not for me, not for her, and not for us." The admission took her by surprise, and instead of finishing her thought, she filled her mouth with champagne.

"Cut yourself some slack," Natalie said, looping her arm around Lennon's neck and gently guiding her back toward the couch. "And while you're at it, cut *her* some slack too. Nothing is perfect from the start—nothing *real*, that is."

Lennon felt the weight of the words. It hadn't been real last time, and she knew it, despite how hard she'd tried. Leigh checked all the boxes of things she was supposed to be, and she made Lennon feel all the right things, but it wasn't real. She tapped her finger anxiously against the glass and looked up at Natalie, discovering she was still talking.

"Like I said, neither one of you is perfect." Natalie paused to sip her champagne. "You're getting to know each other, and you're still feeling this whole thing out. It doesn't have to be a do-or-die thing, and you don't have to make anything perfect." She set her glass down on a coaster before turning to face Lennon.

"You're not in control. You always take responsibility for making sure others are okay, but you don't need to do that here. She willingly jumped into this relationship with you. I know you, and I know you're trying to make sure all the pieces are in place and that everyone is protected from getting hurt. But you can't do that."

Lennon's mind was spinning, but it had little to do with her barely touched champagne. "I feel like I'm at a therapist's office," she blurted.

"Am I analyzing things correctly?" Natalie eyed her knowingly.

"Yeah," she said. "I think you're doing a fine job."

"What does Grant say about it all?" Natalie asked. "I'm sure he's spent a great deal of time with her. What are his thoughts?"

"There's a reason I'm talking to you," Lennon said. "He's so difficult in matters like this. He likes her. But he's also not the best one to get into the mushy feelings part with."

"There are mushy feelings?" Natalie asked, her voice and eyebrows rising in excitement.

"Yeah, I get lots of mushy feelings, because she's good in bed," Lennon quipped, laughing. "Yeah, of course there are a few other feelings tied up in it all." She sighed. "I like her, a lot more than I initially thought I would and certainly more than I intended to. I'm just worried about where it's headed."

"Why are you so concerned right now with what lies ahead?"

"I think she's going to want more than I do. More than I can offer." Lennon frowned. "I feel like a shell of what I once was, like a ghost, and I'm not sure I can do this thing without making things worse for both of us."

"You know," Natalie said slowly, "I know you're going to hate me for saying it, but seeing a therapist might not be a bad idea."

"I've been to therapy," Lennon snapped. "You know that. I've been pretty open about it. I don't need that right now."

"I'm not saying that you *need* therapy." Natalie picked up her glass of champagne and took a sip, eyeing Lennon cautiously. "I'm just saying it might help you to sort out some of the confusion."

And the depression. And the anxiety. And the insomnia. Lennon scowled. She knew Natalie had good intentions, but she was intent on doing this on her own this time.

"We'll see," she said. "But in the interim, I've made it clear we're not getting too serious."

"Why would you do something like that?" Natalie's tone was gentle, lacking the reprimand Lennon had expected.

Lennon ran her fingers through her hair and braced her arms on her knees. "I don't want her to get too attached to the idea of us as a happily ever after," she said. "She just got out of a relationship where she was planning to get married. I'm still a little worried she's just overinvesting in a rebound, and I don't want her to substitute this for what she had. I'm trying to protect her from the confusion and misplaced feelings we all get after a long-term relationship fails."

"But..." Lennon held up her hand to stop her from responding. "I think it's best for both of us. For now, it serves as a reminder to both of us to look at what we have—not an illusion of what might be in the future or what we might be trying to replace."

"Okay," Natalie conceded. "You do you, and I'll be here whatever happens. Even if you're cautious, *I'm* happy for you."

"Thank you," Lennon said, raising her glass in the air in a mock toast fashion. "Let's find something else to watch," she said, glancing back at the television. "This clearly hasn't kept our attention."

Natalie rolled her eyes but didn't argue. As she was reaching for the remote, she stopped and turned her attention back to Lennon. "You do know you can come talk about this kind of stuff whenever, even when Grant is in town."

"I know," Lennon said, taking a drink of her champagne so she didn't have to keep talking.

"One more thing before we get to the movie," Natalie said, eyeing Lennon wryly. "You mentioned she's good in bed. I want to hear more about that."

Lennon laughed. Clearing her throat, she considered her options and decided to let her best friend in on the secret. "She made me orgasm on the very first try," she said, blushing slightly.

Natalie's mouth fell open. "And you've waited until now to tell me that?" she asked. "That's never happened for you."

"I know," Lennon said with a slight smile. *This* was what she missed so much from their college years, before commitments, the real world, life, and significant others. They'd always shared everything, and this should be no exception. "You know as well as I do, I usually have to wait quite a while before anyone figures it out, but she did. And she's figured it out every time since. It's amazing. Mind-blowing even."

"Keep going," Natalie said, scooting closer.

"It's changed somewhat," Lennon said, unable to hide her smile as she mentally relived their encounters. "The first night was wild. But I think that's because we didn't think there was going to be another night. We let it all out and had a great time. And for a while, it was that crazy, no-holds-barred sex. There are times now when it's tender, but it's always passionate, and it's always great."

"Sounds like you could add that to her strengths list." Natalie chuckled. "For what it's worth, I think she sounds like a keeper."

"We'll see," Lennon said, still grinning. "Now that I've indulged you, let's put on a movie."

"Fair enough," Natalie said, settling back into her spot on the couch and flipping through channels.

Despite the fact that Natalie had done as Lennon requested and had changed the channel to *Dirty Dancing*, one of Lennon's all-time favorites, she couldn't focus. Natalie's advice and analyses were zinging through her mind at neck-breaking speed, as she grappled to make sense of even a single thought.

By the time she left Natalie's house, she was no less certain she wasn't making a mistake. But she was certain there was only one place she wanted to be while she figured it out—in Alex's arms.

CHAPTER FIFTEEN

The tiny air vent overhead whirred loudly but did little to cool the dense air created when a hundred people were crammed into a tiny space or to dissipate the sickly sweet and generally unpleasant aroma generated by a thousand different smells colliding in the cabin.

Lindsey Daniels pinched her nose and tried to focus on anything else. In the seat next to her, her four-year-old, Connor, bounced and played, talking to the sweet older woman who sat by the window. After a three-hour layover in Dallas, they were on the second leg of their journey, and Lindsey wanted nothing more than to place her feet firmly back on the ground. At this point, she had lost all excitement about their trip.

The beach, Florida, seeing her sister—all of it somehow had lost its luster after traveling all day with a toddler, no matter how much she loved his sticky little face. Dabbing her napkin in her water, she tried for another time to clean off whatever substance he had on his face.

She had agreed to this trip, looked forward to it even, but after glancing at her watch and realizing they still had another hour in the air, she again wished her sister had thought it through before picking up and moving all the way across the country. No longer could she and Connor come over and hang out. No longer could they easily help one another out when they were in a tough spot. No longer could they truly be close, even though they had promised each other as much in the handful of phone calls they'd exchanged since Alex moved. With a mother who had checked out when they were teenagers and a father who'd long since passed, Alex was all she'd had. She glanced down at Connor, wondering if she would have felt less resentment toward Alex if she'd have found someone of her own to love. Not that she would have changed the one-night stand that brought Connor to her, but it would have been nice to have some help and companionship. She reached down and fished a coloring book and a baggie of crayons out of her backpack and placed them on Connor's tray table, hoping to keep him occupied for a little while longer.

She took a sip of her water and glanced down the aisle of the plane. In another time and place, when her son wasn't as tired and frustrated as she was, she would have gotten lost in people watching, imagining their backstories and where they were headed. She wondered what people might think of her story. No doubt, she looked frazzled. Connor was a spirited but good-natured kid, but at four even he wasn't a saint enough to handle air travel well. She had bags under her eyes, her dark hair was somehow both frizzy and flat, and she was pretty sure the brown stain on her white tee was chocolate milk from breakfast with Connor. No one would have guessed she was headed off to what was supposed to be a joyous reunion with her sister on the beach.

A beach getaway. A vacation. It all sounded so much more romantic than chocolate milk stains, crushed up crackers, crayons, and twelve hours of travel.

Rubbing her temples, she let out a deep breath. Time would tell, and she'd get to see firsthand this weekend, but she hoped this move was worth it for Alex. She truly wasn't fretting about the inconvenience of long-distance travel as much as she was about the fact that it felt like Alex was running from her problems. Her little sister had admonished her during their last phone call—her firm command to "Stop worrying so much" was still reverberating in her head—but that was easier said than done.

As if he knew distraction was needed, Connor dropped his crayons and started to whine. She turned her attention to him, deciding her sister's issues would have to wait until later.

* * *

The slap of her footsteps on the pavement, combined with the sound of Alex's beside her and the way their shadows bounced in tandem on the sidewalk, soothed Lennon as her playlist switched to a new song. It was very simplistic, but it was sweet. Humming along to herself, she continued living up to their deal—running, no talking.

As their run came to an end, she glanced up at Alex. Even drenched in sweat, she was radiant. Placing her hands above her head, Alex nodded breathlessly.

"We need to do that more often," she said, struggling to get air.

"We do," Lennon agreed. "And we will."

"Especially this week, since we'll be feasting," Alex said, jokingly running her hands over her intentionally pushed out stomach.

"When does your family arrive?" Lennon switched her music off and stopped to stretch.

Alex looked down at her watch. "They'll be here around four."

"Good." Lennon wiped the sweat from her brow and nodded in the direction of the condo. "Since we have some time, we can whip up some breakfast."

"I haven't gone to the store yet, but I might have stuff for a smoothie," Alex said, unlocking the door and motioning for Lennon to enter first. "I was hoping we could tackle the shopping together."

Lennon sucked in a pained breath. "Shopping on the day before Thanksgiving?"

"I'll make it worth your time," Alex said, looking at Lennon seductively.

"I'm sure you will," Lennon said, hopping onto the counter as Alex gathered fruits, greens, and yogurt from the fridge. "And I'll go, but I'll have to complain a bit."

"That's all I ask," Alex said, laughing as she tossed the ingredients into the blender and added a heap of protein powder.

"Should I be nervous about meeting them?" Lennon asked, fidgeting in her seat. She brought her hands together in her lap and then placed her palms on the counter beneath her.

"It seems like you already are." Alex laughed. "Don't be, though. I like you, so they will too." She raised her voice to be louder than the blender.

"We'll see," Lennon quipped, hopping down from her place on the counter to grab two glasses and place them in front of Alex. As Alex poured their smoothies, she turned to face Lennon, offering her best pleading look.

"I've met your family. At least I think Grant counts as your family, right?"

Lennon accepted the glass Alex offered. "I guess he's close enough."

"Okay, good. Then I met one of your closest family members the first night I met you, and I lived to tell the tale." She took a drink of her smoothie and put her free hand on her hip. "Can you do this for me?"

"Of course," Lennon said, kissing Alex on the cheek. She straightened her shoulders, hoping the move made her look as confident as she wanted to be. "I'm more afraid of the grocery store today than I am of meeting them."

The words dripped from her tongue easily. She could only hope they were smooth enough to hide the anxiety that was roiling inside her. She smiled and pulled Alex in for a kiss, wondering for the hundredth time that morning how she'd gone from hooking up with a woman she'd met in a bar to meeting her family for Thanksgiving.

Her thoughts jumped to her own family and how uncomfortable it would be if things were reversed. They weren't crazy about her being gay, let alone bringing home a new woman.

Thankfully they mostly hung around their house or with their church crew on the outskirts of town, where she'd grown up, so she didn't have to see them unless she wanted to. Over the years, she'd taken special care to avoid the shops and restaurants her parents frequented, so she could keep her distance.

"Where'd you go?" Alex asked, placing her finger under Lennon's chin and lifting her face upward.

"Nowhere," Lennon lied. "I just need to hop in the shower, and I'll be ready to brave the store."

Alex opened her mouth, and Lennon was afraid she'd offer to join. Any other morning, that would have been exactly what she wanted, but this morning, everything was too jumbled. Needing her space, she exited the room quickly and turned on the water in the bathroom before Alex had a chance to say anything.

After the shower, she emerged, refreshed, refocused, and smelling of the musky patchouli soap Alex kept in the shower. "I'm one clean hippie," Lennon called out as she rounded the corner from the hallway to the living area.

She heard Alex's laugh from the kitchen, its sweet sound bringing a smile to her lips. "I'll be the judge of that," Alex said, raising an eyebrow in approval when Lennon entered the room. "Wow!" She let out a whistle. "Look at you! Quite the transformation from just a while ago. Come here and let me get a whiff."

"Stop it," Lennon said with a laugh, but she leaned in for an embrace anyway. "I'm a new me after that shower."

"You peruse the list on the counter, while I shower," Alex said, still eyeing her with lust. "Then we'll be ready to go." She headed toward the bathroom.

"Good God." Lennon's eyes widened as she took the list in her hands. "This is longer than a CVS receipt."

"I know," Alex said, turning back and offering a sheepish grin.

"Don't worry about it," Lennon said. "We'll knock this out."

She took a seat and waited while Alex showered, reading the list another time, making note of each item to avoid heeding the alarm bells ringing in her head at the prospect of getting in too deep, too fast.

When Alex finally emerged, Lennon stood and grabbed her wallet on the console by the door. "Let's get started," she said, holding out Alex's jacket for her. "Before too long, it'll be a bloodbath in every grocery store."

They gathered their things and headed for the car. Once inside, Alex handed the auxiliary cord to Lennon. Flipping through her phone, she chose a playlist and plugged it in.

"Here you go," she said with a nod. "This will get us in the spirit."

As fast-paced 90s dance music pounded through the speakers, a slow smile spread over Alex's face. "I'm so thankful you're coming with me," she said, casting a sideways glance in Lennon's direction.

"I'm just here for the comedy relief," Lennon said, glancing out the window. "That," she raised an eyebrow, "and for the booze selection, of course." She turned the music down a notch. "Do you want me to come up with a signature drink to pair with dinner?"

"That really would class things up a notch, wouldn't it?" Alex's eyes sparkled. "I'd love it."

Lennon tapped her chin, mentally making a list of flavors she'd like to complement.

"Thank you," Alex said softly, breaking Lennon out of her thoughts.

"What for?"

"Everything." She reached over, placing a hand on Lennon's thigh. "Thank you for coming with me to the store today and planning a drink. And thanks for meeting my sister and nephew." She glanced at Lennon when she stopped at a stop sign, but quickly looked back to the road. "It's a little less depressing than introducing them to a random acquaintance or two that I've made since I've been here."

"I'm happy to do it." Lennon reached over and gave her hand a reassuring squeeze. "But don't be so hard on yourself. You've made friends."

"*Your* friends," Alex corrected gently.

"You have the adoring publics of all people at the galleries and around town." Lennon racked her brain, wishing she could offer more solace, but since Alex's arrival most of their time had been spent together, despite a few attempts to do otherwise. "Those count as friends. But don't worry about it," she added quickly. "You haven't even been here a full four months. It takes a while to build a circle, and I'll be there."

Alex nodded as she pulled the car into the liquor store. "Want to start here?" she asked, changing the subject.

"It's as good a place as any." Lennon grabbed the car door handle but stopped before getting out. She shifted in her seat to face Alex. "Are you okay?" she asked, choosing her words carefully. "Are you nervous about their visit?"

"I just..." Alex looked out into the distance. "I just think I'm afraid Lindsey will tell me I made a mistake coming out here. Aside from meeting you, selling a few pieces of my work, and enjoying the beach, I'm not sure I have much to show for my time." She knitted her brow. "Yeah. I guess I am nervous."

"I get that." Lennon reached over and looped her fingers through Alex's. "You did what was best for you in the moment, and you're rolling with it."

"Thank you." She squeezed Lennon's hand. "Let's go on inside. There's nothing that we can't drink about, right?"

"Absolutely." Lennon laughed. "Let's go have some mixed drinks about some feelings."

Alex's laugh rang out. "God, I love you." As soon as the words tumbled forth, she snapped her mouth closed. Lennon's mouth went dry, and it felt as if the air had been sucked out of the car. Her mind raced as she tried to figure out what to say—and came up empty. She looked out the window, grabbed the door handle, and quickly exited the car. Following suit, Alex hopped out and met her at the entrance.

"I'm going to browse some beer, as well," Lennon said, holding the door open for Alex before darting off to the beer fridge, her thoughts running rampant. As she glanced from IPAs to lagers, she shoved her hands in her pockets to keep them from displaying her inner panic. It hadn't been a declaration of love. It had come out more like a "God, I love the Beatles" type of statement than an "I'm so in love with you." The world seemed to shift beneath her. She reached for the shelving in front of her and steadied herself. That's what Alex had meant, right? It had to be.

She took three deep breaths but couldn't quell the storm of questions within her. What if *that* was what Alex had meant? Did Alex feel that way, or was it some misplaced emotion? And most importantly, what did *she* feel?

She closed her eyes, tightening her grip on a six-pack of grapefruit IPA. Her world was brighter with Alex around, and the sound of her laughter was enough to make a shitty day better. Their chemistry in bed was unmatched, and conversation was passionate. She'd gone along this far with the relationship because there had been no reason at all not to enjoy the ride they were on. But…*love*? Was it? Could it be?

She cleared her throat, but the sound that emerged came across more like a cry. She realized she'd been gone for too long. Her fingers were cold by the time she grabbed two six-packs, without checking the labels, and headed back toward the bourbon section.

"Figured this was a safe bet," Alex said, smiling as Lennon rounded the corner.

"If I'm ever lost, you can wait for me in a bourbon section. I'll always find my way there eventually," Lennon said, forcing a laugh.

Alex shifted her weight side to side and opened her mouth, but she didn't speak. "Which one?" she finally asked, pointing to the wall of whiskey.

"I'm thinking Old Grand-Dad for sure to mix and a bottle of Whistle Pig for a nicer after-dinner treat," Lennon said, nodding toward her tried and true favorites. She grabbed the bottles off the shelf and placed them in Alex's outstretched hands. "I'm going to grab some ginger beer and some orange bitters." She turned on a heel and headed for another section, Alex following behind her.

As she gathered the items, she wondered if she should address what had been said, but as the silence grew between them, she was certain speaking about it would only make it more awkward.

She glanced down at the items she held, thankful they masked the way her hands were shaking. Her nerves were going haywire. She'd grab the rest of the things she needed at the grocery store, she told herself, focusing her attention on everything but the elephant in the liquor store.

Alex stood wordlessly beside her as she paid and took her bagged purchases. Once out the door, she practically raced for the sanctuary of the passenger seat, where there would be the godsend of a stereo. She quickly deposited the liquor in the backseat, took her seat upfront, cued up her music app again, and hit shuffle. As if coming to her rescue, Celine Dion's powerful voice flooded the car's interior. She closed her eyes, singing along loudly to drown out any questions from Alex or, worse yet, from herself.

* * *

Alex's heart was pounding every bit as loudly as the music thumping from the speakers. She resisted the urge to turn it down. Glancing out of the corner of her eye, she watched as Lennon looked completely lost in the music. Her grip on the door handle gave her away, though. Her knuckles whitened as her voice rose and fell with the high and low notes. Looking away, Alex put the car in drive and headed down the road toward the grocery store.

What had she done? Was Lennon going to bolt as soon as she was taken back to her own vehicle? The chorus of "It's All Coming Back to Me" swelled, but Celine Dion singing about old feelings coming back did nothing to quell her fears.

The beeping of a horn brought her back to reality.

"Dammit!" She swerved out of the way of the car that was barreling toward them. "Sorry," she said, glancing sideways toward Lennon. "I didn't see the four-way stop."

"No worries," Lennon said, studiously keeping her gaze on her phone and flipping through it to select the next song.

After Alex pulled the car into the parking lot, she sat for a moment longer than usual, waiting for her heart rate to go back to normal, waiting for her mind to stop swimming in self-doubt and insecurity. She watched as Lennon grabbed her wallet, got out, and strode toward the store. Her movements were smooth, her shoulders were held back with confidence, and the sunlight glinting down brought out the shine in her lovely blue eyes as she turned back to look for Alex. *Love*ly. There was that damn word again. Without her permission, Alex's mind contemplated a scary thought. Had she said what she said out of *habit*? Or had she actually meant it?

She got out of the car, slamming the door to try to dislodge the thought, and walked toward the store. With each step toward Lennon, toward a meet-the-family Thanksgiving celebration, and toward the words she couldn't unspeak, her legs grew weaker and she became more and more certain there was no way to undo the predicament she'd created.

CHAPTER SIXTEEN

The scent of coffee wafted through the air, mixing with the sea breeze that danced through Alex's open window. She stared at the blank canvas in front of her and adjusted the lamp above her workstation. Three o'clock in the morning might not offer the best lighting for painting, but it offered the most peaceful time to sort through her thoughts.

She dipped her brush into red paint and ran it across the canvas, its bold stroke bringing to life the mounting passion and frustration coming to a head within her.

I love you.

The words echoed in her mind, drawing her back to the last time she'd said them before yesterday afternoon, to a time when she thought they meant forever. Rubbing the spot where she once wore a ring, she shuddered. Letting herself remember, she closed her eyes, no longer seeing Olivia's face, but Lennon's in its place.

Leaning forward, she let her mind shuffle through her thoughts and began painting with reckless abandon. Hours passed by in a blur, and as she set her paintbrush down the sun peeked over the horizon. Leaning back in her chair, she crossed her legs and surveyed her night's work. It was chaotic, passionate, and angry. Within it, an array of faceless lovers swirled around one another until you couldn't tell where one ended and the other began.

She turned the canvas toward the wall. What it meant was not clear. She snorted. It was confusing enough to her, and she was the artist.

She jumped at the sound of footsteps in the hallway, suddenly reminded that she had a four-year-old and his mom as houseguests.

"Good morning," she said, turning around to find her sister standing behind her, eyeing her quizzically.

"What are you doing?" Before she could answer, Lindsey held up her hands to stop Alex from saying anything. She turned on a heel and walked toward the kitchen. "Where's the coffee?" she asked, visibly upset, but clearly having opted to forgo a conversation. For the moment at least.

"In the cabinet above the pot," Alex said, wiping her hands on the towel beside her easel and standing. "I made a pot earlier, but I drank it. I'll make a fresh one. Let me take care of it."

She joined her sister in the kitchen and gently nudged her out of the way. "What's wrong with you?" she teased.

"With me?" Lindsey crossed her arms over her chest, then stepped back, running a hand through her tousled hair. She was quite a sight, pouting in her Wonder Woman pajama pants, no doubt something Connor had picked out at the store, given his love of superheroes. "I should be asking you that question."

"I'm fine." Alex tossed the old grounds into her counter compost bin, poured water into the back of the coffeemaker, and filled the tray with fresh grounds. She looked over her shoulder and made eye contact with her sister. Lindsey narrowed her eyes and shook her head.

"I've seen it before," she finally said with her hands on her hips. "You being up at all hours of the night painting is never a good sign."

"Maybe I'm just working on my craft." Alex worked to keep the edge out of her voice. The last thing she wanted was a lecture or life advice.

"Maybe," Lindsey said. "Or maybe you're wrestling with your demons, fighting off depression, or trying to make a decision." She paused only to reach over and grab a grape out of the bowl on the counter and pop it into her mouth. As she chewed, she eyed Alex intently. "Which is it?" she asked after she swallowed.

"Why not all three?" Alex asked as she turned to grab pancake mix from the pantry. "Where's my favorite nephew?"

"Still sleeping. Stop changing the subject."

"Fine." Alex sighed. "What is it you're after? Want to know that I'm a bit uncertain if I should have moved here and dropped everything back home?" She waited, but Lindsey didn't speak. She angrily snatched a spatula from her utensil holder and set the box of mix on the counter. "I was pretty uncertain for a while. It was a leap of faith…no…desperation." She gulped, remembering the tumultuous nature of those first few weeks. "It was a rough bit of time, and I know you're worried I didn't deal with anything. It's been a common theme in your texts, your calls, and now in your condescending grimace."

"I am *not* being condescending. I am just trying to make sure you're okay."

"I'm fine."

"Fucked up, insecure, neurotic, and emotional?"

"I hate it when you do that," Alex said, moving past her to gather eggs and milk from the refrigerator. As she swung the door open, she looked around it to face Lindsey again. "I'm good. I'm happy. I'm human."

"Human, I can see," Lindsey said. "You'll have to sell me a bit harder on good and happy."

"Please stop." Alex held up her hands to reinforce her point. "Yes, I ran from my problems, and yes, coming out here didn't magically make them go away. I have my old problems and old demons too. To which I've added new problems and new demons. And I'm still here fighting." She grabbed a bowl and cracked the eggs into it in frustration. The box of mix ripped as she yanked it open, sending the flour-like substance all over the kitchen.

"Calm down," Lindsey said, walking toward her.

"Don't," Alex hissed. "I'm fucking happy you're here, okay? I'm really excited to see you and spend time with Connor. I've been looking forward to this, and I want to have a good Thanksgiving."

"I'm not trying to ruin Thanksgiving," Lindsey said, stepping backward as if she had been slapped.

"Then what *are* you trying to do?" When Lindsey didn't answer, Alex let out a sad laugh and grabbed a dishtowel. As she was cleaning up the spill, she thought better of it, but spoke the words anyway. "It's bad enough you offered no real support when I went through a broken engagement, but now you show up here, act cold to my girlfriend, and lecture me on Thanksgiving."

"I wasn't acting cold." Fire flashed in Lindsey's eyes. "I am just being protective. Besides there was something else going on between the two of you last night. She's nice, and she's funny, but I don't know what the hell I walked into. You two barely talked to one another, and what was that whole thing with the limes?"

"She cut her hand while making cocktails," Alex said in disbelief. "Give her a break. Don't you think it might be a little nerve-wracking to have to meet someone's family members, especially when those family members have their claws out?"

"I don't know what to think, aside from the fact that I don't think jumping from one bed to another is the best approach for getting your shit together."

"I don't think I asked for your permission or your approval." Her hands shook with anger, but she pressed on with the task at hand. The silence hung between them as she mashed the remaining pancake mix into the bowl. She frowned. This was the last thing she'd wanted. She knew she should extend an olive branch, but she wasn't sure she wanted to.

"I'm just saying I'm not sure she's right for you."

"Ouch."

At the sound of Lennon's voice, Lindsey spun around, her arm flailing out and knocking the bowl of mix to the ground in a single motion.

"Fuck," Alex muttered. She looked from the mix splattered on the floor to Lennon's pained smile to Lindsey's reddening cheeks and threw the dishtowel on the ground.

"Let me help with that," Lennon said, walking over and dropping to her knees. Behind them Lindsey was trying to form words that sounded like a genuine apology, but Alex held up a hand cutting her off.

"Why don't you go shower and get ready?" she suggested, leaning around Lennon to narrow her eyes at Lindsey. "Go," she mouthed silently, shaking her head in disbelief at her sister.

First there was the "I love you" debacle, and now there was this. If Lennon didn't run for the hills by nightfall, she'd be impressed.

"I'm so sorry," she said when she finally heard the door to her bathroom close.

"Don't." Lennon wiped up the last of the mix from the floor and smiled. The feeling didn't show in her eyes, but Alex figured it was as good as she was going to get in the moment. She leaned over and kissed Lennon softly. "She's right about yesterday and the lime crisis," Lennon said. "I let my nerves get the best of me, and things were a bit awkward. I was probably a bit overanimated."

"Still, she shouldn't have…"

Lennon cut her words off with another kiss.

"Thank you."

"Not a problem," Lennon said, standing and gathering the soiled rags.

Alex opened her mouth, wishing she could say something to break the tension that had been festering there for almost twenty-four hours.

"I said something yesterday," she blurted out.

Lennon's eyes widened and she feigned confusion. "What did you say?" Her voice quivered, giving her away. She knew, and Alex knew she knew.

"You know what I said."

The words hung between them, and Lennon cast her eyes downward. "I do."

Alex's throat went dry and her hands shook. She looked into Lennon's eyes and offered a tentative smile. "I meant it." The words were almost too quiet to hear, but when Lennon stiffened, Alex knew she'd heard.

Lennon's eyes darted around the room, and she shifted her weight to the side. Stepping forward, she set the mix-covered towels and bowl on the counter. "I'm not ready," she said after a moment. She stepped closer to Alex and put her arms around her waist. "I…" she exhaled hard. "I don't know what you want me to say."

"You don't have to say anything," Alex said, thankful that Lennon hadn't made a beeline for the door at her admission. "I was up all night trying to sort out why I'd said it, and I just needed to get it out in the open."

"We've always been pretty committed to laying it on the line." Lennon leaned in for a peck of a kiss. "Thanks for telling me, but I'm not sure what we do from here."

"Same thing we've been doing?" Alex's heart pounded as Lennon looked up at her, seeming to weigh her options.

She nodded eventually and gave Alex another quick peck before breaking contact. "Want me to make French toast?"

"Please." As Lennon set to work, Alex watched her swoop in once more to save the day. Once or twice, she considered addressing what Lindsey had said, but she figured they'd dealt with one calamity this morning, a major one, and that was more than enough.

She busied herself cleaning up the rest of the kitchen and setting places at the table while Lennon whipped up a batch of French toast. She was grateful for the help, although she wished the morning had gone the way she had planned it.

"Are you excited for today?" Her voice shook a little as she filled the silence. Wringing a dishtowel in her hands, she wondered if it would always feel this awkward between them now.

"Sure," Lennon said, offering a good-natured laugh. "How do these look?" She held up a platter of perfectly golden pieces of French toast, surrounded by fresh berries.

"Amazing," Alex said, looking from the French toast to Lennon. "Just like you."

Lennon winked, bringing the platter over to the table. "Should we call them in?"

Alex frowned. "I want the little one, but not his mom." The words came out as a hiss.

"Well, we might as well call both of them regardless," Lennon said, placing the tray on the table. "She took off work to be here, and she made the effort to come all this way."

Reluctantly, Alex turned to call her sister and Connor. She stopped in her tracks, wincing as she saw Lindsey already standing in the hallway.

"I'll get Connor for breakfast," Lindsey said, turning around before Alex could say anything, but not before Alex saw her pained expression.

"Fuck this day," Alex said, throwing her hands in the air.

"Happy Thanksgiving, by the way," Lennon said, her thick laugh spreading through the air and building with each passing second. Before long, Alex couldn't contain herself and joined the laughter. "What are you thankful for?"

"I'm grateful this damn day only comes once a year," she finally said. "Have we lost our damn minds, standing here just laughing for no reason?"

"I think there are plenty of reasons for it," Lennon said as she plated each person's French toast and topped it with fruit, a drizzle of syrup, and powdered sugar. "Besides I like your laugh a lot better than the frustration you've been showing today." She reached over and grabbed Alex's hand. A wave of relief rushed through Alex's body at the contact.

She took Lennon's hand and brought it to her lips. "Thank you," she said, planting a soft kiss on the smooth skin. "You're rolling with the punches, and I think you're the thing I'm most grateful for this morning."

"Looks like everyone in here is in better spirits," Lindsey said, coming up behind them.

"Breakfast!" Connor called, his eyes widening as he jumped up to the seat beside Alex. "Auntie Alex, is *this* for me?"

"It is." Alex's heart warmed as she stared down at his big brown eyes. His goofy smile grew and she leaned down to kiss him on the top of the head. "Lennon made it." She pointed across the table with a smile.

He reached down and grabbed a syrupy piece and shoved it in his mouth with his bare hands. "Thanks!" he said, grinning with syrup dripping down his chin.

"Connor," Lindsey chastised.

"I've got it," Alex said, holding up her hands to stop any more drama from taking place in her kitchen.

"Here, kiddo," she said, handing him a paper towel and raising an eyebrow in his direction playfully. She ignored Lindsey's continual chatter and focused instead on the silly faces he was making.

As they ate, Lindsey made small talk with Lennon about the bar and the beach. Lennon filled her in on kayaking and fishing, as well as the intricacies of making a good cocktail, and by the time breakfast was finished, the awkwardness of the morning had faded somewhat.

"Can he hang out with you for a few minutes while I put on my makeup?" Lindsey asked, for the first time turning her attention to Alex.

"Of course," she said, grabbing her sticky, grinning nephew and plopping him on her lap.

"I'll take care of the dishes," Lennon said, standing and collecting the plates. Alex wanted to protest, but Lennon nodded to the living room before she could. "Go play."

Squirming in her arms, Connor drew Alex's attention back to him. "I want to play," he said, shimmying out of her grip and running for the living room.

"Okay," Alex agreed, grabbing a container of baby wipes that Lindsey had stashed on the counter the night before. "Let's wipe you down first."

"No," he protested, but he walked back toward her dutifully anyway. He grabbed the wipe and quickly ran it over his face and hands and tossed it to the ground, running back to the living room. "Do you still like cars?"

"Of course I like cars," she said, taking a place on the floor.

"Good!" He grabbed his backpack and dumped its contents on the floor.

Alex laughed. She was glad Lindsey hadn't been in the room for that moment. There would have been a stern response and reprimanding for sure, and that would only ruin the fun she was having with him.

"You get this one," he said, handing her a red sports car, "and I get this one." He grabbed a blue car and held it up toward the light as if it were a trophy. "This one is my favorite."

In the kitchen, Lennon put soft music on the Bluetooth speaker. It was a sweet gesture, one Alex knew was meant to put her at ease so she could enjoy the moment and not feel bad about not helping. As Connor jabbered on, telling her about how fast his favorite car was, she reached out and scooped him into a hug.

"I've missed you," she said, covering his cheeks in kisses.

"Gross! Cooties!" he said, smirking at her as he wiped them off, but then he leaned in and let her kiss him again. She tickled him and then set him down, laughing. Grabbing his racecar, he ran it over her shoulders and face, giggling as she scrunched her lips in response.

These were the moments she missed the most from her former life, although just a month ago she might have thought she missed other parts more.

"Are we going to the beach?" he asked, pointing out her window.

"We are." She leaned over, trying to see how the waves and sand must look from his perspective. "We'll go after lunch."

"Can I swim?"

"Probably not." She winced as his face fell. "It's cold." She wrapped her arms around her body and fake-shivered just to see the smile return to his face. "But we'll find shells and look at the waves."

"I want to swim."

"I know you do," she said, kissing him on the top of his head. "We'll see if we can't convince your mom to let us dip our toes in the water, but we can't get all the way in."

He turned his attention back to his car, and Alex marveled at what a good-natured kid he was. Never one to insist on getting his way, he went with the flow more often than not. "I like your girlfriend," he said out of the blue.

"Oh yeah?"

"She's pretty." He looked up at her and scrunched up his face, moving his eyebrows up and down exaggeratingly, a move he'd no doubt seen some ridiculous adult do.

"She is pretty, isn't she?" Alex said, smiling as she looked back to where Lennon worked in the kitchen. Her athletic body moved to the beat of the music as she stretched to put a mug up in a high cabinet. "I'm a pretty lucky lady."

"Lucky?" Connor cocked his head to the side, his brow furrowing. "Lucky." He said it again, as if trying the word on for size.

"Hmm," she said, buying herself a moment to think it over too. It was too heavy a topic to lay on a child, but she felt like she'd maybe picked up the pieces of something horrific and turned it into a potential happy ending. "I think I'm just happy to have her in my life," she said after a moment.

"Mom makes me happy. You make me happy." He closed his eyes for a minute. "That means I love you, and I love Mom."

It really was that simple, wasn't it? Happiness and love went hand in hand. "I love you too," she said, taking his tiny hand in her own.

"You love her too," Connor said, pointing with his free hand to the kitchen.

His singsong tone made the words seem so whimsical, so free, and so true. She'd said it, and she'd owned up to meaning it. And now Connor was here speaking it once again into the world.

As he returned to playing with his cars, she tried to focus on his rambling stories about dinosaurs and dragons, racecars, and candy bars, but the word "love" was pinging around in her head like a pinball in a machine.

* * *

Over the chatter of the members of her large extended family exchanging animated stories with one another, Lennon leaned back in her chair, sipping a cup of coffee and willing her overstuffed stomach to settle.

"How is work, honey?" Her mom's words cut into her thoughts.

She smiled, looking across the table and staring into her mother's eyes—eyes that matched her own, yet which would somehow always look wiser with their fine crow's feet in the corners and a softness that must have come with extra years.

"It's going well," she said, stifling a yawn. "Sorry," she said, running her hands over her stomach. "Thanksgiving food coma has set in."

Her mom laughed and nodded. "I feel it too," she assured her, before leaning closer, placing her forearms on the table. "I feel like I haven't seen you in ages."

"I know." Lennon shook her head. "I'm sorry about that. Life has been really busy lately."

"Tell me about it," her mom urged, leaving the open-ended invitation lingering in the air.

"Alibis is keeping me pretty tied up," she said, thankful her mother hadn't put on one of her infamous guilt trips about the two of them only living twenty minutes apart. "Business is great. I may hire another staff member, though. I haven't been taking many nights off, and…" She trailed off and shut her mouth. "How have you been?"

Seeing right through her omissions, her mom narrowed her eyes. "And what?" She smiled. "What are you doing on those few off nights, sweetheart?"

Lennon waited. Was it a trap? Had they come to a place where they could now banter about her seeing someone? Had her mother turned a corner, or was she still in denial and hoping whoever she was seeing was a man?

She took a sip of her coffee, buying time, while her thoughts swirled. It hadn't been that long ago that her mom had told her to keep information of that kind to herself. She didn't want to know about who Lennon was seeing, and she didn't need to ask any questions.

"Is there someone?" Her mother's question was a gentle, but pointed one. "I heard you mention to your brother that you were on your second Thanksgiving celebration of the day."

Lennon pressed her lips together and nodded, no longer able to lie to her mother. She watched as her mom balled up her napkin and smiled hesitantly. Her eyes clouded momentarily, but her smile didn't waver. "Tell me about her," she prompted after a moment of silence.

Her. The word resonated within Lennon, the first time in the decade she'd been out that her mom had broached the subject so openly. Maybe there really was such a thing as a holiday season miracle. Or maybe her Aunt Bernadette had been making some headway in softening up her mom.

"She's…" Lennon looked up to the ceiling, searching for the right words. "Pretty great," she said after a moment.

"And?"

Lennon let out a nervous laugh, clasping her hands together under the table to keep from fidgeting. "She's beautiful." Her cheeks blushed as if somehow admitting to Alex's beauty was as bad as coming out to her mom in the first place. "She's one of a kind. She sometimes seems to live in her own world but also adds beauty to the moment she's in. She's a fabulous artist. And she's funny." She shut her mouth before she could continue the tidal wave of praise.

"I'm happy for you." The words were quiet, and Lennon looked into her mom's eyes. She wanted to question, but didn't dare.

"Thanks. It's not anything too serious right now."

"Everything starts somewhere," her mom answered, standing up from the table and crossing the distance to hug her daughter. "I'm going to help clean up the kitchen."

"I'll join you," Lennon said, standing and taking a deep breath. Talking with her parents about her relationships had been something she'd seldom engaged in, much less talking to them about something that she wasn't sure had a long-term future.

As she washed and dried the pots and pans, her mind swam with questions.

What were they doing? Here she was telling her mom about their relationship, and she'd met Alex's sister and nephew. Even if Lindsey hadn't liked her, they'd met, and they'd shared an awkward Thanksgiving breakfast *and* lunch. And with the holidays quickly approaching, it all felt so intimate. Just months ago, she thought she'd be having this celebration with someone else, and while she had no interest in that future any more, was *this* the one she did want? Even if she did, *was* there a future to want?

She thought back to the liquor store and the words that had been spoken there and Alex's admission this morning that they held truth. Beside her, she heard her mom humming along to an old hymn. The sound comforted her, although she'd long ago stopped going to church and listening to hymns on her own.

If circumstances had been different, she might have asked for advice, for some sort of guidance. She ran the dishtowel over the pan she was holding, turning her attention to the bar top in the corner of the old kitchen.

"Are you guys going to help or just sit there?" she asked, playfully tossing the towel at her teenage cousins who sat playing games on their phones.

She laughed as the soundtrack behind her shifted to banter, family gossip, and chatter, and for a brief moment, she let herself imagine how wonderful it would have been to have Alex by her side for this part of the day as well.

She finished up her chores and looked around, smiling at the sight of the clean kitchen, somehow spotless amidst the chaos of the gathering. From inside her back pocket, she felt her phone buzz. Fishing it out, she saw Alex's name flash across the screen.

"I'll be back," she mouthed to her mom, making her way to the door as she answered the call.

The evening air wrapped around her skin, cooler than normal but still damp and heavy. "Hello?"

"Hey, babe." Alex's voice greeted her with such intimacy that she recoiled.

What were they doing? She bit her tongue, suppressing the question. "Hey yourself," she answered. "How's your night so far?"

"Not bad." She could hear Connor chattering in the background and a TV show turned up too loudly. Alex's voice rose over the noise. "Just missing you."

Lennon bit her lip. She'd been thinking the same thing, but to say the words out loud, to suggest that they spend the rest of the holiday together, it was just too much. "Yeah," she said, dragging the word out, unsure what else to add. "I…" A door opened behind her, and two of her teenage cousins ran into the yard, bringing a lively and heated conversation about sports with them. "Sorry, there's a lot going on over here."

"Here too," Alex said. She lowered her voice, and Lennon knew she'd gone to another room. "I was wondering if you wanted to come by later."

"I can't." Lennon's response was too quick. "I'm planning on spending a bit more time with the family, and then I'm probably going to crash out. I'm pretty tired." She had so much more she wanted to say. They needed to talk about things. They needed to figure out what was going on. Was this love? Were they in too deep? Her thoughts jumped back to how freely she'd jumped into things with Leigh and how quickly it had all come crashing down. She shuddered, clutching the phone tighter in her grasp. She thought about asking if they could talk some other time, but the words caught in her throat.

"Yeah, okay." She could hear Alex's voice break with uncertainty and she chided herself.

"I…" Her words trailed off, and she bit her tongue. What was she hesitating for? This should be the place to share her concerns, and she had plenty of them.

"What is it?"

I want to make this work, but I don't know how.

I want some time to figure out if we're headed in the right direction.

I don't want to get hurt, and I don't want to hurt you.

I've been down this road before, and I didn't like where it took me.

I'm drowning in uncertainty and don't know which way to go.

The ugly truths trembled on the tip of her tongue, and she played out how each of them would be received. It was too much. She was being too needy.

"Hey, I'm going to go." The excuse came quickly, silencing anything deeper. "But I hope you have a happy Thanksgiving night with Lindsey and Connor."

"I hope you do too." Alex sighed. "Hey, Lennon?"

"Yeah?"

"What I said earlier…"

"Let's not right now, okay?" Lennon's heart hammered in her chest. "We'll chat in person tomorrow or the next day. For now, I've got to go. Bye."

She ended the call and stared down at her hands. It wasn't a conversation she was prepared for, but she should have handled it better.

"Shit," she muttered under her breath, careful not to be overheard by the lurking teenagers who were now lounging in the garage, no doubt hoping to get into the beer fridge without being caught.

She kicked the ground. It shouldn't be this hard.

CHAPTER SEVENTEEN

Soft moonlight backlit the palm trees along the cityscape visible outside the window and cast a magical glow onto the beach. Lindsey let the atmosphere calm her as she set to work. Using the jigger and shaker Lennon had left behind and recalling as much as possible of what she'd said about mixing flavors for a well-rounded drink, she mixed the liquids and poured them over ice.

She stepped back, admiring her creation. It looked fancy, but time would tell how it tasted. She brought one of the glasses to her lips and slowly sipped.

"Not bad," she remarked, even though she was alone in the room.

With Connor asleep and Alex on the phone, she took her drink and the one she'd made for Alex to the living room and set them on coasters next to the couch. She was about to take her seat when the front door opened.

"This is for you," Lindsey said, grabbing the drink and thrusting it toward where Alex stood in the doorway.

"What is it?"

"It's called the 'I'm Sorry I was a Dick,' and it was just made fresh for you."

Relief flooded her veins when Alex laughed and accepted the drink. She glanced toward the kitchen and nodded in approval. "I see you took to heart some of the advice handed out earlier."

"Yeah." Lindsey eyed her glass. "It's not my normal vodka and Sprite, and it's not just wine. I don't know that it's *great*, but it's drinkable. And it's sincere." She reached out, touching her sister's arm. "I am sorry."

She watched as Alex shoved her free hand in her pocket and nodded. "I'm sorry too. I probably could have stopped it from getting to the point that it did." She walked past Lindsey, waving for her to follow as she took a seat on the couch. "So you really don't like her?"

Lindsey's shoulders slumped. She knew she wouldn't live that down. "It's not that I don't like her," she said, taking a seat beside Alex. She grabbed her glass and took a drink, trying to find the right words. "I just…" She trailed off and looked down to the floor. "I don't want to get back into it."

"Tell me." Alex drew her feet up under her legs and took a drink of her cocktail. "It's not a trap. I'm curious, but before you answer, you should know Connor thinks she's pretty."

"Well, he's not wrong there," Lindsey said, leaning in closer, hoping her eyes shone with sincerity. "She's beautiful, and I can see what you see in her. I just have to wonder about the timing of it all."

"I get that." Alex's eyes darkened momentarily, but she recovered quickly. "The timing isn't great. It probably doesn't look awesome on paper. I'll be the first to admit that. But it's working, or at least it *was*. It's all a little screwed up now, but…"

"Why?" Lindsey cut her off. "Is it because of me?" She threw her hands in the air. "I knew I should have stayed out of it, and now I've showed up on Thanksgiving and ruined your newfound happiness. I'm so sorry."

"No." Alex's laugh caught her off guard. "It's not always about you." Her tone was playful, but her gaze level. "It's my fault," she added. "I messed it up. Not you."

"What happened?" Lindsey asked, clutching her drink to her chest.

"I told her I loved her." Alex's voice was unapologetic and honest. "And then I doubled down and told her I meant it."

"And?"

"And here we are talking about how I might have fucked it up." Alex downed what was in her glass and handed the glass of ice back to Lindsey. "I'll have another if you don't mind."

"Damn," Lindsey said. "Connor is down for the night, and you and I have nothing to do but drink about this." She downed her drink to follow suit. Rising, she nodded at her sister. "We'll figure it out over some drinks."

Lindsey took both glasses and headed for the kitchen.

"Just bring the bottle," Alex said, smiling sheepishly. "No sense in making it fancy."

Lindsey reached for the bottle, but stopped short. It was her job as an older sister, wasn't it, to be the voice of reason? Her hand hovered over the table as she deliberated, but she grabbed the tequila anyway.

"Bring my cards too," Alex said. "Let's drink and read each other's fortunes."

"We can read *your* fortune," Lindsey said, slipping the cards under her arm. "I'm pretty sure mine is going to be all about *Paw Patrol* and mac 'n' cheese for quite some time. With yours, there's at least the possibility of passion."

"Passion has never been the problem." Alex's voice was quiet and thick with emotion as she reached for the bottle in Lindsey's hands. She unscrewed the cap and pressed the bottle to her lips. After taking a long swig, she passed it over to Lindsey. "You're up."

"Jesus," Lindsey said, leaning back in disbelief. "Not even a wince! Who are you, and what have you done with the girl I knew back in California?"

For a second, Alex jutted out her chin defensively and then offered a sad laugh. "I guess it comes along with the territory when your main point of human contact owns a bar."

"You have made other friends, haven't you?" She worked to keep her tone even but knew her concern had seeped into her voice.

"In passing." Alex reached again for the tequila bottle. "There's a gallery owner who I'd consider a friend, and my neighbors are nice people."

"This," Lindsey said, resting her head in her palm, "was what I was afraid of. You ran out of town as quickly as you could, and I don't blame you. An ended engagement is fucking tragic." She paused and placed her palms on her knees, leaning in for added effect. "But how can you say you love her when your heart wasn't even patched up enough yet to give away?"

Alex swallowed hard. Staring down at the bottle, she toyed with the edges of the label and opened her mouth to speak but shut it when she didn't have an answer.

"I'm not…" Lindsey's words were cut short when Alex cleared her throat.

"Do the cards," she said, nodding to where Lindsey had set them on the coffee table. Without another word, she tipped the tequila bottle up in the air and downed what would have easily been a shot. Lindsey grabbed the cards and shuffled them.

"I'm not sure I remember how to do them correctly," she said, though throughout their teens they'd done Tarot readings at least once a week.

"Doesn't matter." Alex looked up at her. "A half-assed reading is as good as a real one. After all, it's just meant to make you feel better, or to feel worse, or to screw up your day entirely." She placed her head in her hands, before looking back into Lindsey's eyes. "It's kind of like love that way. Even if you don't know what you're doing, or even if you're broken, you can lie to yourself the same way those schmucks do who pretend to have it all together."

Lindsey had so much she wanted to say, but she bit her tongue and opted instead to shuffle the cards. "Here," she said, holding the deck out to her sister. She watched as Alex's eyes darted back and forth across the cards Lindsey had fanned out in front of her. Tapping her finger against the edges, she selected one to the far left.

Nodding, Lindsey laid the card out on the table. The upside down magician. She knew what it meant, but the words hung in her throat.

Alex laughed. "Uncertainty," she said, beating Lindsey to the punch. "I'd say that's pretty spot on for a bunch of hocus-pocus."

* * *

AC/DC blared through his speakers, and Grant rolled down the windows for the drive home. Bobbing his head to the music, he smiled. It had been one hell of a day, and he was full and happy. As he pulled into the driveway, he put the car in park and glanced toward the porch. Lennon was standing outside, leaning up against one of the columns.

The porch light illuminated her silhouette, and Grant paused for a moment to study her. Cigarette pressed to her lips, bottle of whiskey in one hand, and clad in her favorite black leather jacket, she looked like the poster child for what the Kids After-School Specials warned about. He laughed at the thought. She'd been that for him ever since their teen years and he for her. Together they'd been a shiny pair of rebels, just clean enough to never get caught in their shenanigans, but always too wild to keep tabs on. He laughed, thinking back to their high school years and every phase of life that had come since. It was always the same old song and dance of squeezing every ounce of thrill they could find out of life, all while making sure they toed the line enough to not stray too far into their rebellion. She'd been as much as any the reason he never left this place.

He rolled up the windows and shut off the car, noting that she hadn't so much as glanced in his direction. He tapped the wheel, torn between wanting to be supportive to his best friend and wanting to bask in the afterglow of a turkey feast for just a little while longer. Pressing his lips together, he let out a sigh and hopped out of the vehicle.

"Looks like the bitch is back," he sang, hoping to keep spirits high. "Is this Breakup Barbie I see?" He gestured to her exaggeratedly. "Or are you just off parole for the night?"

"Very funny," she said, looking him up and down. "And what are you? An overgrown Jack McFarland?"

"Claws are out," he said, raising an eyebrow in amusement. "For the record, I'm more of a Grace, but you already know that. Regardless, what's going on with you? Why are you out here looking like an outlaw instead of at your girlfriend's house making a turkey or turkey basting or something." He laughed boisterously at his own joke.

"You still have no idea what lesbians do in our spare time, do you?" she asked dryly.

He shook his head and leaned up against the column opposite her. "No and I have no desire to learn. There are far too many vaginas involved for my liking." He reached for the bottle of whiskey and took a swig. As he swallowed, he looked down at the label. "I see you've brought the good stuff," he said, gesturing to the Pappy Van Winkle label. "And you're just out here downing two-hundred-dollar whiskey like it's a fucking bottle of Jack?"

When she offered nothing but a grunt, he walked past her into the house and returned with two whiskey glasses. "Let's at least give this the respect it deserves," he said, pouring two generous portions. "And then you can stop dodging the question and tell me what's going on."

"God you're persistent." She flicked her cigarette to the ground. Stomping it out, she turned to face him.

"And you're smoking again?" He worked to keep judgment out of his tone but failed miserably.

She attempted to form a smile as she sat on the porch swing. "I'm smoking, I'm drinking whiskey I paid for, and I'm having my own Thanksgiving party. I'm thirty-three fucking years old and can make my own decisions. You're welcome to join, but I'm going to need you to settle the hell down with the judgment."

"Okay," he said, taking a step backward. "Sorry." This was the part where normal friends would probably hug, he figured, but instead, he plopped down beside her and grabbed her pack of cigarettes from the porch swing. Lighting one up, he inhaled sharply. "Damn." He savored the heavy feeling of the menthol smoke at the back of his throat. "I've missed these."

"Same." Lennon grabbed another one and lit it. "That's why I'm smoking them. They bring me joy, and they're something that's always been constant. No matter how much time goes by, you can pretty much count on an instant shot of happiness when the stream of nicotine hits."

"You're not wrong," he admitted, taking another drag. "I shouldn't have done this, but I'm just here to be supportive."

To his delight, Lennon laughed. "You and Gretchen Wieners are just *such* good friends," she joked, referencing *Mean Girls*, a film that they'd watched nothing short of a hundred times together.

"That we are." He let the silence between them grow, knowing her well enough to know she wouldn't be able to hold out long.

"She loves me," she said after a moment. She took another long drag, exhaled a thick stream of smoke, and sipped the whiskey in her glass.

"And you don't love her?" He waited. She slumped into her seat. "Oh God," he said, standing to look her in the eye. "You do?"

Lennon stood up, moving past him, and started to pace. "It can't be love, can it?"

"I'm many things, but I've never been a relationship therapist."

She handed him her glass in response and continued to pace. "Love isn't supposed to be this confusing." She was mumbling, and he was grateful he could only hear bits and pieces of it. Knowing she wouldn't actually wait for his response or advice, he busied himself pouring another drink, topping off hers, and enjoying his cigarette.

He handed hers over the next time she passed by, still mumbling about how she shouldn't have to work so hard for something that wasn't supposed to be serious. She stopped and faced him. "The timing is all wrong. But does timing matter? It does, doesn't it?"

"What do you want me to say?" He eyed her cautiously over the brim of his whiskey glass. "Do you want me to tell you that the two of you jumped into this headfirst, all while telling each other—and everyone in earshot—that it was nothing? Well, you did."

Her eyes flashed with anger, and he knew he'd hit his mark. She needed to be mad at him to figure out how she felt. Somehow she'd turn that anger into introspection. He didn't understand it, but it worked for both of them.

"Do you want me to tell you that watching you two together feels like I'm watching you pour vodka on a bonfire and then acting surprised when it blows up? Because that's what it looks like. Is it passionate? Yeah. Is it beautiful? You bet. Is it dangerous? Probably."

He took a deep breath, knowing he was speaking truths she didn't want to hear. Bracing himself against her furrowed brow and killer stare, he pressed on. "I can tell you I've worried about you at times, because it seems like you go all in all the time. But also I see the conflict in you and know you feel deeply about her. I can tell you that much, but only you can tell if you actually love her." She stared him down, and he was grateful looks couldn't do physical damage. "I know I risk being uninvited to this Thanksgiving soirée of yours, but I have to ask. Are you more afraid that you love her and it won't last or that you love her and it will?"

He expected anger. He wasn't prepared for the tear that slid down her cheek.

"I don't know," she admitted after a moment. "That's why I'm here talking to you and indulging in an evening with my longest lasting loves."

"We're all three here," he said, holding up the whiskey and cigarette.

"At least some things remain the same."

"These things always will," he said, motioning for her to come over and join him. "Do you want to talk about it more?"

"Let's see where the night goes," she said, taking a seat beside him. "In the meantime, you're not uninvited to my party."

"Good." He nodded, nudging her playfully in the arm. "Because you were going to have a hard time kicking me out."

"Line 'em up," she said, sliding her glass over to him.

Even though he knew it wouldn't solve the problem, he poured her another drink, knowing one way or another, she'd get through it and they'd lead each other to the other side—the drunk leading the drunk.

CHAPTER EIGHTEEN

The rhythmic sound of the waves greeting the shore mixed with the flap of her umbrella in the wind. As salt and sand gently sprayed her body, Lennon felt as if the sun's warmth was bringing her back to life. When she readjusted her position on her towel, though, her head throbbed, reminding her she wasn't the twenty-one-year-old she'd acted like the night before.

Like a bad movie, visions of her downward spiral replayed in her mind. Thankful she'd only spoken with Grant while in her stupor, she shook her head and pulled the bill of her ball cap down further. Between its brim and her large aviator sunglasses, she thought maybe, just maybe she could hide away for the day and let the shame and pain of the hangover subside in peace.

Movement on the horizon pulled her eyes toward it. Propping herself up on her elbows, she saw a stand-up paddle boarder in the distance, someone with long, dark hair flowing freely in the wind—hair that looked so much like Alex's that she might have been conjured up by the most masochistic parts of her mind. She closed her eyes, trying to rid it of the visions of the hair and the hourglass curves. Clearly, even here in her place of refuge, she was going to find no peace.

Rolling over to her stomach, she fished her phone out of her beach bag. She scrolled through her contacts. She pulled up Aunt Bernadette's number, hovering her finger over the screen. Tears formed in the corners of her eyes. She didn't want Bernadette to know she was about to cry, so talking was off-limits. She wiped the tears away and opened her text-messaging app instead of calling.

Have a minute?

She typed the question and hit Send before she could talk herself out of it.

Three dots appeared almost immediately at the bottom of the screen. Then…

Always for you.

She set the phone down on her towel and shook her hands in frustration. Typing shakily, she wrote

I can't talk on the phone, but I need advice.

She paused and thought through how to succinctly say what she needed to. Her shoulders fell as she typed the words.

How do you know if something is worth it?

Person? Dream? What are we working with?

Bernadette was nothing if not thorough, always one to ensure she gave sound advice, based on what was best for the individual situation.

I should have known you'd want more info. Haha. Let's say it's a person. What then?

As she waited for a response, she wished they'd gone to her mother's side of the family for Thanksgiving. Maybe then she would have had a chance to talk to Bernadette while tossing around a football in the backyard or raking up leaves for the kids to jump into. Then maybe the world wouldn't seem so murky.

The three dots appeared and then disappeared.

"Maybe it's not a simple answer after all," she said aloud, closing her eyes and plopping back down on her towel.

She heard the ding that signaled an incoming message but didn't bother to look at it right away. She drew herself up and clutched her knees, coming to a conclusion. She thanked her aunt for her message without even registering its contents. Her mind was made up, and something had to be done.

Pulling up Alex's number, she typed a quick message asking Alex to meet her at the beach. After getting a reply, she lay back down. There was nothing left to do but sort through the remainder of her thoughts and wait the twenty minutes Alex asked for.

When Alex finally arrived, Lennon took a deep breath. She considered standing but thought better of it. Instead, she beckoned Alex over and spread out her spare towel—the one she always kept in her bag to rid her body of sand before getting in the car—beside her. Alex stood a yard away, her tie-dyed sundress blowing in the wind and her hair up in a messy bun on top of her head. Her oversized sunglasses covered her eyes, but from the look on her face, Lennon could tell they weren't sparkling like they sometimes did.

"Have a seat," she offered.

Alex took a step back and crossed her arms over her chest. "Why?"

Lennon looked down at the sand, digging her feet into the warmth it offered. "I think we need to talk."

"I can talk from here," she said, shaking her head. "I mean, based on the non-conversation we had last night, I'm not sure I need to get comfortable. Or can."

"Last night I was processing things."

"And you've processed them?"

Lennon shook her head. "Not all the way, I guess," she admitted. She bit the inside of her check. Maybe this was a mistake. Maybe the whole damn thing had been a mistake. "But I know I need to say some things. Last night, I didn't have the words I needed. I didn't know what to say. That's why I hung up. It was a dick move, but I needed time so I didn't say things I would regret."

"And you're ready now?" Alex leaned back in disbelief. "Am I just supposed to sit around and wait for you to act like a decent human on your time? What about what I need?"

"Stop." Lennon sucked in a sharp breath. "Please let me talk. I'm sorry about last night. That said, I do need to get to the bottom of some things." She paused. "This is hard." She pointed back and forth to the space between them. "You and I. It's hard."

"Yeah, not everything can be perfect." Alex's voice was cold and too high.

Lennon clasped her hands together. "It doesn't have to be perfect."

"Yes, it does," Alex cut her off. "It always has to be perfect with you. You overthink way too much if something doesn't fit in your bubble. If we step outside of some unwritten rule, it's too much or not enough, and I get it. Neither of us came from a perfect situation, and neither of us is perfect. But we can't be."

"I'm not asking for perfection. That's not what this is about." Lennon frowned. "This is about the fact that this isn't working."

Alex flinched, and Lennon briefly wished she could comfort her, but that would only muddle this whole situation even further. Tipping her chin up as if waiting to be hurt, Alex rotated her hand in the air, beckoning Lennon to finish.

"You said some things. You meant those things." She looked out to the water, then back to Alex. "And I can't do it."

Alex's knuckles whitened as she balled her hands into fists. Her lips formed a thin line, but she said nothing.

"This was supposed to be fun and easy, no strings attached, and somehow it turned into this. It's chaos. It's hard, and it's not what I signed up for. I think we both have shit to figure out." She waited. Alex said nothing.

"I care about you, but the timing is wrong. It doesn't fit." She was rambling, but with Alex's silence, she didn't know what else to do. "I don't want to hurt you, and I feel like if we continue down this path, we're just a ticking time bomb counting down toward destruction." She swallowed hard. "I wish I met you three years from now, or you know, however long it takes to find the right time."

A tear slid down Alex's cheek, and Lennon felt a lump form in her throat. Choking it back, she stood. She took one step toward Alex, and Alex's hands flew up to fend her off.

"Don't you dare," Alex hissed.

"I don't want to hurt you." Lennon's words sounded flat, but she stepped back.

"You already have," Alex said, turning on a heel and striding away.

Lennon took three steps in her direction, then stopped. Chasing after her would only prolong the inevitable and would create new opportunities for Lennon to hurt them both. Or for the relationship to vanish into thin air like her previous failed attempts at love. There was still so much she wanted to say, but it was done. A clean break would be best for both of them.

Staring out at the waves, she watched them crash with renewed fury as if somehow even the universe felt the pain that was welling within her heart.

As seagulls gathered nearby, she let their song drown out her thoughts and let the tears fall until she was certain she'd emptied the contents of her heart onto her towel.

Grabbing her phone, she read Bernadette's message.

There's no hard-and-fast rule. If she brings you joy and makes you feel alive, she's probably worth it. Not true in all cases though.

There she had it, just as jumbled as she thought. She didn't want to get into the specifics over text, so she texted her aunt back, asking to meet for lunch.

Within two hours, she was sitting across from Bernadette, trying to make small talk over an appetizer salad.

With her salad fork hanging in midair, Lennon cast her eyes to her phone once more. No messages. Sighing, she set the fork down.

"You haven't actually touched your food," Bernadette said gently. "You've picked up that same bite of salad about eight times." When Lennon looked up and made eye contact across the table, she offered a sad laugh.

"Sorry," she said. She cleared her throat, bidding away the lump that had formed. She wadded her napkin in her hand and dropped it into her lap.

"Do you want to talk about it?" Bernadette asked, leaning closer. "I mean, I'm happy to just be here for emotional support, but if it's just a body you wanted across from you, I'm sure Grant would have obliged."

Lennon picked up her salad fork again, this time making sure the bite landed in her mouth. As she chewed, she stared at her phone screen, willing it to light up. Something. *Anything.* Anything had to be better than silence. Not that she deserved it or would even know what to do if Alex texted.

She stabbed another bite with her fork but set it down, shaking her head as her stomach churned. She nudged her phone to the side and turned her attention to Bernadette. She pushed down her fears. She looked into Bernadette's eyes, the same deep blue as hers. She'd be met with no judgment, no harshness, just love.

"There was someone, and now there's not." Her words were barely above a whisper as her voice filled with emotion.

She blinked quickly, fending off the tears that threatened to fall once again.

"I'm sorry." Bernadette set her fork down and reached across the table, grasping Lennon's hand.

"It's fine." Lennon winced at the lie and looked away from the table. "Actually I don't have to do that with you." She took a drink of her water. "I'm not doing well with it."

"I gathered." Bernadette slid her empty salad plate to the edge of the table, raising an eyebrow at Lennon's still full plate and the untouched breadbasket in front of her. "Judging by the fact that you and I typically carb load like we're competing in a marathon when we're together and by the fact that we typically have normal conversations, I had a hunch." She softened her smile. "But you're right. You don't have to lie or hide the truth from me. Lay it on me. Give me the good, the bad, and the ugly."

Lennon reached up to run her fingers through her hair. Searching for an adequate explanation, she dropped her hand to the table, where it landed on the handle of her fork, flipping the pronged side up in the air and catapulting spinach onto the adjacent table.

She looked around, thankful to find the table unoccupied. Still, her face reddened. "Life's been about like that," she said as she turned back to face Bernadette.

Bernadette gave Lennon a goofy grin. Rising from the table, she walked over and used her napkin to snag the rogue piece of spinach. Dropping it onto her empty salad plate, she smiled at Lennon. "Sometimes we can fix the mess," she said, taking her seat again. Reaching across the table, she patted Lennon's shoulder. "Tell me what's going on."

Lennon closed her eyes. She didn't want to be this person, crying and spilling her guts over a woman when she'd sworn off love just months earlier. She sniffed and jutted out her chin, feigning the toughness she wished she felt inside. "I think I fell in love," she admitted. She wished Bernadette would say something, but an ever-patient listener, her aunt waited. "And then I messed it up."

She pushed her salad plate away. "Honestly I don't know if I messed it up, or if it was predestined for disaster from the beginning." She put her hands in her lap. Shuffling her feet under the table, she wished she felt comfortable in her skin. "It wasn't ever meant to be, and I think the hardest part is knowing that I let myself get tangled up enough in something only to get hurt when that's the exact thing I swore I wouldn't do."

"We can't always protect our hearts." Bernadette's tone was soothing, and she propped her chin on her palm. "In fact, the best things in life have the chance of hurting us. If we avoided them, we wouldn't really be living."

"The best things in life are the certainties," Lennon said. Thankful to see their waiter nearby, she signaled to him. "I'm going to need a glass of your house cab."

"Make that two," Bernadette added as he gathered their salad plates. "Solidarity," she said, turning her attention to Lennon. When he was out of earshot, she leaned in closer. "Look, I can't fix what happened, and you can't change the past. I know you want things to be a certain way, but they can't always be."

"Why does everyone keep saying that?" Lennon growled, her irritation mounting. Leaning back in her chair, she took a deep breath. "Sorry." She looked down in shame. "I didn't mean to take my frustration out on you, but that's the second time today I've been told that I need things to be a certain way or need things to be perfect."

"I'm not blaming you. I do it too. You and I have always been very similar. It's that whole OCD and anxiety cocktail we've got running through our veins. There's a roadmap that only we can see. It's precise, it's calculated, and we're certain it's our map to success, love, happiness, you name it. It's the way. The only way." Bernadette shook her head. "But it's not, and if we stick to that rigidity, we lose out on so much."

"Thank goodness," Lennon said as the waiter set down their wineglasses. Bernadette was supposed to offer insight and love, not a slew of tough-to-swallow pills. Downing a gulp of wine as if it were water in the desert, she turned her attention back to her aunt. "Speaking of love, how's Mr. Dan Hayes?"

Bernadette's cheeks flushed crimson, and she raised an eyebrow. It looked for a moment as if she might not spill the beans. "They're good." She placed her palms on the table. "They're perplexing enough that it makes me want to run away screaming half the time, and I'm not sure where we stand. But I'm having fun."

"That's what matters," Lennon said, feeling hypocritical as the words escaped her mouth. Her brow furrowed as she considered if there was a difference between her situation and Bernadette's. It was one thing to not know where a relationship stood but to be having fun. It was another when it crossed the line, though. It was okay to run then, wasn't it? Or was Bernadette right?

By the time their entrée arrived, Lennon's mind was churning as hard as her stomach, and she was no closer to figuring out what to feel.

CHAPTER NINETEEN

The typical buzz of an airport—the quick-paced clicking of shoes against the floor, the hum of fluorescent lightbulbs overhead, and the rapid-fire pace of conversations buzzing about in a variety of tones and accents—swirled around Alex as she people watched. Lindsey and Connor had long since disappeared from view and she knew she should return to her car to avoid paying another five dollars for an extra half hour for parking, but she was glued to her spot.

All around, she saw families, couples, and friends. Sure there were lone travelers, but for the most part, everyone seemed to have someone. There were warm embraces at the baggage claim to her right, and laughter filled the air somewhere behind her. What must it be like to have that sort of connection all the time, to have something steady?

She took a deep breath, inhaling the bittersweet taste of togetherness and turned, leaving it all behind her. It wasn't hers to enjoy, and it wasn't right to impose upon the moments of others. Emptiness set into her heart as she pulled out of the parking garage. She reached down to turn up the radio, but her phone lit up instead.

Smiling so her voice would be light, she hit the Answer button.

"Hi, Patsy," she said, greeting her favorite gallery owner.

"Hi, hun!" Patsy's voice filled the line with every ounce of enthusiasm Alex needed. For the first time in the last four days, a genuine smile passed over her lips. "Did you have a good Thanksgiving?"

"I did," Alex lied. "What about you? Did your kids come into town?"

"They did, and I ate too much. Had a great time spoiling those grandkids. Goodness me, they are a handful, though." She cackled and coughed. "But anyway, darlin', I wanted to talk to you about doing a full gallery takeover shortly after the beginning of the year—about six weeks. Would you be willing to do that?"

"Wow," Alex said, mentally tallying her work. "How many pieces do you need? I'm honored but I need to make sure I have the inventory."

"Six to seven for showcase, but you'd need to bring along a variety of smaller pieces if you have them."

"Any boundaries or censure?" She had more than enough of her pieces with her to make it worth Patsy's time, although some were darker and some were more sexual than the usual beach tourism vibe.

Patsy laughed heartily. "That's what I like about you, Alex. You're always pushing the boundary and making me think about things." She made a clicking noise, as if she was considering her answer. "You can be edgy, sexy even. I'm not here to limit you. You know the deal. If I need to put an eighteen and up sign on the door, I will. It'll be a night event, where we can put it all up. We'll keep the exhibit up throughout the month, though, so if we need to have a separate section so as not to offend the average family on a holiday vacation, we'll figure that out."

"Perfect." Tears formed in Alex's eyes. She'd always wanted a full gallery opening and exhibit dedicated just to her work, and here she was, living her dream. But at what cost did it have to come? Did she have to do it all alone? She looked out the window to the clear skies, working to remove the negative thoughts and simply enjoy the moment. "When should I stop by so we can go over the specifics?"

"Come on by today if you're free. And feel free to bring that pretty lady of yours if you'd like."

The words, while meant to be sweet, were like a punch to the gut. Alex hoped her reply sounded lighter to Patsy than it did to her. "I'll be there shortly."

She thanked Patsy and hung up the phone. Making a quick stop at her house to use concealer on the bags that had formed under her eyes, she placed her hand over her heart, willing it to settle into a normal rhythm. She was sure Patsy would bring up Lennon again, and this was a professional visit. She was going to have to hold it together.

Taking a quick trip through her makeshift office, she snapped photos of her best pieces and headed for the door. By the time she stepped inside the gallery, she had a renewed focus. This wasn't about anyone but herself. This was her and the dream she'd held since she was a child.

Beaming with pride, she made small talk with Patsy, scrolled through the photos, and selected the pieces she wanted for the show.

"Do you have any questions?" Patsy asked as she made the final notes in her planner.

"Not that I can think of." Alex tapped her fingers on the counter, wracking her brain to see if there was any additional information she needed.

"If anything comes up, you can call," Patsy assured her. "In the meantime, would you care to join me for a cup of tea?"

Patsy had been all business thus far, and Alex had escaped any personal inquiries. She thought about bowing out gracefully, but she hesitated. She needed people in her life, and Patsy was about the only one she had left that wasn't connected somehow to Lennon.

"I'd love that," she said, hoping she hadn't let enough time pass to make it sound awkward.

Completely unfazed, Patsy nodded decisively. "I'll put on the kettle." She disappeared into the back of the shop, and Alex took the moment to settle into normalcy. Walking around the gallery, she stared at the pieces now on display. Some were complex, and some were simple, but she knew each piece meant something different to the one who created it. She ran her finger along the wall underneath a piece that spoke to the chaos within her. Its deep reds and blacks spoke of torment and passion, mingled as one. It was an emotion she knew all too well.

"Always waiting for the peace to come," she whispered. Relieved to hear Patsy return, she pushed the painting and her feelings to the back of her mind.

"You look pale, dear," Patsy commented, setting a teacup down in front of her. "Anything you'd like to talk about?"

They'd only had a handful of conversations over the months, usually whenever Alex came into the gallery to check on her work or to drop off more, but they'd struck up an unusual friendship.

"There's no use hiding it," she said. "You remember Lennon?"

"Of course." Patsy took a seat. "Last time you were in here it was Lennon this and Lennon that. You went on and on about her." Patsy leaned in and cocked an eyebrow. "There was a special light in your eyes when you mentioned her."

Alex winced. "No need to remind me of that," she said, taking the mug in her hand. "It's over. So I've just been a bit down."

"I see." Patsy took a sip of her tea. "Drink up," she directed, nodding in Alex's direction. "The tea will warm up your tired soul a bit. Then go sort the rest out on the canvas. It's the best therapy…well, that or screwing a stranger."

Alex's laughter exploded like a volcanic eruption, uncontrollable and forceful. She walked over to where Patsy sat, put her teacup on the counter, and drew the older woman into a hug. "Thank you," she said. Taking a step back, she stood taller. "I'm going to be okay. I just have to find my own way for once."

"You've got a good head on your shoulders." Patsy gave her a reassuring pat. "Just be sure to take it with you."

Alex nodded. They finished up their tea in silence, and Alex thanked her again before heading for the car.

As she left, she made up her mind. There was no need to dwell. Some things worked. Some things didn't. She was going to take hold of her life and make decisions that were best for her and no one else.

Back at the condo, she boxed up things Lennon had left behind. She gathered her perfume bottle from the bathroom, the pair of boxers she liked to sleep in when she stayed over, her favorite T-shirt, and a pair of running shoes. Opening her bedside drawer, she paused. She reached in and grabbed the strap-on. How was she supposed to go about returning a sex toy that had been inside her? She pressed her lips together and shook her head. It wasn't hers, and she wasn't going to keep around any mementos. She placed it in the box. Closing her eyes, she could see the visions of the passion they'd created together. Exhaling hard, she taped the box shut. Those were memories that she wasn't ready to relive just yet—if ever. It would be best to put them out of her mind for now, and it was certainly best to have them out of her house.

She loaded the items into her car and checked her phone. Lennon would be at the bar, thankfully. After a quick drive across town, she left the box on Lennon's doorstep. With only a fleeting glance backward, she turned and took steps toward a fresh start.

* * *

The water was rising higher as the vessel was tossed about on the angry sea. Lennon's heart beat faster as she looked from side to side, wishing there was some comfort to be found in land nearby. Her breathing accelerated, and she looked down to her shaking hands. There was nothing, no one to save her. Standing, she ran to the helm of the boat, looking desperately but finding no one in sight.

As a large wave crashed into the boat, she was launched forward, eyes widening as the next wave came to swallow her.

With a jerk, Lennon sat up in her bed. Taking a deep breath, she looked around. Her black curtains on the windows, her oak dresser across from the bed, and her deep maroon sheets below her gave her comfort. Placing her palms over her eyes, she focused on her breathing while reminding herself she was in her own room.

With her eyes closed, she saw the boat and the stormy seas again. Clutching her chest, she fought off the panic she had felt seconds earlier—and the panic that still raged from the revelation that she had seen that same boat, those same seas, before.

Her memory flashed to the tortured painting that hung in Alex's living room, and she sighed. Flopping back down on the pillow, she turned to her right and reached for the empty space. The scent of Alex's perfume still lingered in her memory, although she had since washed it off the pillowcase.

"So much for having my bed back to myself," she muttered, rubbing the spot that had been Alex's.

She glanced toward the box in her bedroom floor. It held belongings that she'd left at Alex's, and it had been dropped off days before. It was still untouched, because she wasn't sure she was ready to face it all.

She could hear Bernadette's words about giving things a chance and Grant's that she'd be okay on her own. She cleared her throat, putting on a resolute face even though no one was around to see through the façade. She *was* stronger than this. She had to be. After all, she had never intended to give that spot to Alex anyway.

It was supposed to be fleeting, and it had been. That was the end of it.

She silently urged her mind to quiet down so she could go back to sleep. Instead visions of Alex's smile and her deep brown eyes danced through her imagination. She opened her eyes wide and rose from the bed.

"Fuck." She spat the curse as she flipped on the lamp beside her bed and reached for her phone. Checking the clock there, she slammed it back down on her bedside table. "Four fucking a.m. on my day off, and I'm wide awake," she seethed, plopping back down on the bed. She clasped her hands together, unclasped them, then sat on them. Restlessness built inside her, and she knew she had to do something. But what?

Leaning forward, she placed her head in her hands. "It wasn't supposed to hurt this time," she whispered through a ragged breath.

Sitting upright, she stared at her reflection in the mirror of the closet door. "Get it together," she commanded, narrowing her eyes. She nodded. It was time. It had to be done.

She reached into the top drawer of her bedside table, her hands trembling. She pulled out the single piece of paper stored there and held the flimsy paper in her hands, feeling as if her heart was physically breaking. She didn't need to read it again. She knew what it said. The simple words scrawled across the page in Alex's loopy handwriting had been emblazoned in her memory from the time Alex had presented the note, alongside a small, handpicked bouquet of flowers, just before Thanksgiving. "*You make bad days better and good days great. I'm thankful for you.*"

She could see it, complete with the little heart and Alex's signature beneath it. Holding the paper between her left thumb and fingertip, she reached for the lighter on top of the table.

Having only used the lighter for candles and an occasional bowl when she wanted to unwind, she flicked it to make sure it still had enough fluid. The flame blazed, and she nodded again, setting her lips into a thin line. There could be no mementos, no trace, if she truly wanted to move forward.

She flicked the lighter again, watching until the flame danced closer to the paper. Right before it touched it, though, she dropped the paper.

"I can't," she said, keeping her tone quiet. With a defeated huff, she flicked the lighter off, scooped the paper off the floor and stuffed it back into the drawer.

"Fuck," she said again, biting a bit off one of her fingernails as her nerves mounted. Pushing herself off the bed, she dressed quickly, donning leggings, a hoodie, and running shoes. If nothing else, she decided, she'd conquer the heartache by making her body focus on physical exertion.

After two miles of listening to her feet hit the pavement, Lennon felt no better, but she did feel tired. Making her way back to the house, she thought about waiting until daytime and calling Natalie or about asking Grant to go out for brunch. She leaned against the closed door.

Then again, it had been more than a week, and she'd been managing just fine on her own. One bad dream and a couple of tears wouldn't change that. She was going to get through this, and no one would see her in this state. They had seen her heartbroken because of her own stupidity too many times before. They didn't need to be her support system through this.

"It was supposed to end," she said aloud. "It was always destined to end, and now it has. Get over it." Her words came out as a harsh hiss, and she nodded. That's exactly what she would do. And she wouldn't drag anyone else down while she worked through it.

She took a quick shower, made a veggie omelet, and drank a cup of coffee. After watching the sunrise and devouring a couple of chapters of the novel she'd been reading, she couldn't stop herself. She knew she was headed for another mistake, but it was the only method she knew.

She fumbled with her phone, reinstalling Tinder and browsing the matches it showed her.

"What are you doing?"

She jumped at Grant's voice behind her, dropping her phone. She picked it up. "I believe it's called 'moving on' in most cultures."

"Moving on?" He raised an eyebrow and took a seat beside her. "I thought you said you were fine." The teasing tone of his voice should have put her at ease, but the hairs on her arms stood up and her body stiffened in defense.

"I *am* fine." She clutched her phone to her chest. "I have a lot to figure out, but I'm pretty sure sitting around here wallowing isn't going to make it any better."

"Want to talk about it?"

"I don't know what I want." Lennon stood, shaking her head. "It's a clusterfuck. I want to hate her for making me feel things I wasn't ready to feel. I want to set the world on fire, because I hurt, and I didn't want to hurt again. I want to get my shit together so I'm not getting myself into this same scenario every time. I want to get back to casual flings. This was all so stupid, and I should have seen it coming."

Grant's brow furrowed, but he recovered quickly. "I'm glad to see you delving into all that darkness."

She opened her mouth to speak, but her retort would have just fallen flat, she knew. There were no words to fix the situation or to pull from the air the words she'd already spoken so he wouldn't make a bigger deal of it than it already was. She eyed him. He could deal with her admitting the obvious—that she was hurting.

"What's going on in your life?"

"The Grindr well has gone dry, so I'm choosing to focus on myself right now." He couldn't hide his smile.

"Things are going well with the muffin man, aren't they?"

"They are," he said, smiling and putting a hand on his hip. "But that's not our focal point right now."

"I want to hear all about it." She waited, a mixture of curiosity, happiness, and jealousy filling her heart. She pushed the ugliness of jealousy to the backburner. "Tell me about your happiness," she insisted.

"We don't have time," he said. "We'll hop into all of that later. For now do you think swiping right is really going to make this all better?" He patted the place she'd left behind on the sofa. "If it is, I'm always happy to offer an opinion on swipes."

Despite the war waging within, she laughed and took a seat beside him. "I don't know that it'll help, but maybe it won't hurt. Who knows? I just know I have to get out of this funk. I can't keep thinking about her. I can't keep feeling things for her, and I can't keep wondering why I was so stupid to jump into something again."

"You mentioned wanting to hate her," Grant offered with a shrug. "Maybe that wouldn't be so bad. It's what I do when I end a relationship."

"I don't know that I *can*." Lennon closed her eyes and saw the raw emotion that shone so frequently in Alex's eyes—sometimes a flare of passion, sometimes a wild and unpredictable storm wrecking everything in its path. She shook her head. "Maybe I can."

"Give it a shot, and then maybe that'll stop you from bringing her back around as a friend later on." He ran his fingers through his beard and laughed. "I don't know what it is with you lesbians, befriending your exes and inviting them to barbecues like it's nothing. If you hate her, you can at least leave her in the past and move forward." His lips formed a tight line as he took in Lennon's pained expression. "She is a great person, and she was fun to have around, but if it didn't work, there was a reason."

"Maybe you're right." She jerked her chin in the direction of their record player. "Aren't we a little overdue for a breakup party?"

"Are you still into those?" Grant's eyes lit up. "I thought you hated when I tried to throw my little soirées to celebrate your new beginnings."

"Maybe it's time I try a different approach this time around."

"That's the spirit!" Grant patted her leg and stood. Smiling at her, he turned and strode to choose an album. Selecting an Eagles album, he hummed the opening notes and danced into the kitchen.

Lennon could hear him talking still but closed her eyes and focused on her breathing. Drowning out the background noise, she drew in a deep breath, held it, and exhaled. She wasn't helpless. She wasn't stupid. She'd made mistakes, and people—including her—had been hurt in the process. But she was going to find her way to the other side of this dilemma.

Dilemma. The word lingered in her mind. What was the root of the problem? Maybe that was her starting point. Was it her need to be loved, to have a partner in her life? Was it her eagerness to avoid feelings to resist heartache and the fact that her two desires could not coexist within the same reality? Was it her utter failing at achieving either of the goals? Was it that she was thirty-three and still trying to solve the puzzle that was her heart?

She picked up her phone. Scrolling through, she swiped right on two out-of-towners in for the week. As she eyed the profile picture of one, it all seemed so superficial—the bio that was clearly exaggerated, the perfectly filtered selfies that were no doubt a result of a hundred tries, and the generic hobbies listed. *Sure, Stephanie. Everyone loves the outdoors and getting drunk on patios.* There was a photo with a dog, one of her in a tight, low-cut shirt, one that looked like a sorority party, one on a kayak, and one where she stood in a group of girls doing a duck face.

She groaned. Staring into the blue eyes on Stephanie's profile picture, she wondered what going out with her would be like, but she didn't have to use too much imagination. Lennon would dress in jeans, a patterned button-down, and Chucks—just enough to show that she'd put in effort, but minimal enough to show that she didn't care all that much. Stephanie would probably show up in a simple flowing dress, judging by the array of photos on her profile. She'd choose something that fluttered in the wind and showed off her cleavage. Lennon would compliment her, and Stephanie would know she had her hooks in right where she wanted them for her vacation fling. Conversation would be casual and easy. There'd be nothing to lose; both would know why they were there. It was always like that with tourists.

They'd grab lunch, probably at the taco stand. They'd drink a couple of beers and have taco platters. Afterward, there would be a stroll on the beach, where Lennon would take her hand. They'd dip their toes in the water, and Lennon would pull her in when she complained of the water being cold. They'd make out on the beach. Lennon would bring her home, or they'd go to her vacation rental. They'd share the night. Lennon would dip out before it got awkward. If Stephanie stayed in town for more than a day or two, she'd end up in Alibis. Lennon would send her a drink on the house and keep to small talk. Stephanie would go home, and Lennon would be here—unfulfilled and still sorting through things. Stephanie would be just another Band-Aid, a way to kick the real problems down the road.

Her phone dinged with a match and a message. Her hands shook as she selected the app on the home screen. She pulled her fingers back, hovering above the screen, before gritting her teeth and hitting "delete."

"Just another tequila sunrise," Grant sang from behind her, oblivious to the battle she'd just been through. Coming up beside her, he handed her a picture-perfect orange drink.

"This looks amazing," she said, accepting the glass and smiling at him. "I don't know what I did to deserve you."

"Likewise," he said, taking a sip of his drink. "Ah," he said as he took a seat. "To facing old demons, to surviving the present, to embracing new beginnings." He raised his glass in the air and clinked the side of it against hers.

She narrowed her eyes. Had she been talking out loud, or had he somehow just read her mind? He took a swig of his drink, and she followed suit. It didn't matter. He was right, and his toast was exactly the mantra she needed for the day.

The sharp taste of tequila stung her mouth, jolting her body more awake. "Nothing like the taste of tequila in the morning for some therapy," she said with a low laugh. The words hung heavy in the air between them. Maybe tequila wasn't the only therapy she needed.

Her eyes darted to the mirror that hung above the fireplace. She stared at her reflection for the second time that day. Whatever the future held, she knew any real change would have to start with her. Warding off those thoughts for just a moment more, she smiled up at Grant. She had this, and for the moment, she would be grateful.

CHAPTER TWENTY

Afternoon sunlight streamed through the curtains as the receptionist hurriedly clicked the keys on her keyboard, and Lennon closed her eyes, pressing her fingers to her earbuds. Letting the music take over her racing thoughts, she focused on the comforting and whimsical beat of Fleurie's "Wildwood." As the indie artist sang about the love that captivated her heart and mind, Lennon hung her head.

Like a bad montage from an old movie, the memories flooded back. At each step of falling, she wished she could have pulled back and talked some sense into herself. How was she supposed to love someone else when she was *this*—this jumbled excuse of a woman who held so tightly to control but somehow still managed to ruin everything? As the beat picked up, Lennon remembered the feel of Alex's hand in hers.

She squirmed in her seat. She hit the Next button and let out a frustrated laugh as the opening beats of Taylor Swift and Bon Iver's "exile" filled her earbuds, as if on cue, ready to fully devastate her heart. She hit the Pause button but didn't pull out her earbuds, just in case she needed them to fend off a conversation from a well-meaning stranger.

She massaged the back of her neck. This wasn't about Alex. It was about her. Crossing her arms over her chest, she focused inward.

Breathe in. Hold. Breathe out. She cycled through the familiar mantra and focused on feeling the connection between her feet and the floor, pulling herself away from tortured thoughts that felt so unceasing, so loud. She looked around the room. She'd been here before. How long had it been? Maybe if it hadn't been so long, things wouldn't have gotten so out of hand. Running a hand through her curls, she shook her head again. That didn't matter.

Taking conscious steps to relax her mind, Lennon studied her surroundings more closely. The old wooden chairs upholstered in white leather weren't overly comfy, but they generated a sense of nostalgia. She'd sat here time and again, as she took the first steps toward getting the help she needed, first when the stress of college, working, and coming out to her family had been too much, again during the first year of opening up her own business, when she was convinced her slew of bad dating decisions meant she was unlovable, and finally when she was attempting to untangle her feelings of rejection from her family and deal with the anxiety of not fitting their mold. The stack of magazines on the shabby chic, farmhouse table next to her were still outdated, but were new since she'd been there last, and a sandalwood vanilla candle burned on the receptionist's desk, offering clients a dose of aromatherapy.

The petite blonde behind the desk smiled at Lennon again over her glasses, and Lennon offered a polite smile in return. Inwardly she groaned, wondering how crazy she looked to the young woman. She tapped her foot and chewed a bit on the side of her cheek. Could be she *was* crazy. Or maybe just too broken to deserve something good.

Melanie, Kacey, Leigh, Alex. There were more women dotting her timeline, of course, but they all blurred together, a long line of leading ladies with doomed fates. Each one a blazing disaster of heartache and regret. And here she was, dramatic, flawed, the only common denominator. She'd been good at so many things, but not this. This wasn't school. This wasn't work. This wasn't her bar. She couldn't just fix it by holding on tighter and working harder. The sharp taste of blood filled her mouth and she grimaced.

As if by some cosmic good fortune, the door swung open and Dr. Constance stepped forward, breaking her from her cycle of destruction. She adjusted her clear-framed, oversized glasses and looked across the room until her soft green eyes rested on Lennon's. She smiled and grabbed the chart from the hanging folder by the door.

"It's good to see you again," she said, waving for Lennon to follow her down the hallway and into her office.

Lennon's heart filled with gratitude. She wasn't sure how Dr. Constance so quickly put her at ease, but she was thankful that she wasn't made to feel guilty. She wanted to hug her, to somehow use her to hold on to the last bits of her sanity like she would a life preserver. It *had* been quite a while—almost two years—since Lennon had canceled her last appointment, declaring herself "better," whatever that even meant anymore. She winced at the memory of how she strode out of the office, flipping her aviator glasses over her eyes, rolling down the windows of her truck, and racing out of the parking lot. She'd felt free. She'd felt alive and ready to face anything—her demons be damned. But it didn't last. She bit her lip and closed her eyes. They'd get to all that, she was sure.

"It's good to see you too," she managed as she followed the doctor's lead and walked through the open door.

Once in the office, she took her place on the comfortable and simple blue upholstered couch. This was exactly where she needed to be. The simplicity of the clean décor, the plants growing in the corner, and the smooth hum of instrumental meditation music in the background all combined to bring her closer to peace.

"I've needed this," she noted, placing her hands on her knees.

Across from her, Dr. Constance took a seat and eyed her with compassion. "How've you been, Lennon?"

Lennon cast her eyes downward. Nothing in the simple, yet tasteful, paintings on the walls or the gorgeous oak bookcases would make the answers any easier to find. She pulled at one of her cuticles.

"Up and down, I guess." She slowly brought her eyes up to meet Dr. Constance's gaze.

"Last time we talked," Dr. Constance said, peering over her glasses onto her file and making a note with the pencil in her hand, "you and I were talking about your family and your anxiety. Is that where you wanted to pick up today?"

Lennon's eyes darted from side to side. Her family had been the source of much of her anxiety in the past, but so much had changed since her last visit.

"I don't really know," Lennon admitted. She stared at her shoes. "I don't know where to start."

"That's okay." The doctor crossed her legs at the knee. "Why don't you just tell me how you're feeling today or what's been going on in your life since we last talked?"

"It's probably going to be a bit jumbled." Lennon wracked her brain. Where to begin?

"We've got time." Dr. Constance nodded, urging Lennon to continue.

"After I left your office that day and decided you'd cured me, I was on top of the world. Simply admitting that it was just my anxiety, that I wasn't broken had felt like such a breakthrough. It was a weight lifted off my shoulders to remember that the constant state of fight-or-flight wasn't normal and that there was something I could do about it. It was freeing. It helped me see what was happening, and when depression reared its head, I was ready for that too. I was doing great…"

Her voice trailed off, and she felt tears welling. Smoothly, Dr. Constance handed her a box of tissues, giving her the silent encouragement she needed.

"My victories were short-lived, and I should have come back then." She brought her hands up to massage her temples.

"It's okay, Lennon." Dr. Constance's voice was soft and kind as she made notes in her folder.

Lennon braced her arm on the side of the couch. "I guess maybe I need to stop treating therapy like it's a car detailing service that I use only when things get so chaotic I can't stand it anymore." She dabbed the tissue to the corner of her eye. "Once I decided to take a step back from working toward a picture-perfect life, I took a step back from it all. I really took a hard look at my life. I spent time on my own, and I realized that I didn't really know who I was underneath it all. I'd found so much of my identity through dating and the women I spent time with. You know my family is difficult, so my people were my friends and the women I dated."

She shifted while she relived the parts of her story she wanted to forget. "When I stripped it all away and had to face myself in the mirror, it wasn't even that I didn't like what I saw. It's that I didn't know what I saw or who I was, and I just wanted to feel something—anything. I felt empty. All I was and all I saw were what everyone wanted me to be. Somehow I got lost. I threw myself into work, I worked out excessively, and I tried to fight through to find something worth holding on to. It all felt so empty, and somehow I went right back into the darkness of constant anxiety and constantly trying to live up to some fantasy that I'd set in my head. I was lonely and felt like I'd never deserve the love I sought. And then, I met someone." She paused, thinking of Leigh. There was still a pang in her heart, but it wasn't because she still loved her. It was regret, plain and simple. She regretted staking so much of her peace in another.

"Tell me about her."

Lennon cleared her throat. "It was never really about her, I guess."

Dr. Constance raised an eyebrow, and Lennon nodded. "She was everything I thought I needed. It was easy. It was bliss. I wasn't alone. She gave me the bare minimum, but it was still more than I'd let another give me before. I thought it was real—real enough to commit to forever. But it slipped away as quickly as it came, and there was nothing I could do to hold it together. No amount of me working on myself had helped to make my relationships less doomed. I was still the failure, and that's when things got really dark."

She pulled the edges of the tissue. "Sorry, that sounds really dramatic." She flicked her fingers in dismissal.

"It's not dramatic," Dr. Constance said gently. "Remember the rules in this office?"

Lennon nodded. "We don't apologize for speaking our feelings."

"Right." Dr. Constance smiled. "And, we don't have to worry about anything sounding perfect or making sense. If I need clarification, I'll ask. In the meantime, continue."

"Thanks," she said with a nod. "I guess when I realized I couldn't fix that—that I couldn't fix anything—and that all my relationships met an untimely end, I fell into a pretty deep depression. But it wasn't like they show in the movies."

"It rarely is."

"Yeah," Lennon agreed. "Life went on as normal. I went on as normal. Day to day, you'd never have noticed a difference. But I drank. My God, did I drink. And I slept around. I stayed busy. I worked hours I had no reason to work. I dove into as many interests as I could, all to find some kind of fulfillment, but never once did I slow the fuck down to heal." She paused and contemplated apologizing for her language but remembered Dr. Constance didn't mind.

"Lennon, you're so hard on yourself, even now," Dr. Constance said, shaking her head gently. "You don't realize that you're recognizing these things on your own, and that in itself is a powerful step toward healing and growth."

"Oh, but it didn't stop there," Lennon said. She grimaced. "I met someone when I was at the lowest point of my high-functioning depression, and I wasn't smart enough to stop it before I ended up screwing it all up and hurting us both." Fresh tears sprang in the corner of her eye, and she dabbed the tissue against the spot. "She didn't deserve what happened. It was just doomed from the start."

"Why do you say that?"

"You know that whole thing about chemistry and timing, how you need both of them? Well, we had the chemistry, but more than that, we had *love*." Her voice cracked as she said the word. She swallowed hard. "We just had it at the worst possible time. And now I'm back where I started, alone and trying to hold together everything as it crumbles. I'm not sure that there's anything left in there worth salvaging."

In the brief silence that followed, Dr. Constance scribbled some notes on the paper and looked up, making eye contact with Lennon. "You've brought up a lot of things, and I hope we can spend the next several weeks going through them. For today, I'd like us to strip everything away. We'll dive into everything with both women and how you see your relationships and your part in them. But for today, I want to focus on how you see yourself. You mentioned that you struggled with finding your identity."

Lennon nodded. She always wanted to argue at this point. She wanted to focus on the heavy-hitting issues. Her defenses rose as she realized that the problem really *was* her. She willed her inner dialogue to chill.

"How does that sound?"

In spite of herself, Lennon agreed. "Let's do it." Her voice was too eager. She groaned to herself. Even in therapy, she wanted to please. She watched as Dr. Constance wrote down more notes. Was it possible to get a good grade at therapy? If so, she hoped the notes were positive. She thought about sharing those thoughts with Dr. Constance, then decided she'd spilled enough for one day. She'd given the doctor a lot to unpack.

As they worked through a visualization exercise, Lennon closed her eyes, determined to put herself fully into dealing with her mental illnesses. She'd skirted her issues long enough. For once, she was going to do the work and hopefully find something other than the emptiness she'd been trying to fill for thirty years.

As the session came to a close, she found herself wishing that she could stay for a bit longer, could shelter inside the sanctuary of the office, where it felt so normal to talk about her feelings and to sort through them, where for once she didn't view her problems as weaknesses. She listened while Dr. Constance gave her homework exercises for the week and stood reluctantly, thanking the therapist for her time, before walking out into the parking lot.

Practicing the mindfulness they'd discussed, she took a deep breath and let the sunlight warm her skin. She wanted to bask in the moment, but she was acutely aware of the people on the sidewalk around her.

Hurriedly, she made her way to her truck, her hands trembling as she fastened her seat belt. She looked down at the book in her hand. "*Peace Within*," she said aloud, dropping it onto the passenger seat. How long had she been seeking just that? It wasn't going to be a quick fix. She replayed Dr. Constance's words in her head. She was on a journey—a long one at that. She glanced in the flip-down mirror, wiping at the smeared mascara on her face. Therapy was supposed to make her feel better, she knew, but somehow she felt more raw and more vulnerable than ever after today's session.

We have to stick with this. Dr. Constance's words replaying in her mind, she stuck her key in the ignition and Noah Cyrus's "Lonely" poured through the speakers. As the girl sang about being lonely and pretending to be someone else, Lennon's body shook and something that was half-sob and half-scream ripped through her core.

* * *

Lennon sat up, letting the morning sunlight stream over her body and listening to the birds singing softly outside her window. She stretched and reached for the leather journal on her nightstand. A slow smile spread over her face, and she felt the cracked places in her soul soften. For the first time in a month, she felt free. The new year ahead brought with it a litany of new chances. She took a moment before the world started for the day to breathe deeply, gather her thoughts, and write about how she felt.

She set the journal back in its place, rising and savoring the feeling of the hard wooden floor beneath her feet. Looking around the room, she took note of the changes she'd made over the past few weeks. The brightly colored sticky notes with positive affirmations, the calming décor, the incense burner that looked like an intricate angel wing with half a stick of sandalwood hanging in its holder—it all seemed a bit over the top, she'd be the first to admit. But she didn't care anymore.

None of this had been easy. She'd clawed and fought and pushed to get here, and she was damn proud of how far she'd come. She wasn't done, but she wasn't giving up. She was on a journey, and she was relishing the beauty of that journey—even when it was painful.

"Broken, but not gone," she whispered, running her fingers along the beading in the weighted blanket on her bed. It was her favorite of the self-care purchases she'd made and one of the most effective.

She craned her head toward the door and heard Grant shuffling around. Knowing she wouldn't be disturbing his sleep, she reached over and hit Play on her phone.

Camille Trust's commanding voice knifed through the speakers, and Lennon stood. It was a breakup song, sure, but something about the lyrics of "Move On" just resonated within her soul and lifted her spirits. Dancing through the room, she grabbed her robe and seductively shimmied her hips in the mirror—a show for no one else but herself.

The hem of her ribbed white tank top kissed her skin just above the line of her navy blue boy shorts, and she winked at her reflection. If nothing else, *she* and she alone would appreciate what she saw. That was what it was all about anyway.

Confidence rising, she shouted along with Camille, "I'm fucking fantastic!" Moving in rhythm with the sultry beat, she belted out the words until she was breathless. Collapsing in laughter at the sheer frivolity of the moment, she pulled out her meditation cushion from underneath her bed and set the playlist to instrumental music.

Life would not get her down; her depression and anxiety would not define her. She would not stay broken, and she'd do what she had to every day to make sure of that. Positioning her feet under her crossed legs, she straightened her shoulders and centered herself in the here and the now—and in the moment's beauty.

CHAPTER TWENTY-ONE

The upbeat dance music pulsing through her home speakers was breathing fresh life into Alex's veins. She finished her winged eyeliner, smiling at her reflection. Taking a step backward, she indulged her vanity for a brief moment, delighting in the way her contoured blue dress clung to her curves, showing off her hips and accentuating her breasts. She gave her best sultry pout and shimmied her hips. She looked and felt her best. From her bright red lips to her fuck-me stilettos, she looked the part of a model, and she knew it. Slowly, she ran her finger across her neckline, over her cleavage, and down across her body. Her body tingled, and she tensed. It had been far too long since she'd had the type of touch she craved. Before her mind could drift to the face that matched the touch she longed to feel, she clicked her heel against the hardwood floor of her bedroom and tossed her hair. With one glance at the clock, she laughed. Biting her lip, she gave in to the mounting tension.

Careful not to dishevel the look she'd worked so hard on, she laid back on the bed. Closing her eyes, she slid her fingers lower, teasing herself as she hovered just above the ache. Arching her hips, she slid her lace underwear to the side. She let out a soft moan as she teased the entrance. Her breath hitched in her throat as she plunged one, then two fingers into the wetness. Pumping with fury, she forced away thoughts of anyone in particular and let the primal instincts of her body take over. She brought her free hand up to massage her nipples beneath the thin material of her dress and cried out as she quickly finished, letting the cry echo off the walls as a badge of pride for not needing anyone else. She was her own woman.

Licking her lips, she let out a jagged breath and smiled. With one final glance in the mirror, she grabbed her purse and her special occasion pack of cigarettes from her vanity. If ever there was a deserving circumstance for her favorite occasional vice, this was it.

As she lit up on the front porch, warmth tingled through every inch of her being. Maybe it was confidence, maybe it was relief at finally having given in to her body's desires.

Flicking the ash, she looked out at the fury of the waves tossed against the sand. Its power reminded her of the passion between lovers. She blew out a thick plume of smoke. Maybe she hadn't scratched the itch all the way, and a good roll in the sheets would clear her head completely. Maybe she'd bring someone home tonight to satiate the need. Lifting her chin, she took another long drag. If nothing else, doing that was taking back control of her body, her heart, and her mind. She tapped her heel on the wood of the porch and ran her finger along her bottom lip.

Tonight was a celebration. There was no room for brooding, just as this was not the time for the isolation she'd imposed upon herself or for the anger she felt within. No. That would no longer do. She put the cigarette out and tossed the butt into the ashtray she kept on the porch just in case. In her car, she spritzed her favorite rose water perfume, turned the key in the ignition, and cranked the music. This gallery opening was the culmination of weeks—years, really—of hard work, and she was going to relish every second of the celebration. She deserved it. Turning up the music so loud she felt the bass thump within her bones, she put the car in drive and let the music take the lead over her thoughts.

As she pulled into the gallery parking lot, she flipped down the visor mirror for one more look. Smiling devilishly at her reflection, she ran a mental list of what the things she deserved might be: a successful opening, paintings sold, being the center of attention and actually enjoying it, champagne, friendship with Patsy and socializing with others, and sex—hot, passionate sex.

She bit her lip, fighting to hold her hormones at bay—and wondering when she'd morphed into an insatiable beast. She figured it had to have been around the time she swore off sex and the drama that surrounded it, doing so because apparently she couldn't have a one-night stand in this town without falling in love.

Alex closed her eyes, calling to mind the words of a guided meditation she'd listened to once that had stuck with her. She could embrace the fact that relationships didn't work out and that the failing of a relationship wasn't a failure on her part. Pulling in another deep breath, she held it and reminded herself that she still deserved the good in the world—and that the good did still exist. She exhaled and raised her head. There would be sex, and if it came with drama, it was drama she was free to embrace.

She eyed the entryway. A handful of people had already gathered, and it was still almost twenty minutes until start time. A tall, slender blonde sauntered by on her way to the front door and Alex leaned back in her seat, enjoying the opportunity to take in the view without being seen. She wasn't her normal type, but Alex decided she certainly warranted a conversation at the very least.

She glanced past the blonde and through the large windows of the gallery. She felt the smile on her face grow and the tension fade from her body. This was her dream. Her artwork was displayed on the walls for all to see, enjoy, and buy. As for the blonde...she might see about talking to her, but she might also just enjoy a night that was all about her for once.

Stepping from the car, she was grateful for the slight breeze and chill in the air. After the months of humidity, it was a nice change. She made her way around to the back of the building, where she knew Patsy would be waiting. Her body tingled in anticipation, as she quietly opened the back door.

"Hello," she called out softly.

"Hello to you," Patsy said joyfully, rounding the corner of her desk. "Were you able to catch a glimpse from outside? It's incredible. It all came together so well. I hope you are as excited as I am." The older woman's words all came out together in a mesh of excitement, not leaving any room for Alex to interject.

Alex laughed, wrapping Patsy in a hug. "It's perfect," she said, reassuring her with a squeeze. "I'm honored."

"*You?* You're honored?" Patsy gestured around at the walls. "I'm the one who's honored to house…*this*." She turned in a circle with her arms outstretched, sheer awe etched into her face. "Truly, you are a talent, Alex."

"Thank you." Alex's cheeks heated slightly under the weight of the compliment. "Shall we let the people in?"

"Soon," Patsy said, holding up her hand. "But first, we celebrate."

She walked back toward her desk, beckoning over her shoulder for Alex to follow. At her desk, the corners of her lips twisted into a mischievous half grin. She reached under the desk, and Alex craned her neck, catching sight of a mini fridge.

When she stood, brandishing a chilled mini bottle of champagne, Alex laughed. Patsy opened the bottle and split it evenly between two chilled glasses. "To you, your insane talent, and how jealous I am of that body in that dress," Patsy said, handing over the glass and eyeing Alex up and down. "You're a vision."

Alex felt tears welling, but she pushed them aside. "Patsy," she said, her voice breaking. "Thank you," she managed, clinking her glass against the older woman's. "I appreciate you more than you know."

"Feeling's mutual, hun," she said, raising her glass once more before downing its contents in one swallow. "Go on now," she urged, nodding at Alex to follow suit. "Get a little bubbly buzz on before you go greet the masses."

She did as she was instructed, delighting in the way the tiny bubbles fizzed in her mouth. With a smile, she set the glass back on Patsy's desk and followed behind as she made her way to the front of the gallery and welcomed the crowd. One by one, people made their way inside. Alex stood back, not wanting to ambush them like an overeager puppy dog.

She looked at her work on the walls and fear gripped her. What if they hated it? What if she was a fraud? She steeled herself against the negative thoughts, the imposter syndrome that threatened every artist, she was sure. Turning her attention to the large piece in front of her, she looked at it as if it were the first time she'd seen it. The silhouette of a woman, tired and ragged but strikingly beautiful, was reflected in the otherwise calm and serene waters of a wooded lake. She ran her finger along the wooden frame surrounding the painting, remembering the depths of feeling that had brought this one to life.

"This is pretty impressive," said someone behind her with a deep Southern drawl. A broad-shouldered, dark-haired man stepped to her side and pointed at the painting, his hand wrapped around one of the glasses of wine Patsy had been handing out at the door.

"How so?" she asked, raising an eyebrow. It always did her good to hear feedback from others, to see what one of her works meant to them.

"It's somehow troubling and peaceful at the same time," he said, taking a slow sip. "I enjoy it, although I don't know if I'm supposed to."

Alex laughed. "Sounds about right. Just like a woman, huh?"

He pressed his lips together, eyeing her with curiosity. "I don't think we've met," he offered, extending his hand for a handshake. "I'm Jameson."

"Nice to meet you." Alex accepted the handshake but cringed inwardly at the way he massaged his fingers around her hand. Pulling back quickly, she offered a polite smile. "I'm Alex, and I'm glad you're enjoying the show."

He opened his mouth to respond, and she could see the come-on coming from a mile away. Before he could speak, she took a step backward and glanced at the front door. "If you'll excuse me, I have to check with Patsy on something, but it was great meeting you."

Not waiting for a response, she made her way toward Patsy.

"You already have a couple of interested buyers," Patsy said quietly as she continued to pass out wine and greet the guests.

"I have interest, that's for sure," Alex muttered, accepting a glass of wine and shaking her head as she took a drink.

"Anyone giving you problems?" Patsy asked, giving Alex a once-over. "I'll take care of it, if need be."

"Gallery owner, bartender, and bouncer? You're the whole damn package, Patsy."

Patsy laughed and waved her hand through the air. "Well, you're not wrong," she said after a moment, "but I mean it. This is your night, and nothing—and no one—should ruin it for you."

"Nothing will ruin it," Alex assured her. "I'll make sure of it." She paused and laughed. "Or I'll have you handle it. One way or another, this is a great night. It's *our* night." She patted Patsy's shoulder and turned to mingle in the crowd.

As she made small talk with the guests, she stopped to chat with casual acquaintances like the checker from the grocery store, one of Lennon's regulars at the bar, and her neighbor from a few doors down. By the time the event drew to a close, she'd sold three of her larger pieces and two of her smaller ones and had a meeting set for the following week for a custom order. The remaining pieces would remain in Patsy's gallery until they sold. She breathed a sigh of relief as she watched the last guest leave.

Glancing up, she saw the blonde waiting outside, staring through the glass and watching her. She rubbed the back of her neck. They'd made small talk, but her earlier plans had been derailed by a busy evening of working and mingling. Now, she considered her options.

"You never know until you take a chance," she heard Patsy say behind her.

"What are you talking about?" she asked, turning to face the woman.

Patsy stopped gathering the empty wineglasses and held her free hand up. "I'm just saying is all," she muttered as she turned back toward her desk. "Why don't you go get some fresh air, and then you can help me clean up after?"

Alex chuckled. She should have known Patsy would have her figured out. Maybe she was right. She opened the door, breathing in the ocean breeze as it prickled against her skin.

"It's a gorgeous night," the blonde said, looking over from where she was leaning against the side of the building.

"It is."

"And that was a hell of a show."

"Thank you," Alex said, taking a step closer. "I don't think I got your name."

"I'm Elle," she said, smiling as she handed over a folded piece of paper. "I don't think you got my number either."

Alex leaned back and nodded, accepting the offering. "Bold," she noted. "I like that. I'll keep this handy."

Elle toyed with a strand of her hair and smiled as though she was proud of herself. Alex considered the possibility of what their night might hold.

"Do you want some company when you finish up here?"

Alex looked up at the stars. Here it was, what she had fantasized about earlier, hers for the taking. She didn't even have to try. "Not tonight." The words were out of her mouth before she could stop them, had she wanted to. She wasn't even sure what she wanted to do. "It's going to be a late one for me," she added. "But I will hang onto this," she said, waving the paper in the air, "and I'm really glad you stopped by, Elle." She turned to walk away, but stopped, wondering if she'd been too harsh. She looked over her shoulder. "Have a good night."

"You too," Elle said, her stare unwavering, even though Alex could hear the questioning tone of her voice. Alex waved and walked back into the gallery, locking the door behind her.

Busying herself by picking up glasses, she waited until she could see that Elle had left before she took a seat on the lounge chairs at the entrance. It wasn't that Elle wasn't attractive or that Alex didn't feel the ache for a touch. It just wasn't what she wanted.

Was it not *who* she wanted? Alex stood, shaking her head. It wasn't about that. She could separate sex from feelings, or so she'd thought. She looked out at the moon and smiled. It wasn't about Lennon. She allowed the name to roll around in her mind. It was about her.

"What happened out there?" Patsy said, rounding the corner. "Did I misread her signals that badly?"

Alex laughed. "No, you didn't."

"Then why are you still here?" The older woman raised an eyebrow.

"Because I have to clean up," Alex said, grabbing a handful of napkins and reorganizing the stack.

"That's a half-ass cleaning job if I've ever seen one," Patsy said, huffing as she crossed her arms over her chest. "What's the real reason?"

"I think..." Alex shook her head. "I think I've been on this track of thinking I *needed* someone to complete me, when in fact I'm the whole damn package too."

Patsy took a step closer, wrapping Alex into a hug. "That you are," she said as she released her and took a step back. "Now let's do some *actual* cleaning and get out of here."

* * *

Slipping out of her dress, Alex rolled her shoulders and felt her body relax. She walked to her kitchen and poured a glass of water, gratitude filling her heart. It had been a good night, and for that, she would continue to be thankful.

Standing in the center of the room, she looked through the condo. Whether or not it always had been, this *was* her home for now. She closed her eyes, feeling that she was at home, spiritually and emotionally. Her thoughts wandered to Elle, to Lennon, to matters of the heart.

Taking a sip of water, she made her way back to her bedroom. "It'll sort itself out," she whispered in an attempt to ease her mind's worries. How and when wasn't her concern right now.

She glanced at the clock. It was already eleven. She should get some sleep, but her mind was abuzz with the night's activities and her feelings of euphoria, confidence, and even a bit of the confusion she still felt.

Music would help. It always did. She fished through her purse, grabbing her phone. As she pulled it out and illuminated the screen, her hand froze at the sight of Lennon's name on the screen.

Of course tonight couldn't go as smoothly as she had hoped. She set the phone on her dresser and walked away. Opening a window, she took in the breeze. Running wouldn't give her the solace she needed. It never had.

She walked over to the dresser and placed her palms on the smooth wood. With a silent pep talk, she picked up the phone and slid the button to unlock the home screen. Her fingers hovered over the button, hesitating briefly, before clicking the message icon.

I know this is out of the blue, but I read about your opening in the paper. I'm happy for you. Hope it's everything you dreamed of and more!

She looked at the time stamp. It had been sent hours before the show even started. It was simple, but Alex knew it had come from a place of sincerity. All of Lennon was sincere despite the hard exterior she tried to put up.

It was late. Lennon would probably be at work. Somehow that made texting her easier. She bit her lip and typed out a response.

Thank you. That means a lot. It was great.

Alex added a smiling emoji and hit Send.

Almost immediately, three little dots appeared on Lennon's side of the conversation. Alex knitted her brow in confusion. A lot could happen in a month's time. Schedules changed. Or maybe Lennon was on a break.

I'm really glad to hear it. You deserve it!

Alex started to reply, but Lennon was typing again.

How are you?

Alex rubbed her forehead, staring at the follow-up message. How *was* she? Unnerved at how not unnerved she was, but also unnerved. She couldn't type that…or could she? She'd never hidden anything from Lennon, but that was before. This was different.

I'm good. A little surprised to hear from you, but doing really well.

It was as close to the truth as she was willing to give in the moment, and even that felt too vulnerable.

I know. I'm sorry. Can I get you breakfast tomorrow to celebrate your opening as well as to catch up?

She waited a second to see if Lennon would send the age-old lesbian "as friends" addition, but she didn't. Alex raised an eyebrow. She set the phone down and steadied herself, considering her options. She'd followed her heart's urgings once already tonight with Elle, and if she was really honest with herself, she knew where her heart was on this one too.

Sounds good to me.

As soon as she hit Send, she winced. What if it was a mistake? She covered her mouth with her hand, contemplating her response. It was breakfast—not a drunken night at a bar or a dinner. Both of those held too many implications.

How do you feel about smoothie bowls?

It wasn't just breakfast. It was a healthy breakfast. That felt safe enough. As they hammered out the details and made a plan for the next morning, she unclenched her jaw. After all they'd been through, it was still Lennon, and if it all went to hell, at least she'd enjoy a hearty, healthy breakfast to start her day.

CHAPTER TWENTY-TWO

Lennon tapped her foot in rhythm with the music playing overhead and focused her attention on the ornately decorated acai bowl in front of her. She looked up, making eye contact with Alex. Those brown eyes seared into her skin, and her heart rate accelerated. She knew she should say something but shoved her spoon into her mouth instead. She'd been the one to ask if they could hang out, and now she was freezing under pressure.

There was no pressure, she reminded herself, aside from Alex's bemused expression and eyes that danced with questions.

"So how have you been?" she managed after she swallowed the bite.

"I've been good," Alex said with a laugh. "But we've already established that…three times. Why is this awkward?"

"I guess it doesn't have to be," Lennon said, exhaling. "I don't know. Sorry. I guess I just still feel some guilt for the way I left things."

"Water under the bridge right now." Alex waved her hand as if to wipe clean Lennon's conscience. "Tell me about what's going on at the bar."

Lennon's forehead crinkled. She didn't deserve all the grace Alex was showing her at the moment, but she brushed the thought aside. "I'm actually taking some steps back from things," she said. Alex eyed her with curiosity. "I can't control everything, you know?" She winked, but then broke eye contact. She didn't want to appear too flirty. "And, I mean, if I hire the right people, the owner doesn't have to be underfoot all the time, right?"

"That's good." Alex flashed her a smile, unfazed. "I'm proud of you."

The weight of the words, along with the dazzling smile caught Lennon off guard. She took a drink of the water in front of her.

"How was the gallery show?" She managed the question before shoving another bite from her smoothie bowl into her mouth.

"It was…" Alex's voice trailed off. "There really aren't words. It was wonderful. I've been a part of shows in the past, but this one felt like I was celebrating a house I'd built from the ground up in record time. I was in a new place, surrounded by mostly unfamiliar faces, making it my own. And it was only my work on display. It was powerful."

As Alex talked, a war waged within Lennon, who was caught somewhere between reason and passion. For once, she was acutely aware she didn't *need* Alex—or anyone else for that matter. She could and had been standing alone, albeit only for a month and a half, without a bed to fall into or a pair of arms to hold her carefully curated illusions in place. But her thoughts stretched far beyond need. She wanted Alex. She wanted her in every way. Lennon shoveled another bite into her mouth, unsure of what she could or *should* say. The thoughts in her head swelled louder. She longed to take Alex in her arms, to feel those soft lips on hers, to moan as those long, slender fingers caressed her body. She wanted to talk with her and laugh into the night. She wanted to hold her and fight beside her in every situation. She wanted to bask in the beauty of watching Alex come to life in front of a canvas. She wanted to cheer her on, to make things right, to be a better version of herself—the version that didn't run from the magic the two of them created.

She had thought she was over this or she would have never invited her to breakfast. The lump in her throat swelled as she fought through the confusion for words that felt appropriate.

Alex furrowed her brow and leaned her forearms on the table, a clear nonverbal inquiry as to what Lennon was thinking.

Lennon cleared her throat, wishing she could make sense of it all. "This is good," she finally blurted out. "I'm glad we picked this place."

"Yeah," Alex said. Her face fell, and Lennon's stomach sank. She wasn't brave enough to even scratch the surface of the depth of emotion she felt. It would be too catastrophic for both of them. Alex had spent over a month away from her, and here she was—confident, poised, ready to take on the world.

Hell, she already was taking on the world. Lennon put her hands in her lap. Alex had always been taking on the world. Maybe she'd just been too caught up in whatever was between them to see the sheer insanity of the fact that she was able to be part of this woman's larger than life presence. She was better for their time apart too. Maybe that was supposed to be the sign.

Alex cleared her throat, and Lennon snapped her head back up. "Sorry," she said. "I have a lot on my mind this morning."

"Care to share?" Alex's raised eyebrow shot tingles through Lennon's body. How many times had that eyebrow shot up in suggestion of the sex that would follow? She looked down at the floor. It would do no good for her to read too much into the small gestures. Alex had already said she was happy. They both were.

"I'm thinking of remodeling my patio." Lennon inwardly cringed as the words came out of her mouth. Where in the hell had she pulled that from? "But it's not just that. Work, life, it's all been busy. But I just want to enjoy this moment, catching up with you. I feel like there's so much I want to know about how you've been, what you've been up to, what you've painted. I know that there's been a lot going on for both of us."

She was rambling. She shut her mouth, only to open it and take a final bite of her meal. She wanted so badly to say what was on her mind, to open up. Her heart raced as she considered the possibilities.

"Are you nervous?" Alex shifted in her seat. "You know it's still me, right? I don't think I've ever seen you act quite like this. You don't have to be nervous. There's not really much to hide or shy away from anymore. I mean, you've seen me drunk and throwing up. You've seen me cry. You've seen me naked."

As she spoke, those memories filled Lennon's head. "I have, indeed." She pushed her bowl to the edge of the table. "I've missed talking to you," she said, softly uttering the first truths in a few minutes.

"I've missed it too." Alex reached across the table, her fingers brushing Lennon's hand. Lennon felt the touch, searing into her skin. Her breath caught in her throat, but she didn't move. Savoring the contact, she brought her eyes up to meet Alex's. They were entering the danger zone. The shimmer in Alex's eyes told Lennon she knew it too.

With a sad smile, Lennon slid her hand into her lap, breaking the contact. Alex leaned back in her chair. "It's been good to catch up," she said, keeping her tone light, but Lennon could see disappointment cloud her expression momentarily. She knew her face mirrored the expression.

"It has." Lennon checked her watch. "I should probably get going." *Where?* She didn't know, but she had wasted enough of Alex's time. Her stifling uncertainty was something she had to live with; it wasn't Alex's burden. "Can we do this again soon, please?"

Alex's lips formed a tight line, then she nodded.

Lennon stood. She wanted to go in for a hug, but it felt out of place somehow, as if the contact of their bodies against one another would be a dose of lust-filled nostalgia too pure and too much for her addicted heart to handle. "Thanks for hanging out," she said awkwardly. "I'll call you."

She grabbed her bowl and turned to toss it in the trash. As she opened the door to leave, she felt the sun's warmth on her skin and hesitated briefly. What would it be like to feel that warmth flood through her entire body? Behind her, she heard Alex's chair scrape across the floor. She looked over her shoulder and watched, her heart falling as Alex scooped up her trash and shook her head. Lennon wanted to move forward, but she stood motionless. How many times had she almost told Alex how she felt, how she was scared but ready to dive in? And how many times had she fallen short of the action?

"Did you forget something?" Alex asked, eyeing her cautiously as she prepared to leave as well. A slight chill had replaced the warmer tone her voice had held only seconds earlier.

It was now or never. Her heart raced as the words caught in her throat. Alex's eyes darkened, and she shrugged. She moved to step past Lennon, and Lennon cleared her throat.

"Don't." The plea was soft, but stern. She reached for Alex's hand, following her out the door. Alex spun on a heel, turning to face her.

"What? Do you want to talk about your patio some more? Do you need an opinion on a stain color? Or do you want to race like some scared kid out of a breakfast you requested?"

"I don't know how to say everything I need to." Lennon looked to her feet, trying to find some shred of the confidence she'd had whenever they first met. She shoved her trembling hands in her pockets and swallowed, wishing her mouth didn't feel so dry and her words didn't feel so stuck. "I feel so many things that I don't know how to put into words."

"Well, you've got to try," Alex said, her tone softening. She took a step closer and looked deep into Lennon's eyes. Her expression was unreadable.

"I don't want to race away from you in any fashion. I'm scared, but I've let my inability to communicate, my need to be in control of all things, and my fear of getting hurt stop me from taking this chance fully. I'll be damned, though, if I keep missing out on you because of my stupidity."

She stared into Alex's eyes, making a silent plea. She put her hand on Alex's hip.

"Is this smart?" Alex asked, a string of additional questions dancing in her eyes.

"I don't know," Lennon said. "But I know I won't ever forgive myself if I don't take the chance." She took a step closer. When Alex nodded, her heart beat faster. Gently pulling her closer, she placed her hand over Alex's heart. "If we do this, this time it's for real."

"It always has been real. And I'm going to feel so bad for us if we fuck it up this time."

"Maybe we can't," Lennon said, wrapping her arms around Alex's waist, her hand pressing into the small of her back and pulling her forward. "If every path keeps leading me back to you, maybe we don't have the power to fuck it up."

"We've both tried, though, haven't we?"

"Maybe some things are stronger than our will to self-destruct," Lennon said, smiling as she traced Alex's jawline. "I do have some amends to make, though."

She cleared her throat and felt the sting of fresh tears. "I'm not running anymore, and as long as you'll have me, I'm going to spend my days by your side."

Alex tangled her hands in Lennon's curls and crushed her lips against Lennon's, stopping her words. A guttural sound, half moan, half sob escaped Lennon's lips as she returned the kiss.

As she pulled back, tears rolled down her cheeks. "This is what it feels like to come home, isn't it?"

"I think it just might be." Alex smiled, never moving her lips from their resting place against Lennon's. "Later, I'll throw you a homecoming party, but right now, I just want to get lost in the magic that we create."

"The magic," Lennon repeated. "That's part of what I was going to tell you in there when I started mumbling about the patio. I've been working on a lot, Alex, and part of that is letting go of the need to control. I realized that I've been chasing magical moments as if there's some secret to life that makes it worth the living, when all along, I was the magic. You were the magic. The world around us was magic and that feeling of insane gratitude and ecstasy when we're together. That's the real fucking magic, and it's not something I can find, create, or control. It's something that just is—and when I tried to control it, I messed it all up in my head and for both of us."

"You had some help." Alex took a step back and looked her up and down. "But this isn't some bar hookup anymore."

"Oh yeah?" Lennon looked inside the smoothie shop. "You mean I don't get to take you home from here?"

"I thought you said you had somewhere to be." Alex narrowed her eyes comically. "You really *were* just trying to run away from here, weren't you?"

"I felt like I had to."

"Why?"

"Because if I didn't"—Lennon looped her finger through Alex's belt loop—"I was going to do this." She pressed her mouth against Alex's and ran her tongue along her inner lip. Pulling back, she bit Alex's bottom lip and deepened the kiss. "And I knew I wouldn't be able to stop."

"Good thing you never have to," Alex said, returning the kiss. She glanced back toward the shop and laughed. "But we probably should take this elsewhere." She nodded in the direction of the shop owner, whose eyes were wide and glued on the two of them.

"How about I take you home?" Lennon's voice was husky with desire.

"Isn't that my line?" Alex laughed, grabbing Lennon's hand and following her toward her parked truck. "I walked here anyway, so you can drive me home."

On the drive to Alex's house, Alex rested her hand seductively, possessively, on Lennon's thigh.

Lennon's body ached to feel Alex's touch, but this was about more than sex. Once inside the house, she fought the urge to throw Alex against the wall. Instead, she took off her coat and stood, savoring every detail of the moment. Alex's long hair framed her face, her soft brown eyes twinkled in the midday sunlight, and the air held a mix of tension and vulnerability.

"Come with me," Alex invited, holding out her hand and leading the way to the bedroom. With each step, Lennon surrendered her need to be in control. Inside the bedroom, Alex turned to face her. Swiftly grabbing her by the hips, Alex picked her up and laid her on the bed.

Lennon gasped in surprise. Newfound confidence shone in Alex's eyes as she straddled Lennon, hovering above her body briefly before crashing her lips down on Lennon's. She ran her tongue along Lennon's bottom lip at the same time hitching her hands under Lennon's hips and pulling down her jeans. Wasting no time, she removed her underwear and hungrily pulled Lennon's shirt over her head.

Lennon looked down, her naked body waiting for Alex, fully dependent on her next move. She trembled, fighting the urge to flip Alex over and take control of the situation.

"You're mine." The words came as a husky growl.

The weight of the words hung in the air, as Lennon's body shook with need. Her wetness building, she reached up to grab Alex's neck and pull her closer, but Alex leaned back. "It's all or nothing, baby."

"It's all yours," Lennon said breathlessly. "I'm all yours." She let the words resonate. "I want you."

"You've always had me," Alex said, tracing her finger along the outline of Lennon's breasts before grabbing a nipple in her fingers. "But now it's your turn to give."

Lennon's mind searched through the times they'd been together. She'd been a giver, hadn't she? "What?"

Alex gently placed a finger over Lennon's lips. "Not like that," she said, as if somehow reading Lennon's mind. "Like this." She took one finger and plunged it inside Lennon. "I want you to give yourself to me."

Understanding dawned, and Lennon nodded, breathless as Alex pumped in and out of her. Alex had fucked her before, but that's not what she wanted today.

"I want you to give me the parts you've never given, to bare your soul to me here, to let go and let me in."

"Fuck me," Lennon moaned, teetering on the edge of control, her walls gripping Alex's long, slender finger. Alex pushed another finger inside, leaning down to kiss Lennon as she steadied the slow, deep thrusts.

She'd always needed to hold on to some illusion of control, but it wasn't just here. Alex needed more, Lennon knew. She needed her to drop the walls she put up around herself. She stared into Alex's eyes and nodded. Wordlessly, she threw her head back.

"I *need* all of you," Alex said. Sweat dripped from her brow as she positioned her hips over her hand, driving her fingers in deeper as she put her body into the motion.

"You have me," Lennon said, arching her back as she felt something inside her break. She was no longer in charge. "I want you to fuck me. Ruin me. Undo me. Take me and make me yours." She moaned as she thrust back into Alex. "I was always meant to be yours."

She looked up. "It's all yours," she moaned, as the most powerful orgasm she had ever experienced ripped through her body. When the sensations subsided, Lennon fell back limp. Alex slowly withdrew her fingers and brought her lips up to kiss Lennon on the forehead. She pulled her into an embrace and wrapped her arms tightly around her body.

"I meant it," Lennon said, struggling to catch her breath. "Every word."

"I know," Alex said, leaning in for a soft kiss. "I love you, Lennon."

"God, I love you too." Lennon shifted her weight and propped herself up on her elbow. Basking in the simplicity of loving and being loved, without walls and restrictions, without expectations, she smiled up at Alex.

She drifted off to sleep, lost in the comfort of Alex's arms. When she woke, it was dark out.

"How long was I out?"

Alex kissed her lips softly and pulled her close. "I fell asleep, too, but it's been a while." She stretched and sat up in the bed, an accomplished look on her face. "Here," she said, standing and handing Lennon a robe. "Toss this on and meet me outside on the porch." She shimmied out of the room, and Lennon sucked in a sharp breath. This woman was a goddess, and she was going to do everything it took to make sure this feeling—this bliss—never ended for either of them.

Dressing quickly, she followed Alex's instructions and soon rounded the corner to the porch. Sitting there on the porch swing with two tumblers of whiskey, Alex motioned Lennon over. "Come sit with me," she said, her voice barely above a whisper. She patted the spot beside her. Lennon smiled as she took the seat, wrapping herself beneath the blanket Alex offered.

"See the moon?" Alex asked, pointing the beautiful sight in the sky. "They say moonlight makes all things new."

"Fitting," Lennon said as she accepted the glass of whiskey. "To moonlight, new chances at a beginning…"

"And a new year, since we missed that celebration," Alex said, holding up her glass.

"We did. To a new year, a new beginning." Lennon paused, looking deep into Alex's eyes. "And no endings in sight."

As they clinked their glasses softly together in promise, Lennon could have sworn the stars shone a bit brighter.

Lennon and Alex's Playlist

Listen on Spotify: https://cutt.ly/HjR9teS or search for Playlist "Lennon and Alex"

The XX – "Islands"
Joni Mitchell – "A Case of You"
4 Non Blondes – "What's Up"
Ingrid Andress – "Lady Like"
Amos Lee – "Arms of a Woman"
Stevie Nicks – "Silver Springs"
Lady Gaga – "Million Reasons"
Poison – "Every Rose Has Its Thorn"
Kathy Mattea – "Walking Away a Winner"
Patty Griffin – "Heavenly Day"
Celine Dion – "It's All Coming Back to Me"
Fleurie – "Wildwood"
Taylor Swift (ft. Bon Iver) – "exile"
Camille Trust – "Move On"
Noah Cyrus – "Lonely"

Cocktail Recipes

Unsung Heroes

3/4 oz. beet juice
1.5 oz. bourbon
3–4 oz. ginger beer
1–3 dashes of orange bitters (to taste)
squeeze of lemon juice
fresh ginger

Combine bourbon, beet juice, and orange bitters. Shake with ice, and strain into a lowball glass, top with ginger beer and lemon twist. Add a dash or two of bitters to taste. Garnish with fresh ginger.

Unsung Heroes (Mocktail Version)

3/4 oz. beet juice
1.5 oz. Lyre's American Malt
3–4 oz. ginger beer
squeeze of lemon juice
fresh ginger
orange wedge

Combine Lyre's and beet juice. Shake with ice, and strain into a lowball glass, top with ginger beer and lemon twist. Garnish with fresh ginger and orange wedge.

Midnight Rambler

1.5 oz. Old Grand-Dad Whiskey
2 oz. limeade
1.5 oz. blueberry simple syrup
¼ cup cubed pineapple pureed

Blueberry Simple Syrup
12 oz. fresh blueberries
½ cup sugar
½ cup water

Limeade
6–8 limes
6 cups water
1 cup sugar

To make blueberry simple syrup, combine 12 oz. fresh blueberries, ½ cup sugar, and ½ cup water in a small saucepan over medium heat. Cook 15–25 minutes. Stir occasionally, until syrup is thick. Strain and let syrup cool for at least half an hour.

To make limeade, squeeze 1 cup lime juice from fresh limes. In a separate small saucepan, combine 1 cup sugar and 1 cup water to make a simple syrup. Boil, stirring often, until sugar has dissolved. Cool and pour into pitcher with lime juice. Add remaining sugar and water and stir.

Combine whiskey, limeade, simple syrup, and pureed pineapple in a shaker. Shake, strain, and serve in 8 oz. mason jar over ice. Garnish with a pineapple slice.

The Tipsy Kitchen Witch

3 oz. muddled berry shrub
1 oz. fresh citrus juice (lemon, lime or orange)
1.5 oz. vodka
2–3 oz. club soda

Shake first three ingredients with ice, strain into mason jar over ice, top with club soda, and garnish with fresh blackberry and mint.

The Tipsy Kitchen Witch (Mocktail Version)

3 oz. muddled berry shrub
1 oz. fresh citrus juice (lemon, lime or orange)
1.5 oz. Seedlip Grove 42
2–3 oz. club soda

Shake first three ingredients with ice, strain into mason jar over ice, top with club soda, and garnish with fresh blackberry and mint.

Muddled Berry Shrub
1 cup strawberries
1 cup blackberries
1 cup blueberries
1 cup raspberries
2 cups apple cider vinegar
2 cups sugar
1 cup water

Combine berries, sugar and 1 cup water in saucepan. Boil and rapidly reduce to simmer. Stir occasionally for 15–20 minutes. Add apple cider vinegar and simmer for 5 additional minutes. Cool and strain syrup. Enjoy over ice, in soda water, or as part of your favorite cocktail. For added flavor, muddle berries along the bottom of the glass in your shrub or cocktail.

Bella Books, Inc.

Women. Books. Even Better Together.

P.O. Box 10543
Tallahassee, FL 32302

Phone: 800-729-4992
www.bellabooks.com